BULLIES LIKE

ME

FROM *USA TODAY* BESTSELLER

Lindy Zart

bullies like me

Lindy Zart

Published 2016 by Chameleon Writer

Copyright 2016 Chameleon Writer

Cover Design by Sprinkles On Top Studios

Formatting by Chameleon Writer

Edited by Wendi Stitzer

ISBN 13: 978-1-945164-09-5

To all the kids who treat others like they're nothing: I didn't write this story for you. I wrote it for all the kids who are mistreated by their peers. We don't forget, even if you do. And if we make it out of high school alive, we can make it through anything.

One

Alexis

I GRAB THE ONE-EYED PINK teddy bear and bring it close to my face. It smells like baby powder, and even now, after everything—especially after everything—it makes me feel safe. It seems silly, to put such faith in an inanimate object, but that hasn't stopped me from sleeping with the bear tucked between my arms each night since my first here. I was stunned that my dad even packed it, and then I was tremendously grateful. I never thanked him; he wouldn't have acknowledged it if I had.

"What do you think, Rosie? Should I stay or should I go?" I ask the question in time with the song by The Clash.

A throat clearing from across the room startles me enough that I accidentally send the stuffed animal flying through the air. I spin around and watch as Nick Alderson's hand shoots straight up and catches Rosie, his eyes never leaving me, his expression never changing. An invisible charge shoots from him to me, locking us in each other's direct hemisphere.

"Hi." I wave weakly, and then hasten to inform him, "It was a rhetorical question. The staying or going one."

Nick looks into the bear's lone eye. "Was it directed at me, or the bear?"

"It doesn't matter, obviously. Rhetorical question, right?" I move to tuck hair behind my ear before realizing there isn't any long enough to do that with anymore. "And of course I should go." I lightly slap my palms against the sides of my purple cotton pants. "I mean, look at me. I am as sane as can be."

"Well, saner than me anyway." Nick looks up, holding my gaze with his ocean eyes.

I open my mouth, but don't reply. I don't know why Nick's at this place, but he seems pretty levelheaded to me. We've talked about a million things, but never that. Then again, I've never told him what I did to get here either. There are some things you just don't want to talk about.

He tosses the teddy bear to me. I lift my arms, but it somehow goes through them instead of into them. Nick lowers his head to hide a smile. I remember the first time I saw him. I was walking from the center's library, looking at the book in my hands instead of where I was going. I ran into him. Literally.

Nick picked up my book, asked me my name, and gave me a smile that turned his average features into something more. His pretty, long-lashed eyes don't hurt either. When I saw him, it was like I woke up from a dream. He's a patient like me, only he seems to be A-OK with staying here indefinitely. Maybe forever. Seeing how comfortable he is here, and with the staff, it seems like he has been here for a long time.

He's seventeen now. Since the facility focuses on thirteen to eighteen year olds, I wonder if they'll kick him out once he turns nineteen. I wonder if I'll still know him by then. My heart throbs, once, to let me know how much it doesn't like the thought of not knowing Nick.

"Are you ready to go?" he asks, moving farther into the room.

I gesture to the bed where an opened red suitcase rests. It's the most colorful thing in the tiny room with a single bed and dresser. I'm not sure how I qualified for my own room, but I'm glad. I retrieve Rosie and set her on top of the folded clothes. "Yep. All packed up."

"I don't mean physically."

My eyes instinctively rove over his face. I watch with fascination as a faint blush creeps along his skin. There is nothing romantic between us. Nick and I are just two head cases who found friendship with one another. And yet, it feels like there is, or could be. Something hidden just beneath the surface, something waiting to be revealed. But I'm leaving—I have to leave—and Nick...Nick will be here. If he ever does leave, I don't even know where he'll go.

Inside these walls we formed a make-believe world for the two of us. It isn't real, but I wish it was.

"Yeah. I mean, why wouldn't I be?" I avert my face, wishing I'd spoken with more confidence. I glance at him.

Looking uncomfortable, he shifts his feet. "It's a lot different out there than in here."

My focus drops to the white tiled floor. "Is that why you stay?"

I look up when he doesn't answer. Stricken blue-green eyes stare at me, and he takes a step back. It's like looking at a turbulent, broken sea. "Sorry," I mutter.

He shakes his head of messy brown hair. There is faint blondness interwoven through the strands, like his hair was once naturally highlighted. Like he used to spend a lot of time under the sun. "Don't be."

There was a catch in his voice, one I pretend I didn't hear. I answer his earlier question softly, honestly. "I'll never be ready to go back to that school."

He tilts his head, not asking what I mean, even though the question is etched onto his features. I told Nick the school here sucked, and that's as far as I took it. He never pushed, but he wonders. Well, I wonder about a lot of things concerning him too. Why he's here. Where he's from. What secrets he keeps hidden. If he thinks about me as much as I think about him.

I swallow, looking to the doorway behind him. "But here? Yes, I'm definitely ready to go from here."

"It's just a school, Alexis," he tells me, sliding his hands in the front pockets of his fleece pants. Nick only wears fleece pants. Today they are black.

And this is just a building as well, I want to tell him, but I don't.

"I know." Just a school full of people who almost killed me. I turn to zip up the suitcase. I don't want him to see my face right now. He'll wonder at the darkness there, because I can't ever keep my thoughts from my face.

I unclench my fingers from the sides of the suitcase, and fight to keep my voice even. "Dr. Larson said I could have it approved to finish my schoolwork for the remainder of the year from home. But I can't do that. I have to go back."

"Why?"

I rapidly blink my eyes, images flying through my mind. All of them bad, all of them real. Twisted smiles and mocking laughter and beautiful ugly girls. Blackness. Hopelessness. The sensation of drowning in a version of myself I can't escape. My throat tightens.

8

Why am I going back? Because if I ever want to move on, I have to. I don't have a choice. I focus on my breathing before answering, making sure it's even.

"I don't know." I do know.

Nick's silence is loud. Grating. I hear him sigh behind me. "You'll still talk with Dr. Larson?"

Suitcase in hand, I face the one good thing I've had since I moved to this state. "Every week for at least two months. That was the deal."

He hesitates, and then steps forward. I lift my face. His throat bobs. I hold my breath, wondering what he's about to do. Nick yanks me to him and crushes me within his strong arms. His hug is rushed, awkward, and everything. "Take care of yourself, Alexis."

Even with my bag in hand, I manage to cling to him harder and longer than I should. He smells good, like clean clothes and something honeyed. "Will I—will you still be here, do you think, when I have my sessions? Will you be around? They are every Wednesday at four." Hope is threaded through my words.

Will I see you again?

Nick steps back, avoiding my eyes. "I'm not sure where I'll be."

As if aware of my heart falling, he briefly touches my shoulder. The smile he gives me is sweetness mixed with sadness, and my vision goes a little fuzzy at the impact it has on me. His bottomless sea-colored eyes and rare smiles are magical.

"Right. Of course. I'm sure I'll see you sometime." I give him a bright, phony smile. "In fact, we'll probably see each other all the time, actually, so much that we'll get sick of seeing each other, and we'll hope to never see one another again." I don't sound one bit convincing, and my attempted smile falls flat. I haven't gotten sick of his company once in the two months I've been here.

Another smile dances across his lips before dipping into nonexistence. He puts more distance between us, and I feel the cold where he stood. "Dr. Larson knew I was coming to say goodbye. She asked me to tell you that your dad is on his way to pick you up."

I nod, turning my attention to the hallway beyond the doorway. My stomach somersaults. Am I ready for this? I guess I have to be. It's time to go. Straightening my shoulders, I take a deep breath and march from the room. Nick briefly locks gazes with me as he turns in the opposite direction, disappearing around a corner. Probably to go hide in his room until it's time for his chores.

I blink and face forward, telling myself I'll make sure I see him when I come for my therapy. I'll seek him out like I did after that first time we met. I was relentless, searching every hall and room I could until I found him helping out in the kitchen. I saw something in him I see in me. Raw, hurting need. And I saw something else. Just a flicker of it. Just enough to grab my attention and keep it on him.

Something that made me want to hope when I was sinking in the opposite of it.

A few people call out a greeting as I walk, and I give them a quick, fake smile that is over before it really touches my lips. A silent girl with troubled eyes shuffles past, and I avert my gaze. The more disturbed ones make me nervous, and I know why. Because not so long ago, I was one of them. I was a complete mess.

Two more kids walk by, engrossed in a conversation about Star Wars. *May the force be with you.*

It always smells like coffee in the halls, and everything has a new, orderly feel to it. As far as decorative pieces, there isn't much on the walls, but the few paintings are light, airy scenes obviously garnered to elicit feelings of tranquility. To my eyes, the place is fancy-looking with its cream and tan walls, open spaces, and leather furniture. They must get great funding. I snort. I guess so, since there will always be screwed up kids.

In one of my more bored hours, and there were a lot of them while here, I read up on the history of the place. It's called Live— rhymes with give—and it's a small rehabilitation center for mentally unstable teens. Run primarily by Dr. Larson, it's been around for six years, and has patients from all over the United States. There are staff members here twenty-four hours a day, along with doctors of varying degrees popping in and out as required.

It focuses on individual, group, and family therapy, among other positive movements, like activities and implementing self-goals. There are also daily chores for the capable kids that result in either helping or befuddling the staff, depending on the kid. I had kitchen duty—because I requested it, knowing that's where Nick would be— in the morning and afternoon, which consisted of me helping with the meals, setup, and cleanup.

Except for my obligatory meetings, counseling sessions with Dr. Larson, and designated chores, I spent most of my time reading in my room, or in the library. Usually with Nick. And even though this place has teens teeming about, I never connected with anyone, except for Nick. I found him, and I didn't need or want to find anyone else. Not that we did anything other than talk, and possibly stare at one another for a beat too long. My mouth twists. At the Live treatment center, our free time isn't regulated, but even so, there are always people around, and the cameras, watching.

Some of the kids here are crazy; some are violent; some are despondent. All are lost.

I SEE MY DAD BEFORE he sees me, and I flinch at the sight of his shrewd blue eyes surveying the waiting area. Bald and of medium height with massive shoulders, burly arms, and not much neck, he reminds me of a bulldog. Other than one family therapy session, the only time he's set foot in the center is when I was initially brought in. That visit was to bring me the small amount of clothes, and Rosie, packed inside the bag presently clutched so tightly within my hand that it's cramping.

That's okay, though, because that one time he came to sit through a counseling session with me, he hardly spoke. I didn't want to sit in a room with him again after that and have him wordlessly tell me all the ways I've failed him. He's embarrassed of me. He has to be. Nothing else makes sense for his outright avoidance of me. Because, as you know, when someone tries to kill themselves, they're doing it to annoy people.

I just needed a little attention, so I swallowed some pills.

"You're going to be okay, Lexie," a kind voice says from behind.

I start and swing around to find Dr. Hilary Larson watching me. Everyone calls me Lexie, and because of that, soon after exchanging names, Nick told me he was going to call me Alexis. With a smile, of course. I like that he's the only one who uses my given name. I like the color of his eyes, and I like the unruliness of his hair, and I like that when he looks at me, he *really* looks at me.

I like too many things about him.

"Jumpy today?" She smiles, looking over my shoulder.

The smile falters. I probably wouldn't notice if I wasn't staring so hard at her. I don't want to turn around. I don't want to face my dad. I feel him behind me, his eyes boring into the back of my head, judging. I can hear his thoughts, even though he doesn't bring voice to them. They always center on: What would your mother think? Well, I don't know what my mother would think, because she took off about three years ago. Leaving no word, no letter—just a big, fat, unfillable void. And an uncomprehending Nathaniel Hennessy. My dad never got over it.

He changed.

And I changed.

"Yeah," I croak. "Super jumpy. It's all the excitement of going home, and getting back into the school routine." I can't even drag enthusiasm into my tone. The house doesn't feel like home; this town isn't mine. And the school? It's so much worse.

Her gaze moves back to me. She leans closer, bringing a lemony scent with her. "You can do this, I know you can. And you have me. You aren't getting rid of me just yet. I'll see you next week."

Dr. Larson has medium length hair she calls river water brown and warm brown eyes. I think her hair is pretty, like milk chocolate, chocolate chips. When she wears heels, she stands taller than most of the men here, and definitely taller than me. Easy to have happen when you're not even five feet one. With her gentle eyes and quick smile, Dr. Larson made my therapy tolerable, even though I had to endure hours of talking about my thoughts and feelings. It's hard to explain things I don't entirely understand myself.

"And the one after that." I smile weakly.

"And the one after that," she adds with a wink.

I fidget and blurt, "Is Nick going home soon?"

Dr. Larson straightens, her eyes instantly shadowed. "You know I can't discuss patient details with you."

"Right." I rub the palm of my free hand against my leg. "I just…I just hope I see him again, that's all."

"I'm sure you will," is all she says, and it's enough.

"Lexie." My dad's voice is firm, and demands attention.

I turn and meet his eyes, attempting a smile. I give a small wave when that fails. "Hi, Dad."

I remember his face at the hospital. It was impassive, pale. Like all the emotions and life were drained from him. He was a wall, and I gazed at him, unable to break through. Other than color being added back to his flesh, his expression isn't all that different right now.

He studies me, frowning as he takes in the choppy strands of light brown hair framing my face. At least my hair's grown out some, not to mention been professionally evened out, since I decided to give myself a haircut. "Are you ready to go?"

"Mr. Hennessy?" Dr. Larson moves to stand beside me, offering a hand with short, uniformly cut nails polished in pale pink.

My dad takes the offered hand, giving it a brusque shake before releasing it. "Dr. Larson."

"If you'll come with me for a minute, we'll go over the paperwork you're required to sign, Lexie's treatment plan, and discuss a few other things before her release."

An annoyed look passes over my dad's craggy face, but he doesn't say anything, merely nodding and gesturing for Dr. Larson to lead the way. The doctor gives me a pointed look when I try to stay behind. I grudgingly follow the adults into a nice-sized room with comfortable beige chairs and flower paintings on the walls. There are tulips, daisies, roses, and more I can't name, all in blurred, muted shapes and colors.

The lemon smell is stronger in the office. A chair and desk are on the far side of the room, and I admit, I never once saw Dr. Larson sit at it when we met. She always sat across from me in one of the brown chairs with a welcoming smile and few words, allowing me to speak my own.

"Please, take a seat, both of you."

We sit, Dr. Larson gathering a file from her desk as we do. For the first time since I've been here, I realize how much I'll miss certain parts of the treatment center. The feeling of belonging, even if it was in a place full of distressed kids. Dr. Larson's quiet thoughtfulness. The silent calm in my head. Nick. Sometimes, I was able to forget about my life before this. Nick is right; the world outside the wooden fence surrounding the center is harsh, and I don't know how I'm going to face it again.

You will, because you must.

"—important that Lexie feels like she has someone to talk to. A regression is the last thing we want. She's come so far."

I look up, wondering how much of the conversation I missed.

15

Red faced and scowling, my dad shifts in his seat. The legs creak, and I hope the chair doesn't collapse under the weight of his large frame. It would be the chair's fault, of course, not the extra servings of food my dad likes. "I know how to take care of my daughter."

Yes, just ignore me and tell yourself I can survive.

Dr. Larson levels her gaze on him. "I'm glad to hear that. Communication between parents and their children is vital for them to have a healthy relationship."

I tilt my head and study the red and pink petals of a painted rose on the wall to the right of me. I wonder what it's like to live with Dr. Larson. A vision of her and a faceless husband come to mind. They're sitting at the kitchen table, eating breakfast.

Faceless Husband: I ate the last of the cereal.

Dr. Larson: How do you feel about that?

I smirk, quickly forcing it back when my psychiatrist turns her attention to me. I realize she's waiting for something. Probably an answer to a question I didn't hear. "Um...what?"

"I asked if you were all set."

I hop up and grab my bag. The sooner I get out of here, the sooner I can move on to worry about something else. Like school. I look to my left. "Ready, Dad?"

He gives a brief nod, Dr. Larson shakes my hand, and we go.

Hollowness grows in the pit of my stomach as I step through the front doors and face the parking lot. I tell myself I'll be okay, but I'm not sure I will be. The sky is painted in wispy gray clouds, and the tips of my ears immediately sting from the cold. They're used to having hair cover them; now there are short layers flittering about my head that offer little protection. The chill and wetness in the May air quickly work their way through my hooded sweatshirt and lounge pants.

My dad catches my shiver, shaking his head. I only wear jackets when not doing so would be life-threatening, like when it's below zero out and the wind chill is strong and cold enough to rip the skin from your face. This forty degrees weather doesn't have anything on me, but even so, I flip the hood of the sweatshirt before trekking in the shadow of my father's footsteps.

He silently unlocks the white Ford Explorer and takes my suitcase from me, setting it in the back before moving to the driver's side. It isn't like we've ever been all that close, but something happened to my dad when my mom left. Light left his eyes; words no longer passed his lips. He got colder. I don't know if it's because I look like her that he distanced himself from me, or if it was because he just couldn't handle it all. All I know is, on the day my mom left, I lost my dad along with her.

It was an avalanche of unexpected occurrences, with me at the bottom of it all. My sister Jenna left to live her own life across the country, my mom decided she no longer wanted a family, we moved to a new town, and inside the school where I was friendless and vulnerable, the hell truly began. If even one thing had happened differently, it all could have been different. But, here we are, with me leaving a mental institution. That gives you a good idea on how well it all went.

I pause with my hand on the door handle, looking back at the brown and red brick building with lights shining from most of its windows. I'm waiting for something I shouldn't, waiting for something that won't be there. Still, I delay my departure. I know I don't have long before my dad becomes impatient. *One more look.*

Shifting my eyes from side to side, I search for a form in the gloom. It is as I am turning in dejection that I see him, a shadow that separates from the tree he stands beneath. Half of my mouth lifts as Nick's hand does, and I nod once, climbing into the Explorer.

As we leave, I think about the town. There are fourteen thousand people in Enid, Illinois, and during the months I went to Enid High School, a handful of them made my life hell. Overall, the whole school experience was abysmal, but two girls in particular made my time there unbearable. Just thinking about their uncaring cruelty makes my skin clammy and my head hurt. They ridiculed me, singled me out to beat down. Melanie Mathews and Jocelyn Rodriguez. Sixteen years old, in a new school, and I was bullied. Hurt, disbelieving, I became a person I didn't recognize.

I became someone who wanted to die.

And that makes me angriest of all. That I gave them that power, that I let them decide my value. Monday, I'm going back to the school that took my soul. I have to. It's the only thing that makes sense, the only thing that makes it all endurable. Because I have something I need to do, and one month to do it. I'm taking back what was taken from me.

I'm going to make my bullies pay.

Two

Melanie

THE SCHOOL IS HOT, SMELLY, and mine.

I may be a junior, but with only a month of school left this year, I'm as good as a senior. Feeling my chest expand with importance, I turn to my locker as the first bell rings. I smile as endless greetings are called out to me, even though I don't call any back, or bother looking to see who they're from. This place is a madhouse of sounds with all the kids trampling up and down the halls, and it stinks like a collection of body odor and soap. After checking my hair and makeup in the small mirror on the inside of the locker door, I grab my books for my first class, and meet up with Casey Reed and Jocelyn Rodriguez near the door to the English classroom.

"Nice haircut," Jocelyn calls out to a younger classman with short, curly red hair, smiling the whole time. "Who did it? You?"

The girl stops abruptly, and is shoved forward as the person behind her keeps moving. Sidestepping the redhead with a glare and an unfriendly comment, the boy continues. Unsure of Jocelyn's intentions, the girl's eyes dart around the hallway before landing on Jocelyn. "N-no. I go to Claire's on Fifth Street."

Jocelyn nods. "That explains it."

Face crumpling, the girl hurries down the hall.

"That was mean," I tell Jocelyn, even though I don't care. Her hair does look really bad.

Jocelyn turns bored brown eyes to me and smirks. "Now she knows to not go there again, right? I was helping her out."

"And of course, that was the only reason you said it."

"Of course."

With long, wavy hair the color of ebony, a flirtatious personality, and long legs, Jocelyn gets her fair share of boyfriends. Even some of mine.

Jocelyn focuses on Casey. "Mel, tell Casey it's not okay to date Lucas Haskins."

I sigh and take my friend by the shoulders. When her wide hazel eyes meet mine, I shake my head. "It's not okay to date Lucas Haskins. He's a total nerd, Case, you know that. We have standards, and dating nerds goes against them. You'd be a nerd just like him if you did."

"I know, but—but…he's nice and…" she trails off meekly.

"He has to be nice. He's a nerd. He has nothing but niceness to offer," I explain patiently, dropping my hands from her shoulders.

Quiet, and overall, uninteresting, if Casey didn't dress as well as she does, or wasn't a cross country star, chances are, she wouldn't be one of us. It helps that her family has money, and with her silky blond curls and creamy skin, she's pretty. Pretty is always good. And sports are important here. The three of us bonded during sixth grade basketball, and we've been friends ever since.

"You know the rules. Two against one, Casey. He's non-date worthy," Jocelyn says apologetically, even as her dark eyes dance.

Casey pouts, her blue-eyed gaze locked on the blond-haired boy in question as he struggles to remove books from his backpack. Lucas is smart, has never played a single sport in all his years at school, and knows more about science than any normal person should. Nothing about him comes close to being popular. He doesn't know how to dress either. His outfits consist of gray or khaki slacks, polo shirts in various colors, and white tennis shoes. I honestly don't know a single thing about him that could be considered attractive.

The last warning bell rings.

With a blushing face and agitated movements, Lucas looks around as he tugs at the books crammed inside the bag. Anyone can see he overfilled it, the dork. As if hearing my thoughts, his eyes shoot to me before moving to Casey. With a silly smile, he lifts one hand to wave while the other continues to work on his books. Casey waves back, quickly dropping her hand when Jocelyn narrows her eyes at her.

Surprise flashes across Lucas' face as a book dislodges from the bag and smacks him in the face. The back of his head bangs against the locker, the sound sharp and loud in the emptying hallway. He slides to the floor, looking dazed.

Jocelyn and I look at each other and laugh.

"Total nerd," I remind Casey as I step into the classroom.

Sighing, she gives Lucas one last lingering look before following us.

Even with it being a Monday, the noise level is high in the pastel green room, as is the scent of perfume clashing with someone's body odor. Crinkling my nose, I look around the room, spotting the culprit. Winston Zander. I shudder. He's overweight with acne covering his face, and he sweats, all the time. With his greasy brown hair and dirty clothes, I swear he must not know how to bathe, or use a clothes washer.

Digging around in my sparkly teal wristlet wallet, I find a miniature bottle of body spray and go to war with his stench as I walk by. Vanilla subdues the stench of rankness, but doesn't entirely snuff it out. When Winston turns clueless gray eyes on me, I make a face and give the bottle a few extra squirts. Maybe he'll get the hint.

"Looking good today, Melanie Mathews," Clint Burns calls out, wiggling his eyebrows when I look at him.

Other than a look of disdain aimed Clint's way, I don't bother acknowledging him. You'd think he'd have gotten the hint by now that I'm not interested, and never will be. Clint might be good at basketball, but his ears stick out too far and his teeth are crooked. And he's not that smart. Too smart is bad, but being barely smart at all is just as bad. He has no right being as cocky as he is, not with those flaws. And he made out with Becky Sloan at my last party, the biggest slut in the whole school. No, thank you.

I take a seat as far from the smelly kid as I can get. Jocelyn sits across from me, and Casey takes the seat ahead of me. We've been separated in multiple classes for talking when we're supposed to be working, but we always sit by each other anyway. The teachers hate it, and yet, they allow it.

"All right, class, settle down," Mr. Walters calls, gesturing with his hands. With thinning brown hair, glasses, and a long nose and chin, he isn't going to win any hot teacher contests.

Jocelyn leans over, her dark hair curtaining the side of her face, and whispers, "What are we doing this weekend?"

Casey twists in her seat, looking to me for direction. Honestly, I'm not sure Casey is able to have a single decisive thought on her own. She needs me.

"I need a new dress for my end of the school year party. Shopping?" I suggest, and get two nods.

"Girls." Mr. Walters watches us, along with the rest of the class.

"You can go shopping with us too, Mr. Walters," Jocelyn says with a coy smile.

"That won't be necessary, but thank you for the offer."

Someone oinks when he turns his back to grab a folder from his desk, and Mr. Walters' neck blossoms into a nice shade of pink to match his button-down shirt. I snicker along with half of the class. He faces the classroom, stony-eyed and tight-jawed, his gaze sweeping over the students. The oinking has happened every morning this past year; he should be used to it by now. Really, what does he expect with a first name like Wilbur?

"That's enough," he snaps, glaring directly at the offender. Even though he knows who is responsible, Mr. Walters has never actually caught Jeff doing it.

Jeff Oliver averts his gaze, but does nothing to hide the grin on his face. Now there is a guy worth my time. Just smart enough, a total jock, and nice to look at. Chestnut hair with a hint of a wave, strong jaw, toned body. He looks up, catching my eyes on him. Dark blue eyes. I smile faintly. Jeff winks before facing forward. We've barely talked since he came to the school in eighth grade, but over the last couple of weeks, I've been eyeing him.

I catch Jocelyn's knowing look, and my smile grows. I think I've found my next boyfriend. The smile disappears when my friend gives Jeff an appreciative glance. *Don't even think about it.* Like she can hear my warning, Jocelyn smiles widely at me. All I see are white teeth, and my hands tighten around my textbook.

"We're having one final project of the school year, and it's a big one. It's going to take the next four weeks to complete, with presentation expected the last week of school." He pauses. "Listen carefully."

As he explains the short story we're all being tortured into writing in groups of three and four, I shift in my seat. Heat sweeps along my back, and I look over my shoulder, feeling like someone is watching me. I clash gazes with a girl who looks vaguely familiar. Her hair is shorter than I'd ever cut mine, but it actually doesn't look bad on her—not that I'd ever tell her that. It makes her pale blue eyes stand out. Her pale blue eyes that won't look from my green ones. I frown. Why is she staring at me like that? People generally avert their gaze once eye contact is made. Maybe there's something wrong with her.

"What?" I finally snap. "What are you looking at?"

Her eyebrows shoot up, like she wasn't just ogling me and has no idea what I'm talking about.

"Hello. Yeah, you. Why are you staring at me?"

"Melanie, is there a problem?"

I face the front of the classroom and briefly meet Mr. Walters' gaze. My skin heats up as all eyes swivel to me. "No," I mumble.

"Good," the teacher says, and continues rambling on about the lame project.

Jocelyn gives me a questioning look.

I jerk my head back and she shifts her eyes behind me. Seeing the short-haired girl with the unnerving stare, she shrugs like it's no big deal and turns around. Tapping my pencil against my notebook, I try to focus on what Mr. Walters is saying, but now I'm paranoid.

Even if she isn't looking at me, it seems like she is. Like tiny bugs are digging into my skin. I shoot a look over my shoulder, annoyed to find her eyes still on me. Whoever she is, she better disappear once class is over.

"Stop it," I hiss.

The girl finally looks away, but not before I catch the small, satisfied smirk on her face.

Three
NICK

SOMETHING IS DIFFERENT ABOUT ALEXIS the next time I see her. It isn't anything she says, but it's the vibe coming off her. She *hums* with energy. Her cheeks are flushed, her eyes sparkle, and I want to press my lips to hers to steal some of her vibrancy. That, and I just want to kiss her.

"I take it you had a good session with Dr. Larson?" I doubt that's it.

She sits down beside me at the table in the library, pushing my book back and forth along the surface of the table before I stop her with the touch of my hand. I look at my hand covering hers, and I swallow around a dry throat as I drag my eyes up. Electricity crackles between us. Alexis smiles, showing dainty teeth. My pulse quickens. I start to smile back, but she tackles me before I can complete it, working her arms through the space between my arms and my body. She smells like peaches. I try to swallow again. Can't.

It comes out muffled, but I hear it.

"I've missed you."

I close my eyes and let those words sink into me.

The library has dim lighting, and other than three or four other kids and one staff member, it's ours. I always sit in the back, far from the entrance, and behind a row of books. Even with the cameras set up and recording every room in case of any incidents, it feels like we're alone. I want Alexis to stay with me until she can't.

"That's not why you're so happy." I want it to be.

Alexis sits back, disentangling our limbs. She picks at the fabric of my pants. "Red and black plaid today. That's new."

"My mom sent them." I flush, not sure why.

"Well, I know what to get you for your birthday," she jokes, her fingers tailing down the material toward my knee. My muscles tense. Realizing what she's doing, Alexis snatches her hand back and picks up the book. I can tell by the way she's looking at it with absolute fixation that she's not really seeing the words.

Something falls to the floor across the room, and we both jerk at the unexpected noise, smiling as our eyes meet.

"My dad and I had pizza last night," she blurts.

Eyebrows lowering, I say slowly, "Okay."

"Right." Alexis turns back to the book. "This town has around fourteen thousand people, right? And only one really good pizza place. Giovanni's."

"Which is where you got the pizza?" I guess.

"No." With her smile in profile, she tells me, "My dad got the pizza from Garfield's, which is an Italian restaurant that has pizza, but they don't specialize in pizza."

I sit back, wondering where she's going with this.

"He thought it was Giovanni's." Alexis lifts her eyes to me, and they sparkle. "That's my story."

I nod. "I enjoyed it thoroughly."

Alexis laughs, and I go still to better allow it to wash over me.

"What is this about?" She frowns at the black-covered book with silver lettering.

"Robots programmed to kill anyone over the age of eighteen, and a nineteen-year-old girl trying to destroy one before it can get to her."

"Huh. Why are the robots killing people over eighteen?"

"Because in this futuristic world run by robots, people lose their worth once they reach adulthood. They're considered old and obsolete."

"Sounds like a happy place."

I want to kiss the smile from her lips. As if sensing that, Alexis is silent and still as she watches me. I drop my eyes, breaking the invisible pull of her. She exhales slowly.

"Things are...going okay for you?" I ask quietly.

"Yeah." She nods, setting down the book. "Not bad, actually. Better than expected."

"Good." My brows furrow as I examine the way she shifts her eyes, looking everywhere but at me. I press my fingers to the tabletop, watching as the tips go white. "And the school?"

Alexis shrugs.

I relax my hands. Knowing she doesn't want to talk about it, I drop it. We both have limits as to what we'll discuss. I don't make her talk about what she doesn't want, and she does the same for me. Before Alexis came here and shoved her way into my world, I was a nonentity. Just barely functioning. Just barely alive. All it took was one interaction with her, and I was altered. I wanted to live again. I don't want there to come a time when we no longer talk, because one of us couldn't leave secrets alone. I don't pry. I let her have her secrets, and she allows me mine.

"Nick."

I look at her.

She hesitates, capturing her lower lip between her teeth. I study the motion, enthralled by it. "Are you here because you want to be, or because you have to be?"

I go cold, everything in me halting. Breaths must pass through my nostrils; my lungs must work, but I am unaware. I stare at Alexis, not really seeing her. Seeing a ghost instead. My hand clenches, and I bow my head, studying the tense veins that run along the back of it. I can't answer that. I won't.

"I...I'm sorry," she stammers, getting to her feet. "I just, um, I thought maybe...maybe sometime you could, you know, go somewhere with me. Like, spend the day with me or something. If it was okay with...whoever." Dismay clings to her words. "Never mind. Forget I asked."

I stand as well, wanting to be close to her. I always want that. I take the hand she keeps running through her hair, and I squeeze the cold fingers. Alexis goes quiet, looking at me in a way that makes my heartbeat stutter. "I would like that. If you let me know when, I can set it up with Dr. Larson."

Joy splits her face with a grin and Alexis tightens her fingers around mine. "We're going to do terribly dull things together, Nick, but you'll love it."

I laugh softly, releasing her hand. "I believe you."

"About the dull part, or the loving it part?"

"Either. Both."

"Are you free Saturday?"

I'm free every day. Alexis' dad came once during her two months here. No one's come to see me since I was first admitted last year. I just nod, pressing down a nauseating combination of panic and hope. I haven't stepped off the center's grounds, I think, ever. This place is a prison of my own making, and for good reason. Forcing myself to focus on what is before me instead of inside me, I study Alexis' pink lips, her naturally arched eyebrows, the way she's looking at me right now, and I breathe.

I think I could do just about anything, with her beside me.

"I'll pick you up at eight." She pauses. "Do you have anything besides pajama pants to wear?"

I laugh again. "What's wrong with my pajama pants?"

"Nothing. They're nice, and look super comfy. I just thought we could go for a walk, or maybe hiking. It's supposed to be in the sixties. If you want to wear fleece pants, then go for it."

"I'll figure something out," I say, smiling. I hope my smile appears more encouraging than it is. The thought of being out in public isn't a pleasant one. *Worry about that later.*

"If you…" Alexis takes a deep breath and locks eyes with me. She looks nervous. "If you ever want to call me—you know, if you're bored or have free time or whatever—you can. It's a landline. My dad won't let me have a cell phone; he thinks they're more trouble than anything."

Making a face, she tugs something from the pocket of her jeans and slaps her palm to my chest. "I'm usually home every night after six. Call me, but, um, only if you want."

I reach up, and she drops her hand when I take the paper she placed there, but not before the imprint of her hand is branded to the skin above where my heart beats. I look at the slanted name and numbers, committing them to memory.

"I will," I promise.

Relief loosens her shoulders, and she laughs shakily. "Cool."

"Nick, you're due in the cafeteria in five minutes for supper chores," Jackie calls from the desk near the doorway. Other than the doctors, we only know the first names of the staff. Safer that way for them when we're discharged. Most of us are harmless. Most.

I look at Alexis, apology lining my face. "I have to—"

"Right." She backs away. "I'm not supposed to linger anyway. Dr. Larson's orders." She smiles, but it doesn't quite reach her eyes.

"I'll walk you to the door."

Alexis shakes her head before I finish. "No. You'll be late. I'll see you Saturday. And maybe I'll talk to you before then."

When she smiles shyly, my body tautens and I even find myself leaning toward her. Needing to feel her lips on mine. I used to dream of blood, but now I dream of Alexis' lips. She stares back with wide eyes. Her lips part, beckoning me forth whether she is mindful of it or not.

She's everything I want, and she is not mine. Forcing myself to take a step from her, I raise a shaky hand to my head and dig my fingers into the back of my neck to keep from reaching for her.

The light in her dims, and she blinks like she's coming out of a trance.

"Have a good night, Alexis," I say quietly.

Swallowing, she jerks her head in a semblance of a nod and practically flees from the library.

THE CAFETERIA IS FULL OF kids and staff, and conversation and laughter are at a loud volume. There are only around thirty kids present, but it seems like there are triple that. Voices echoing, building on the resonance of one another. It makes my head swim. I serve food, refill tubs when they get low, keeping my eyes down to avoid conversation. I don't like to talk to people all that much; I don't like a lot of noise. I like to be alone, in the quiet.

Most of the kids here seem normal. You wouldn't know they had any problems, especially seeing them as they are right now. But I know the boy with skin the color of coffee beans sitting in the left corner of the room was sexually abused by his uncle, and cuts himself. The girl I am presently serving mashed potatoes screams in the night, every night. I catch her unfocused gaze before hurriedly looking away.

"What about the butter?"

I look up, taking in the pale-faced boy with a stained yellow shirt and dark blond hair sticking up all over his head. I don't recall seeing him before now. He must be a new one. "What?"

"The butter." He looks around, his eyebrows pinched. "The butter should be here, by the mashed potatoes. You need butter with mashed potatoes. Where's the butter?"

I wordlessly point to the dish containing individual packets of butter.

"No." He slams a fist on the table, attracting the attention of nearby kids and Manny, the worker in charge of the kitchen and everything that happens within it. "That isn't the right kind."

I slowly straighten, speaking in a low voice. "That's the only kind we have."

Panic flares his nostrils, and darkens his eyes. With his wild hair and constantly moving eyes, he looks like some feral beast. "No," he mumbles, his voice getting louder, until he's shouting. "No. No. No, no, no! This isn't right. This isn't right!"

"What's going on?" Manny asks, looking between the two of us. With a shaved head, and massive muscles, there isn't much discordance when Manny is around. Dark eyes set in a dark face fixate on me.

"It's the wrong kind of butter," the boy shrieks, throwing his plate of food. It hits the wall, mashed potatoes and meatloaf creating an abstract picture on the cream canvas.

His tormented eyes fall on me and he shoves me. I stumble until I hit the wall behind me, looking at the boy who's lost inside his own mind. And I grieve for him. I look around the room at the silent spectators. I grieve for all of them.

Manny talks into his radio with one hand, the other firmly around the boy's wrist. He efficiently explains the situation, and before I can count to thirty, two giant orderlies appear. The boy will be taken to a cool down room. He will stay there overnight. His family will be notified. He will be discussed, dissected. We all know the drill, most of us having been there before. I've been there.

Everything appears normal, until something like this happens. Then reality sets in. It always does, eventually.

Looking at me, Manny says, "Get the mess cleaned up, Nick."

I nod and move to the closet inside the kitchen area.

"It's the wrong kind of butter. She'll be mad. Mother will be mad. It's the wrong kind of butter," the boy screams, wild-eyed, as he's taken from the room.

33

No one laughs; no one speaks for a good minute. I wipe the wall with a wet rag, and then work on the floor. As I listen to the quiet, it's as if we all say a silent prayer for the troubled mind of the nameless boy. Slowly, cautiously, there are murmurs, until kids are talking again. It's subdued, though, not like it was at the beginning of the meal. We all recognize the present chaos of his mind; we've all been trapped in a place we can't escape. It's dark, and scary. It's a place where screams have no sound.

The rest of the meal goes by without incident. Once the cafeteria is cleared out, with the supervision of Manny, two other kids and I work on getting the leftover food put away and dishes in the washer. Alexis used to help with this, but now there is a boy in her place. Definitely nowhere near as cute as her.

When the tables are wiped down and the floor is swept and mopped, I say good night and go back to my room. Not only smelling of food, but also wearing a good deal of it, I take a quick shower in the communal shower rooms. I get dressed, smiling as I pull on a pair of dark blue fleece pants and a gray tee shirt. I can picture Alexis shaking her head with a little grin teasing her lips.

Back in my room, I don't pick up the new book I took from the library, like I normally would. It's a young adult novel set in a dystopian era—my favorite kind to read, along with science-fiction. Instead I pace from the bed to the dresser and back, again and again. When I first came to Live, I had a roommate. He was eventually sent home and I was never assigned another. I suppose I've been here long enough that I've earned my own room, small and bare as it is.

I've seen a lot of kids come and go during my time here.

My mind is stuck on Alexis Hennessy, making any attempt to do anything worthwhile futile. Since she came to the center, she's taken over my thoughts. But this isn't a love-struck reminiscence. The spark in Alexis' eyes, although nice to see, wasn't completely happy. Some of it was ominous.

She's hiding something, something big. During our conversations in the past, at times I sensed bitterness in her. A certain look, a certain comment would mar her essence. I know it has something to do with Enid High School, and whatever happened there.

I pull out the white slip of paper from the pocket of my red and black plaid pants lying on the floor, staring at the neat handwriting. I trace the letters of her name with my index finger. More than the occasional unrest of her mind, I feel her heart, her goodness. The thought of her losing that makes my hands tremble. I don't understand the course my thoughts have veered down, but I know they have merit.

I take a deep breath, hold it until my lungs burn, and release it. "What's going on with you, Alexis?"

Four
Melanie

WHEN THE FOLDED PIECE OF paper drops to my desk just as the bell rings, I look up in time to see the weird girl, Lexie, disappear in the crowd of dispersing students. Her pace is hurried, like she can't wait to get away from me. The feeling is mutual. It's bad enough that I have to deal with her creepy stares all the time, but Mr. Walters thought to further torment me by putting her in my writing group.

No one wanted to pair up with her, and I completely understand why.

"You coming?" Jocelyn wonders as she twirls a lock of black hair around her finger and watches Jeff saunter from the room.

I shoot to my feet, purposely elbowing my friend as I do, and slide the paper inside my folder. "Yes. And you can quit checking out Jeff Oliver. He's not available."

She turns her gaze to me, and there's fire inside the brown and gold irises. "Says who? He looks available to me."

"You only decided you wanted him because you saw that I'm interested in him," I say in a voice that bristles with anger.

Smiling, Jocelyn glides toward the door. "See you at lunch."

Teeth clenched, I hasten to my locker and ditch my books before heading to gym class. The hallways are full of hurrying kids, with a few who aren't moving at all. They stand or sit, looking dazed and unwashed. Druggies, I'm sure. They probably don't even know where they are. I catch a glimpse of shiny black hair as Jocelyn turns the corner. Sometimes I don't know why I put up with her. She's a snooty, slutty bitch who thinks she can just take whatever she wants.

A boy with two chins and overly large glasses stutters a greeting as we walk by one another.

"Don't talk to me," I say coolly, not even bothering to look at him.

"But I—"

"No."

"You're in my—"

"Don't care," I trill.

Something slams into me from behind and I go sprawling face first onto the hard floor, barely catching myself before my chin hits it. I lie still, gasping for air as my heart pounds at an alarming rate. I shift my eyes to the dirty floor caked with who knows what, my face inches from it.

"Whoops. Sorry. I didn't see you there."

I turn over and lock eyes with Lexie.

"You clumsy oaf," I seethe, climbing to my feet.

"It was an accident," she says in an innocent voice, but her face calls her a liar.

Shorter than me, and more bones than anything else, she wouldn't stand a chance in a fight. Not that I would ever stoop that low. Only losers physically fight. And where does she get off looking like she's entitled to do and say as she pleases around me? She should quiver where she stands.

I glower at her, my eyes narrowing when she won't meet my gaze. Her throat moves as she swallows, and she finally looks at me.

Her eyes don't match her smug expression. It's disconcerting, and irritating. I jab a finger at her face. "You've been giving me shit since the start of this week."

"Have I?" Again, her eyes quickly bounce from mine.

A muscle jumps as I flex my jaw. Is she schizophrenic or what? "You better watch it."

"Definitely. I should do that." She turns on her heel and actually whistles as she strides down the hall.

"Psycho," I mutter.

I brush off my pink paisley print dress, glowering when I see the dirt smudge near the hem. Knowing I'm going to be late for gym class, but not caring enough to do anything about it, I stomp to my locker and work at the combination. I grab the folder with enough force to tear it, and withdraw the paper Lexie dropped on my desk. With fury screaming up and down my veins, I unfold the paper. I jerk back, stunned. It's a crudely drawn picture of me.

My eyes are tiny and squinty, my nose is disproportionately long, and my teeth are pointy and crooked. As I study the picture, feeling like I'm in some reality I don't understand, my face goes hot, and my throat turns dry. It's stupid. A stupid drawing made by a stupid girl. And yet, it bothers me. People don't make fun of me, and they especially don't make fun of my looks. Where did this Lexie girl come from, and why does she think she can treat me like she's above me?

Well, she's wrong. She can't.

I crumple up the paper and let it fall from my hand.

"Miss Mathews, are we lost?"

I spin around.

Principal Stenner watches me from the door to the main office. Short with naturally red skin, a small, upturned nose, and unending rolls, he reminds me of a pig with glasses.

"No. I just had to get something from my locker."

His bespectacled eyes move to the floor. "Would it happen to be the piece of paper you dropped?"

Mortified at the thought of anyone knowing such a thing was meant to portray me, I scoop up the paper and throw it in my locker, slamming the door on it. "I have to go to class."

"That would be a good idea, yes."

Without replying, I walk to gym class. I'll get marked for being tardy, unless I can come up with an excuse, like girl problems. That usually works. I shake off the tainted remnants of the ugly drawing, and the weird girl. Calming down, I realize neither are worth being upset over. She's nobody. I won't let her think otherwise by showing that her behavior troubles me.

I won't allow her to be somebody.

Five

Alexis

NAUSEA CHURNS MY STOMACH WHENEVER I think of my actions at school this last week.

It all sounded flawless as I schemed and planned in my room at the facility, long into the nights. Hunger for revenge spurred me on, and I was downright giddy with it. I was going to do all the things to my bullies that they did to me. I have a checklist. I've been working my way down it this past week, but everything I've done lowers my standards of myself, action by action. It was perfect—until my emotions were added.

Melanie had to have seen the picture by now, and yet, whenever I saw her, she acted as if everything was fine. When I saw the cruel drawing of me, I wanted to weep. It makes me doubt myself. Why was I so weak? Why did I fall so effortlessly? What makes her stronger than I was? I tell myself it's because I have a heart, and she has a hole where one should be. And when I sort of on purpose tripped her in the hallway, even though she did the same thing to me last fall, I wanted to hurl. Big time.

My bravado is all an act, one I don't know how long I'll be able to continue. Each time I do something—even just meeting her gaze—I think I'm going to dissolve in a pool of terror, or heave. Still, I won't lie and say it's completely unenjoyable to watch her try to comprehend what's going on. No one purposely gets on her bad side. No one until me.

I look around the entryway as I wait for Nick to appear. We talked on the phone the last two nights. Neither time was for long, but hearing his voice was enough. He talked about a new book he's reading, and I mentioned a funny movie I watched. He told me about a song he liked and asked if I knew it. I said I did. I brought up the Loch Ness monster, and said I'd like to go to Scotland just to look for it. He said he'd go with me, and then it got quiet and awkward, until we both laughed.

Inconsequential details and musings that seemed monumental, because of who they were shared with. I'm not sure what I feel for Nick—I only know he consumes my thoughts, and when I think of him, my stomach tumbles, and my pulse goes crazy. The thought of seeing him makes me feel sick, and the thought of not seeing him makes me feel sicker. It's weird, and I like it—which is also weird.

It's six after eight, and with each passing minute I don't see him, my anxiety rises. I've waited days to see him, and it seems like it's been forever. I want to tell him everything that's transpired over the past week during school, but I can't. I can't tell anyone, not yet. Maybe never.

I realize that is a sign that maybe I shouldn't be doing what I'm doing, and I make a face. I'm the only one who can stick up for me, and I'm doing it, even if it is late. I'll do this, and then, I'll move on. Simple.

I clench my hands to keep my fingernails out of my mouth—a bad habit I'm trying to break—and instead shift from foot to foot. *Come on, Nick. Where are you?*

With it being as early as it is, and a Saturday, it's quiet in here. Gladys, the middle-aged woman who sits at the desk and runs the main phone line and schedules visitations and other such things, eyes me like she wants to tell me to move out of her personal space. I step back from the desk and force my legs to a chair, even though I'm restless. I sit down, and my legs immediately bounce. I want to track down Nick, but I no longer belong here. I'm not allowed to roam the halls. Time that we could be together is being wasted while I wait.

"I'm sure he'll be down any minute," Gladys assures me before turning her attention back to the computer screen.

I nod to myself, since she isn't even looking at me.

Because of his work as a mechanical engineer in a fast-growing company opening factories in multiple states, my dad moved us to this town in August of last year. I was nervous and sad about leaving my friends in Iowa. I was worried about starting a new school my junior year. But I never, ever thought I had to worry about being bullied.

Maybe I should have been mad; maybe I should have fought back, but really, I was stunned—unable to accept that others could be that horrible to another human being, even as I was proof that kind of stuff really does exist. It was happening—to me—someone never popular, but not unpopular either. I was liked by most in my old school, hated by few, and never once a victim of that kind of spite. I was unable to cope with it. Mostly, I just wanted it to stop, however it needed to happen.

I would lie in bed at night, staring at a ceiling I couldn't see. I dreaded the next day, because, without fail, it always came.

Old you, I remind myself. *You're fighting back now.*

With a small stack of files in her arms, Dr. Larson comes around the corner, smiling when she notices me. I know she has regular hours, and I know she is here way beyond them. This place is her life. I wonder how often she sees her husband. Her brown hair is up in a ponytail and she has on black yoga pants and a pink long-sleeved top. She looks like a college student more than a doctor in her thirties.

"Hello, Dr. Larson." A smile stretches my mouth.

"Good morning, Lexie. Nick told me you were spending the day together."

"Yeah." I shift my gaze behind her, looking for a boy who isn't there, and sigh as I settle back in my chair. "If he ever shows up."

She pauses before taking the seat on the other side of the end table from me. Setting the files on her lap, Dr. Larson turns to me. "This is a big step for him. He hasn't left the center since he was brought here."

A feeling of significance washes over me, warm and dangerous. Thinking I'm special to Nick could have negative repercussions, I know, but I feel it anyway. Nick is doing something for me that he hasn't for anyone else. My impatience evaporates. He's probably terrified. I almost want to find him and tell him to forget about it, that he doesn't have to do this. But I'm selfish, and I want him all to myself for the day without the eyes and ears of Live nearby.

"I like him a lot," I admit in a whisper.

Her smile, although kind, has a touch of sorrow in it. "He likes you a lot too."

As I look at my therapist, I realize she knows Nick and me better than we know each other. She knows his hidden truths; she knows mine. I wonder what she thinks of us as individuals, and together. I

43

wonder if that's why she looks sad. And then I don't wonder about anything, because Nick is standing before me.

He got his hair cut since I last saw him. The sides and back are short, with the top left long. The blond is still there, intermeshed with the brown. His marine eyes stand out, searing me with their intensity. With a racing pulse and a plunging stomach, I tear my eyes from his to take in the faded jeans, black tee shirt, and red Converses. A navy blue hooded sweatshirt is tucked under one arm. He looks like every other teenage boy, and nothing like anyone I've ever known.

I carefully stand, much too pleased with his appearance. It's just jeans. He's just a boy. Just a boy who makes my world spin. He doesn't smile when I bring my eyes back to his. I don't smile either. I am acutely aware of his warmth, his scent. His life. It feels like something's changed between us, and I'm not sure when it happened.

"Well, you two have a good day." Humor hangs from her words that are able to sever whatever spell we're under. Dr. Larson gets to her feet. "Don't forget to sign out, Nick."

He nods, looking ill.

We say goodbye to Dr. Larson and Nick signs himself out, his motions slow, like his limbs weigh more than he can bear. I want to help him, but there's nothing for me to do. I wait by the door, watching the struggling boy. Hoping he'll choose me instead of what's safe. He runs a hand through his hair as he faces me, and with grim determination lining his features, Nick walks to me.

"You look really happy about hanging out with me," I grumble, only somewhat kidding.

Nick grimaces and pushes open the door. Once we're outside, standing under the sunny sky, he takes a deep breath, grabs my shoulders, and levels his eyes on me. "Let's try this again, okay?"

Startled by the heat of his hands on me, burning me where they rest, I nod. "Okay."

"Okay." He nods to himself and drops his hands. Inhaling again, he doesn't speak until he's let go of the breath. He locks me in place with a single look. "I'm happy to be hanging out with you today. If I could, I would hang out with you every day, all day."

A grin grabs hold of my lips, and I swipe a chunk of bangs from his eyes. "I like the haircut—and the jeans."

Laughing, he looks around. "Are we walking?"

"No. I drove my dad's second car." I cringe as I lead the way to the boat pretending to be a car. "It's unofficially mine."

The closer we get to it, I become rattled. It's a rose-colored beast that has low miles and cream leather interior. To another generation, the Oldsmobile would be classy. To mine, it's a laughable means of transportation. I was mocked for driving it, made fun of for the kind of car I drove. Any little thing they could find about me to ridicule, they did. The memory hits me hard, taking my breath and any joy I feel, with it.

I make it through the first half of the day without any incidents, and I think, maybe, finally, I'm simply an outcast, someone too unimportant to bother with, and not a target for scorn. Clint Burns quickly rectifies that misconception. I am in the hallway sitting in front of my locker, pretending to read, and actually counting the minutes until lunchtime is over, when he appears with Casey Reed.

"Hey, Lexie." Clint smiles, stopping by my shoes.

My face instantly burns as I glance up, sliding my legs up and back from him.

"Hi," I say softly, wondering why he is talking to me. My gaze moves to where Casey is standing behind him, biting her lip to keep from smiling.

Clint hasn't said more than a few sentences to me since school started in September and it is now close to the end of October. His presence is odd, and fills me with unease. He crouches down beside me and I want to shrink away, not liking how close he is or how nervous I am.

I instinctively fear whatever is about to unfold.

"So, your car? The pink one out front—that's yours, right?"

My eyes flicker in the direction of my dad's parked car outside the school and disquiet goes through me, like a twisting snake. Did something happen to his car? He'll be pissed if it did, and will probably make me ride the bus, or walk, for the remainder of the school year. If something happened to it, I will cry. I will more than cry, but before anything else, I will cry.

"Yeah. It's my dad's." I focus on him. "What about it?"

He puts a hand over his mouth to hide a grin. "What kind of car is it anyway?"

"Clint, stop," Casey says, but a faint smile hovers over her lips.

Casey is one of those people who isn't exactly mean, but she isn't exactly nice either. She's a follower more than anything, going along with the crowd, falling into place with the majority. I think people like her are worse than the bullies, because they're the ones who might *realize that what someone is doing isn't right, and still, they remain silent.*

I glance at her, but she is already looking elsewhere, tapping her foot impatiently. I look at Clint. "It's an Oldsmobile. Why?"

"Oldsmobile. Really?" He looks thoughtfully surprised. "I didn't know they still made those."

I just shrug, not sure what is the point of all this.

"It's awesome, a really cool car."

For a second I think he is trying to be nice, and I open my mouth to say thanks, but then he ruins it by laughing. He gets to his feet and walks away, Casey slapping him on the shoulder as they go. As they round the corner, she says, "That wasn't nice."

I stare after them for a long time, wondering what it is about me that makes it so fun for them to put me down. I hate this school. I hate the kids in it. I hate this town. I hate my life. I hate it all.

"Where did you just go?"

I rub my eyes with hands that shake, counting to ten before I look at Nick. Concern bleeds from his eyes, and his expression is pinched with worry. Anger and pain echo through me, and I push them both away. "I just...bad memory."

He doesn't let me look from him, his magnetic eyes holding me captive. "I get those a lot. Want to talk about it?"

Thinking about the past does no good. Talking about it does the same. I'm already doing what I have to do. If anything, I wish I could forget the months at Enid High School that sucked the life from me. I'm tempted to ask him if he wants to talk about the bad memories that haunt him as well. Instead, I shake my head and point to the car, steeling myself against whatever reaction Nick is going to have. He's different from my classmates, I know he is, but it doesn't make the apprehension dissipate.

"This is your dad's car?" Nick blinks, and a slow smile takes over his face. He runs a hand along the driver's side door.

"Yeah. It's a real beauty, I know."

"It is," he agrees, awe in his voice.

I tilt my head. "What?"

Nick drops his hand and straightens. "What year is it?"

"I don't know. '87 or something."

His eyes shine. "I like it. This is a solid car."

Feeling unusually uplifted by his response, I unlock the doors and get in on the driver's side, but not before telling him, "You're so weird."

MY DAD IS GONE FOR the day visiting a friend who is in town on business, which makes the idea of being at my house fun instead of nerve-wracking. I can just imagine how my dad would react to a boy he doesn't know being at our house. Actually, if he reacted at all, that would be something. I didn't tell him about Nick coming over, figuring by the time he got home, Nick would be back at the center. It's not like he asked what my plans were anyway.

I show Nick around the grayish blue and faux rock-sided house that looks like a cottage. The purple door is my favorite part of the exterior, and probably my dad's least. I don't know that Nick cares all that much about what my house looks like, but I want to share everything I am with him, even my home. Even the sad. Even the bad, in time.

But I think Nick gets it. His eyes shine whenever they meet mine, seeming to say: *Thank you for showing me pieces of you. I want to know them.*

In my cream-colored bedroom with various vintage framed photographs and paintings on the walls, he picks up Rosie from the bed, the pink one-eyed teddy bear, and smiles. "How long have you had this?"

"Since I was five." I'm blushing. I can feel the heat as it erupts in my face. "My mom gave it to me. She's gone now," I hurry to add, for whatever reason.

Nick's eyes darken and he slowly lowers the stuffed animal back to the turquoise bedding. "I'm sorry."

"Oh, it's okay. She didn't...she didn't die." I can't look at him. The only people in Enid who know what I'm about to confess are me, Dr. Larson, and my dad. And now Nick.

If she hadn't left, if my dad hadn't moved us here, if I hadn't gone to this school.

If, and if, and if.

If I hadn't met Nick...

I pick at the hem of my shirt, focusing on the necklaces displayed on hooks on a wall across the room. Gold and silver and glittering, they are artwork without the prison of a frame. "She just...left. Three years ago. It kind of, I don't know, messed up my dad. Things have been different since then."

Fingers touch my cheek, gently lifting my chin until I can't escape Nick's pretty eyes. Not that I want to. "I'm sorry."

I shrug, but inside, my heart aches.

"My parents are still together."

"Wow." I step back from Nick, needing space to put my emotions back in order. "You know how to make a girl feel better."

"But they shouldn't be," he finishes.

"Why?" I whisper, hearing something in his voice that makes me want to wrap my arms around him. Instead, I cross my arms.

"They don't talk, unless they're fighting. My dad has his life, and my mom has hers, and neither seem to involve their kids." His chest lifts as he takes in air, keeping his head turned from me. "But I do have an aunt, and she looks out for me."

With burning eyes, I grab Rosie and press her against Nick's chest.

Brows furrowed, he looks at me.

"Hug Rosie. You'll feel better."

"You're kidding, right?"

I lift my eyebrows.

Sighing, Nick wraps his arms around the teddy bear. He looks resigned, and then, after a moment, he softens, shooting me an embarrassed look before rubbing his cheek against the fake fur. He looks adorable, and sweet, and I want to hug him like he's hugging the bear.

"You feel better, don't you?"

"No," he mumbles, but there is a smile pressing against his lips, ready to push forth.

"Take her," I encourage. I don't know if he wants my raggedy bear; I don't know why I want to give it to him. But I feel like he needs her more than me, at least right now anyway.

"You're so weird," he gently mocks, repeating my earlier words to him.

"And fabulous. Don't forget that part."

"Weird and fabulous." He nods. "That sounds like you."

Nick takes the bear with him as we leave the bedroom.

When we get to the kitchen, I grab the backpack already packed with food and water. "There's a bike trail that goes through the woods along the edge of town. It starts a few blocks from here. Do you feel up to walking it?"

Nick tells me yes, but his tone is less than convincing, and he won't look at me. I want to ask him what's his problem, but I don't. The insecure part of me tells me it's because he doesn't want to be seen with me, and that he doesn't really want to hang out with me, but I don't want to believe that. I convince myself that he's just used to having walls or a fence around him all the time. I lock the door behind us, pocket the key, and head toward the bike path.

It's perfect weather, cool enough for jeans and a sweatshirt, but warm enough to chuck the sweatshirt once you get moving. I focus on the trees as the wind rustles their leaf-filled limbs, but my senses are all on Nick. I feel each time he looks at me. I hear his breaths as he draws air into his lungs. I even smell him when the wind blows just right. I also know he's uncomfortable, even though I don't know what is causing it. His eyes constantly dart around us, and his gait is tense. His shoulders are stiff. It's like he's making sure there isn't anyone around us, but if someone appears, he's ready to bolt. It doesn't exactly give me a boost of confidence.

"I have an older sister," I tell him to fill the edgy silence.

"I have an older brother, and a younger one," he replies.

"What are their names?"

"Brett. He's twenty-one. And Derek. He's thirteen. Brett's in college, and Derek, well, he's a pain more than anything. What about your sister?"

"She's seven years older than me. Her name is Jenna. I have a niece too. Lucy. She's three, and the sweetest thing you can imagine." I smile wistfully.

I miss my sister and niece. They live in Kansas, and visits are rare. The last time I saw them, I was in a hospital. I remember Jenna's quiet pain, how her eyes cried with words she wouldn't say, and how Lucy didn't understand what was happening. She wanted to be held by me, and she wanted to explore the tubes connected to me, crawling over me and tugging at them until her mom took her back. I swallow at the shame that courses through me, wishing I could go back. Wishing I could make different decisions.

Wishes are wastes of time. And yet, we go on wishing, don't we?

Nick's arm brushes against mine as we cross the street, and he flinches.

I grit my teeth, holding in my irritation until we reach the beginning of the path. Then I slam my hands on my hips and glare at him. "Okay, what is your deal? If you really didn't want to be with me today, why didn't you just say it?"

He opens his mouth.

My glower deepens.

"I don't like being out in public. I don't...like being around people," he says after a pause. "I like to be alone."

I throw my arms up in frustration. "Then why did you agree to this?"

Nick steps closer. "But I like to be with you more than I like to be alone, and even though I don't like to be around people, I like to be around you—probably more than I should. How could I say no to being with you, even if it's in a setting I despise?"

"That's messed up," I say, shaking my head, even as a warm glow fills my insides.

"I'm messed up."

"You're not, not really."

He lowers his head, taking my hands in his. Examining them. It feels like fire and ice when we touch. Sparks and frost. "You have no idea, Alexis." Nick threads our fingers together, lifting our hands between us, and looks at me.

"Tell me," I whisper, feeling like I can't breathe. My air is caught somewhere within the magnetic pull of blue-green seas. Who needs to breathe anyway?

"Someday," he promises, and then, with our hands still entwined, he leans forward and kisses me.

His lips are soft, firm. Magic. Tasting of dreams and hope. And grief too. I'm kissing not only Nick, but his soul as well. I feel his heartbeat with my lips. I taste the feelings he has for me, and they are overwhelming. Catastrophically beautiful. The kiss lasts long enough to rearrange everything inside me, to steal my breath, to give it back. To let me know Nick has the power to ruin me. To let me know I'd probably let him.

"I'm sorry," he mutters with his head bowed, closing himself off to me. Tarnishing the perfect moment. "I shouldn't have done that."

I squeeze his fingers still entrusted with mine, and the gesture forces him to look at me. "Yes." I don't waver—not my eyes, not my voice. Whatever this is, I don't want it to end. "You should have."

Nick pulls back, gently unlocking our fingers. He smiles, stealing the sunshine from the sky. "I'll race you to the bridge."

"What?" I blink, trying to understand the words coming from his mouth. My heart is beating in my ears, and everything is muted. Everything but the stunning boy standing in front of me. He shines.

Laughing, Nick nods his head once. I slowly follow the motion with my eyes, seeing the bridge in the distance. The wide, blacktopped path is lined with towering trees; there is a waterfall of green and brown on either side of us. Birds and insects form a melody of nature. I look at Nick, seeing the trees reflected in his eyes. I'm not fast, and my endurance is pitiful, but I'll race Nick. I'll probably lose. I don't care.

I take off without warning, smiling when he protests. He easily catches up to me, his stride and form that of a natural athlete. He doesn't look winded, while I'm gasping for air. I wonder if he played sports before. If he was popular. If he had a girlfriend. I trip over a rock, kicking it out of the path and into the grass.

Nick pulls ahead of me, and I don't mind. This way, I can stare at him without him catching me. He's not one of those boys who is blindingly beautiful. His attractiveness is quiet, something that is slowly revealed the longer you're around him. The best kind. Like a perfect present waiting to be unwrapped.

My lungs are on fire and my legs are already tired. I think we've run a total of four minutes. Two more and I might collapse. Good thing we're almost to the bridge. Nick reaches it first, silently boasting with his crossed arms and twinkling eyes. He's asking for it. I tackle him, wrapping my arms around his waist and pushing against him. Startled, Nick's arms come around me as he staggers back into the rough bark of a monstrous tree. He smells like deodorant and sweat, and my skin is damp with it too.

Neither of us move.

"You make my heart beat so fast it hurts," he whispers against my neck.

I inhale sharply, my own heartbeat rioting inside me. I wasn't expecting that confession, but I'll gladly take it. I tighten my arms and press my forehead to his. It's the same for me, and that he can feel for me how I feel for him, is amazing. Nick is the nightlight when the dark wants to suffocate me with nightmares.

"You looked so sad the first day I saw you. And you were so skinny." Nick's arms tauten. "I just wanted to be invisible, and then I met you, and I desperately wanted to be seen."

"I felt invisible," I admit.

Nick lifts his head, meeting my gaze. "You're not."

I smile. "I see you." *You're all I see.*

Dropping his arms, Nick walks to the path, keeping his back to me. When he doesn't say anything, I move to his side. Our eyes meet briefly, and I feel his gaze all the way to my toes. Each of us looks forward, and we set out on the trail. The quiet is comfortable this time. We don't touch, but it feels like we are. Even the space between us is some kind of concealed connection. It takes over an hour to get to the end, and once there, we find a patch of fairly even grass on which to rest. Nick and I snack on apples, string cheese, and crackers, washing the food down with water. I'm tired, and alive. Happy like I haven't been since the move here last year.

"What do you want to do with your life? When you're older, and have to be responsible. Do you ever think about it?" I untie the sweatshirt from around my waist and wad it up in a misshapen ball before setting it on the ground. I place my head on the makeshift pillow, hands on my stomach, and look up at the tree-obscured sky.

Nick does the same with his sweatshirt, but instead of looking up, he looks at me. It should make me nervous, but it doesn't. I like that he wants to look at me.

"I don't know," he finally answers.

I turn my head and find his face inches from mine. His smile is faint, and it makes my heart twinge. It isn't a happy smile, touching his lips and nothing else. "Meaning?"

"I used to know, but then...things happened...and now, I don't know what I want to do."

"What did you used to want to be?" I ask.

A self-derisive smile taunts his mouth. "I didn't really think too much farther ahead than college, and playing basketball while there. I'm good with numbers, and being an accountant seemed like a solid way to go, but I wasn't for sure."

I'm not surprised about the basketball. "Why can't you still do that? The basketball, and the college?"

He looks at me evenly, and takes a slow breath. "I'm different now."

My focus drops from his eyes to his mouth. I slowly reach out, and trace the upper curve of his lips, moving my fingers down to his angular jaw. His hand covers mine, holding it to his warm skin, and my gaze is pulled back to his.

"I don't think," he says slowly. "That you would have liked me."

I sweep my thumb across his cheek. "I like you now."

Nick's eyes brighten, and he moves forward. My body trembles, anticipation winding my nerve-endings into knots. A chittering sounds above my head, and we both lurch to a sitting position. Laughing at the bushy-tailed squirrel standing less than two feet from where my head recently was, I look at Nick. With a smile on his face, he takes a cracker from the pack and tosses it toward the furry creature. The squirrel chatters at us before darting for the food. It shoves it in its mouth and runs across the bike path and into the wooded area beyond.

I laugh, and look at Nick.

He smiles.

I throw away our garbage and gather up the sweatshirts, handing Nick's to him. I feel shy now that we're going back. We have perfect moments together, but we always have to go back to the imperfect reality.

Nick grabs the backpack and slings it over his shoulders. I want to ask him to stay with me for the afternoon, but I don't want to smother him. Maybe he'll decide one morning with me is enough, and he won't want to see me again. This could be it for us, our one and only unofficial day date. But the earlier kiss says otherwise. Everything about today says I matter to him. I hold on to that, shoving aside my doubts. Doubts are evil.

"Ready?"

I nod.

The sun is high in the sky by now, warming my head and the back of my pasty white neck. Naturally light-skinned, color doesn't ever stay on my skin for long. I squint as I take in the blue skies, and then glance at Nick before heading in the direction from which we came. Six miles in one day is more than I think I've ever walked. I'd walk a hundred more if it meant walking them with Nick. As if he can hear my thoughts, and thinks the same, his fingers thread through mine. My stomach lurches and I take a shallow breath.

I can tell Nick isn't ready to go when we get back to my house, and the knowledge fills me with a light, floating sensation. We make a frozen pepperoni pizza and watch movies, and it seems like we've done this a thousand times. There is little conversation, but it isn't needed. When it's time for Nick to go back to the center, he takes Rosie from where he earlier set her on the kitchen table. His expression tells me to not comment. I don't. I do smile. Big and wide. I might even beam a little.

Six
NICK

SHIFT IN THE SEAT, all the unspoken questions suffocating me. She wants to ask so many, but it isn't her job. Her job is to listen. She knows it. I know it. I count on it. Still, they gather, and they build, and I feel them clawing at my skin. All the questions she doesn't ask.

"I spoke with the staff on duty last night."

Jerking at the sound of her voice as it breaks the silence, I shift my eyes from my lap and meet Dr. Larson's gaze. Concerned eyes watch me under the hazy glow of dimmed lighting. Her signature lemon scent is overpowering in here, and it feels like the thermostat is set to ninety. It's after five on a Monday night, and she should be gone, but here she is. Trying to fix the unfixable.

How does she do it? Every day, dealing with freaks like me. I twist a corner of my shirt between my fingers, immediately releasing it. And I'm one of the milder ones. I wonder what she thinks about my "case". If she thinks I'm as crazy as I do. I study the notepad on her lap. What words does she use to describe me, and my mind, and my history? My reality?

I've told her everything. She knows it all. But right now, I don't want to tell her another word. Dr. Larson shows more interest in me than she should, and I wonder what others would think. She wants to help in ways she cannot. My association with her could be deemed unorthodox, but then, I'm not really here. I'm a phantom patient with a phantom file. Sometimes, I wish I was the phantom, instead of the dead boy I dream about.

"It was different this time. Nick," Dr. Larson prods, folding her hands over the notepad, like she is shielding the concealed words from my laser eyes.

I had a nightmare last night. That in itself is nothing new. But the details...the details were new, and twisted. So twisted. I woke up screaming, soaked with sweat, and terrified. It was bad enough that Live workers came barreling into the room, not knowing what to expect. I didn't know where I was—I thought I was back at his house. I thought it was that night. When the walls cried blood. When my world was filled with it. I was given an oral sedative to help me sleep. I spit it out in the wastebasket once they left.

"You were screaming in your sleep. Do you want to talk about what caused you to scream?"

"I don't—" My mouth is dry, and when I try to swallow, it takes more effort than it should.

"You don't have to tell me, but it might help," she encourages softly.

"There was blood. Everywhere." I choke on the words. I fist my hands, watching as my knuckles bulge.

Quietly jotting down notes, she nods. "Go on."

I see the bedroom walls smeared with it. I see the words written in it. Red. Thick. Smelling of rust. Blood. It's a nightmare, and it's not. Because it happened. I see the boy, lying on his bed. Dead. Eyes open. Staring but unseeing. The sliced wrists. And I see Alexis in his place, with blood seeping from her veins. I see the dream, and I see the truth. And I don't want to see it anymore.

"It was Alexis," I rasp, my eyes burning from staring so hard at the yellow tulip painting directly across the room from me.

Hand paused above the pad of paper, Dr. Larson slowly looks up. "What?"

"In the dream. It's—it's always the boy, but...last night...it was..." I trail off, unable to repeat it.

"Lexie Hennessy," she supplies.

I nod as the burning in my eyes turns to stinging, because there are tears, and they want to fall. I blink and they do, noiselessly sliding down my cheeks. *It was a dream*, I tell myself. A dream that felt as real as this moment. What if the dream was real, and this is really the dream? What then?

"Why do you think that is?" she asks after a time.

"I don't know." It's a lie.

My legs bounce and I look all around the room to keep from looking at the doctor. I do know why. It's because I care for her. Because I'm scared. Because I deserve nothing good, and I especially don't deserve her. Because I'm worried I'll lose her before I really have her. Because I wonder, if she really knew who I am, if she'd want me. Because I know she wouldn't.

"You two seem to be getting close."

"Yes. No. Maybe." Sweat breaks out on my skin. "Yes."

Dr. Larson straightens in her seat. "And that worries you."

"Yes," I whisper, pushing my palms against my knees to steady the shaking.

"You've been here for a year now, Nick, closed off to most family and friends." She leans forward, her hands clasped before her. "There's nothing wrong with reaching out to someone; there's nothing wrong with allowing them to reach back. In fact, I think this is good, very good."

Her words are steady, but I sense it all the same. Something off. A pause.

Hesitation.

I stare at her intently, to the point where Dr. Larson looks away. "It won't end well, will it?"

She inhales slowly, and the smile she gives me is too bright. "You're both great kids who've had to deal with things most don't. I have every faith in each of you, and your futures."

That wasn't an answer. I would have been amazed if she had given a direct one. I can't count how many times I've wanted to ask Dr. Larson what she's doing here, why she would choose to surround herself with mentally unsound kids who, more times than not, are incurable. I want to ask her why she won't give up on them, on me.

We might get better for a while, but how long does it last? It always comes back to the past, to that moment, or a collection of moments, that altered our world. There's no escape from ourselves, from our minds.

I will never not know what I have done.

"I'm late for kitchen duties," I mumble, standing.

My name on her lips stops me at the door. I wait with my back to her. "Try to remember that it was only a dream."

I open the door. "But that's just it—it wasn't." I step through the doorway and close the door behind me.

The hours in the kitchen go by in a blurred whirl, flashes of people and actions that don't register for more than an instant before another takes their place. Like every night, I take a shower after I'm done in the kitchen. I grab my latest library book before settling in on the bed to read until I fall asleep. It's funny how much I read now compared to how much I didn't before I came here. I had better things to do. I feel my face contort as something coils in my chest.

I don't own any books. Everything I read is borrowed, and must be returned.

I wonder if that's what happiness is like.

From what I've seen, at home and here, it seems like it has to be.

I study the book in my hands. It's a new one, and I've only read the first two pages. In this story, the main character, a girl, has been resurrected from the dead with science. That's as much as I know, but I think I can guess the rest. She's used as a weapon for evil, but only until she begins to remember who she Is. At least, that's how my version would go. Could be she never remembers. Could be she's killed, again, and how ironic is that? To be given life again and have it effortlessly taken back. Like my books. Like happiness. Borrowed.

As if they know me better than I know myself, my hands set aside the book and grab Rosie the pink teddy bear. I stare at the worn stuffed animal, feeling kinship with it. It's important to Alexis, and since she gave it to me, that makes me important too. I wish Alexis was here in its place. I wish I was brave enough to leave here for good.

I put the bear on the bed near my legs and drop my face to my hands. There will be no reading tonight. There will be me, and my maudlin thoughts, and maybe, if I'm lucky, there will be no dreams of Alexis dying.

Seven

Melanie

I LOOK AT JOCELYN AND Casey, being extra careful to not look at Lexie. It doesn't matter—I can feel her freaky presence like it's some kind of plague breathing beside me. "So? What are we going to write about?"

Jocelyn shakes her head, the scent of expensive perfume filling the vicinity as she does. "Don't look at me. I hate writing. I'm doing as little as possible on this project."

"As if that's anything new," I snap. I saw her talking to Jeff this morning. She was standing too close, smiling too wide, laughing too loud. I wanted to claw out her eyes. The urge hasn't lessened all that much.

Her gaze narrows on me. "Something bothering you, Mel?"

Just your face.

"We have to be way behind everyone else." Casey looks around the classroom split into small groups, gnawing on her lower lip with her teeth. Her nude-toned top completely washes out her pale complexion, and seeing that immediately after Jocelyn and Jeff, put me in a better mood.

"All the more reason to decide on what to write about, and get writing." Realizing my jaw is clenched, I work at loosening it.

"How about a story about shopping? That would be fun, right?" Casey suggests, her enthusiasm fading as I turn my attention to her. She shrinks in her seat.

"That's lame," Jocelyn announces.

"We could write about the hideous zit taking over your chin," Lexie says to me in a bored tone.

Jocelyn snorts, clapping a hand over her mouth to keep the laughter contained.

My mouth drops open, even as my fingers reach up to cover the blemish. If I had bullets for eyes, she'd be dead.

Looking disinterested in my rage, she focuses on Jocelyn. "Why are you laughing? Your lipstick makes you look like a clown."

Jocelyn's eyes widen, and I fight a smile.

Lexie looks at Casey, who freezes in her chair with a tiny squeak.

"Too easy," Lexie mumbles.

I slap a palm against my desk, and Casey jumps. Leaning toward the short-haired girl with an obvious death sentence, I hiss, "I don't know who you think you are, but you are not allowed to speak to me the way you are."

"Really?" Her blue eyes flash and she straightens in her seat. "Do you think you control everything and everyone around you? Because I can talk to you however I want, just like you talk to me and everyone else however you want."

The bell sounds as she gets to her feet. She drops a handful of papers on her desk and leaves. An unusual feeling shrieks through me at the sight of them, and I practically dive for the papers, thinking it's another hideous drawing of me, or worse, multiple ones. Ignoring the looks from my friends, I glance down. Relief streams through me, as potent as the other unnamable emotion I had when I saw the papers. It's just words.

"What is it?" Jocelyn demands, reaching out a hand.

"She started the project," I say slowly, my eyes skimming along the first page before moving to the next. Jocelyn grabs the pages from me as I read them.

"About what?" Casey works at putting the desks back in their proper places.

"A girl tries to kill herself and ends up in a mental institution," I tell her, more disturbed by the words than I understand.

I look up, and find both of my friends staring at me.

"She's a total nut job," Jocelyn says with a shudder. Her eyes go back to the piece of paper she's holding, her expression riveted as she reads.

"Did you ladies decide you'd like to have two English classes today?" Mr. Walters asks with a pleasant smile from the front of the room.

"Oh. No," Casey supplies.

His smile disappears. "Then I suggest you leave."

Realizing I'm the only one still seated, I get to my feet and walk up the aisle.

"Melanie," Mr. Walters calls.

I shift my gaze from the last page I hold in my hands to my teacher.

"Your desk."

With an eye roll as I turn my back on Mr. Walters, I quickly backtrack and shove my desk in line with the rest. Jocelyn and Casey wait for me at the door, and I wordlessly take the pages from Jocelyn's hands. When she opens her mouth to protest, I silence her with a cutting look. I'm keeping the papers. I'm dealing with Lexie. I'm not letting Jocelyn have anything—not the papers, and not Jeff.

It's all there in my look. She understands, flipping her hair over her shoulder and strolling toward her next class. She understands, but she doesn't accept it.

Jocelyn and I may end up enemies yet.

After suffering through my art class, I make a beeline for the girls' restroom. First checking that it's empty, I then go to the mirror and study my face. To be popular, you don't necessarily have to be good-looking, although that definitely helps. What you have to have, more than anything, is confidence. If anyone knew I was in here, self-conscious about a pimple, my social status would take a dive. Because when you're popular, even if something upsets you, you have to act like it doesn't.

Turning my face side to side, I decide the zit really isn't that noticeable. I'm letting Lexie get to me. An unpopular girl who has nothing going for her. Nothing to make her even the smallest bit interesting. Why am I making her more intriguing than she is? That isn't acceptable. I wipe the scowl from my face, stiffen my spine, and stride from the restroom, my poise restored.

But when I meet up with Jeff, I swear he's staring at my chin the whole time. I try to cover it up with my hands, becoming flustered the longer we talk, to the point where I flee the conversation in the middle of asking him to come to my party in three weeks. This isn't me. I don't like feeling this way. And when I walk by Lexie in the hall before lunch, unease trickles through me at the thought of what she might do or say. I avert my eyes; I hurry my steps. As if I can outrun her. As if I can make her not exist. If only.

Finally, as I make my way to the lunchroom with paranoia as my companion, I realize what I felt when I saw the papers: anxiety.

Eight

Alexis

IT HAPPENS SLOWLY.

A smile from someone who wouldn't look at me last fall.

Being included in conversation where I was previously excluded.

Noticed when I used to be invisible.

Should I be happy about it?

Should I welcome the attention?

I'm not, and I don't.

Because I was here, in this school, just a few short months ago, and I was never given a chance. I meant so little that no one even remembers me. Cut off my hair and I'm unrecognizable? Is that how it works? No. They never saw me, and so, they can't see who I am now. Why should I give them a chance?

How have I changed since then? I'm bitter, to be sure. Is that what they see? Is that what makes me remarkable to them? A jaded girl with an immovable chip on her shoulder. Maybe I remind them of themselves now. I unclench my jaw and stare at the white ceiling of my bedroom. Being at that school makes me scream on the inside every second that I'm there, and every second feels like a lifetime. I want to let it loose on all of them. I want to tear down the school, and all the kids inside it. I also want to hide, and never step foot inside it again.

I want to cry.

And I want to forget.

Forcing my thoughts from the turmoil of my mind, I get up from the bed and move to the window. I push back the curtain that matches my turquoise bedding, and stare out at the dark blue sky as it fades to black. Lights from houses and businesses join the stars, making Enid bright, and seemingly beautiful. I can't think of a single person here who was kind to me, and that's sad.

I look in the direction of Live, and wonder what Nick's doing at this very moment. When I want to obliterate everything from my mind, I think of him, and it all becomes bearable. His careful smile, the sound of his surprised laughter. How his eyes shine when he looks at me. I focus on that now, and calmness descends.

My path to get to Nick has been wretched, but all the same, I wouldn't know him if things had gone good instead of bad. I guess I should thank my old self for trying to kill herself.

I move from the window and turn off the softly playing music at the sound of my dad's voice on the other side of my bedroom door. I hate to tell him, but I prefer the sound of Sia's voice to his. I walk across the room and open the door. My father's pepper and soap scent fills the hallway as his large form overtakes the doorway to my room. The faint light in the hallway catches his bare scalp, making the skin gleam. After a nearly silent meal of burgers and fries from a fast food restaurant, I escaped to my room. I spend a lot of time in my room.

"What's up?" I ask in a voice more cheerful than I feel. It's pretend, like we pretend everything is okay.

My dad looks at me and away, offering the cordless phone. "It's for you."

I assume it's Jenna, who calls me almost every week. It has to be her, or Nick. My stomach flutters. Either possibility makes me happy, but the thought of it being Nick makes my pulse spin.

"A boy. Nick." He forces his gaze back to me. "Who's Nick?"

Fireworks explode in my chest and I grab the phone. "Uh, just a boy. From the center."

His expression tightens. "Do you think it's wise to continue to be in contact with kids from there?"

"Why? What's wrong with the kids from there?" Yes, there is a mocking quality to my tone. No, I don't care that it is there. As recently as a week or so ago, I was a kid from there.

"You're back in school. Why aren't you hanging out with your friends from there?"

I almost laugh. We both know I don't have any. "There are just too many to choose from, Dad, so I choose none. I wouldn't want to make any of them jealous. That would be mean."

Lips thinning, he studies me, and then he wordlessly walks down the hallway.

It takes me a moment to drag my eyes from the spot where I last saw him. If I had succeeded—if I wasn't here, would anything be all that different for him, I wonder. My father and I, we live in two different worlds, side by side. It takes me another moment to remember Nick is waiting on the other end of the phone line. Taking a deep breath, I close my door as I bring the receiver to my face. It's been three days since I've seen Nick, and waiting one more seems like an eternity. Before I hear him talk, I'm smiling.

"Hello, Nick."

"Hello, Alexis." His voice is warm, missed.

I glance at the alarm clock on my nightstand. It's ten to eight. "You're cutting it close, aren't you? No phone calls after eight."

"It took me a considerably long time to work up the courage to call."

His honesty enamors me to him more. As if he needed help. "Why do you need courage to call me?"

Nick doesn't answer for a long time, and when he speaks, I struggle to breathe. "Because I want to be fearless for you, and that scares me."

I exhale loudly. He's stolen all words but one from my thoughts. "Nick."

"I'm just a boy, huh?" he quickly asks, telling me he wants to move on from his confession. There is a self-deprecating smile somewhere in there.

I freeze, and then fall onto my back on the bed. "You heard all that?"

"I did. I especially enjoyed the large dose of sarcasm directed at your father."

Sighing, I close my eyes. "My dad is clueless."

Nick laughs softly. "What do you expect when you never really mean what you say? That would confuse anyone."

"I mean what I say. Usually." Opening my eyes, I silently count to ten, pulling forth any shard of mettle I can find before saying my next words. If he's going to be frank with me, he deserves the same from me. "And you're not just a boy. You're *the* boy."

A sharp intake of air is the only reply I receive.

Feeling nervous, I tug at a short lock of hair. Did I say too much? Did I say it too soon?

"Say something," I demand, listening to the pounding of my heart. Its beat is too hard, and too loud.

"I want to be that boy," Nick finally says. His tone is careful, subdued. Possibly regrettable, like he's telling me that in spite of wanting nothing more than to be that boy, he cannot.

Be that boy then, I silently urge.

I sit up, holding the phone hard against my ear. There is a framed photograph of me, my dad, Jenna, and my mom on my dresser. I blink at the image. My hair is long and wavy around my shoulders. The smile on my face is the kind I haven't felt the need to express in a long, long time. Jenna and my dad are on either side of me, with Mom on the other side of Jenna. I'm hit with three pairs of similar blue eyes, happy and crinkling at the corners. Mom's eyes are brown. That seems significant, for some reason. One more way she was separate from us.

"Do you ever have bad dreams?" Nick asks quietly.

"Sometimes, I think I'm living them," I admit.

I was ten in the picture, and it was before things went bad. Before I knew they were bad anyway. We're sitting on the steps to the porch of the dark blue house we lived in until Mom left. It is in that house that I had all of my sister Jenna, before she moved to begin her own life. It is in that house that I had what I was allowed of my mom, before she decided we weren't enough. It is in that house that I had my father, before he lost his wife and turned into an unresponsive stone. In that moment, at that house, in that picture, we were a family.

Nick takes a shuddering breath. "Me too. All the time."

Tearing my eyes from the captured memory, I pick at the blue-green bedding that looks like Nick's eye color. It helps me sleep at night, imagining I'm adrift in the depths of his ocean eyes. "What's the matter, Nick?"

"I had a dream about you."

I frown at the caution covering his words, my hand stilling. "I can tell it was an awesome one."

"No." Nick sighs. A tapping sound starts, like his fingertips are drumming against something. Probably the wall next to the phone. "It was scary as hell. It just—I just wanted to hear your voice quick. That's why I called."

"Okay. But that's not why you sound the way you do." When he says nothing, I press, "What happened in the dream?"

"Alexis." Pain echoes from my name.

"Nick."

"I don't want to say."

"Say it anyway."

Time ticks off the clock. I watch it pass, seeing the numbers get closer and closer to eight. When Nick finally speaks again, his voice is hollow. All the life is gone from it.

"You died."

THE GYMNASIUM IS PACKED WITH hot, sweating bodies. An array of scents permeate the air, more so bad than good. I linger off to the side, watching the bleachers fill. The noise level is excruciating to anyone with sensitive ears. It's an end of the year pep rally, and an excuse to miss the last class of the day.

I remember standing here last November for a guest speaker, near the doorway, alone, seeing masses of students and not having a single one to sit beside. I remember Casey stopping beside me, and telling me I should find a seat. I remember telling her I had no one to sit with. I remember her walking away like I never spoke. I remember sitting by myself in a room full of people.

You died.

The words echo through me, more powerful than they should be, bringing chills and apprehension with them. I don't know why they bother me as much as they do—it isn't like I didn't try to achieve the very thing Nick dreamed. Am I not writing the story of my almost demise even now, with the purpose of having it read aloud under the guise of an assignment to an entire classroom? The thing that makes it that much better is the fact that Melanie, Jocelyn, and Casey will have to read it. They are the villains, and they will tell their own tale. It might be sick, but at the same time, it feels good. Really good. Maybe too good.

Not that any of them would have cared if I had died.

And maybe I did die, in a way. Because that girl who lived through six months of hell in this school—that girl vanished.

I pull back my shoulders and stride toward the bleachers, finding a spot behind Melanie and her sidekicks. I swear she stiffens when I walk past, and a part of me wants to smile. Another part of me, though, tiny and almost nonexistent, feels guilt that I'm making someone suffer like I did. Even if she deserves it. Even if she'll bounce right back whereas I did not. I had no one here, and I had no one at home. I had no one at all.

You have Nick now.

Do I? I'm not sure.

"H-hi," a small voice greets.

I turn my head and meet a pair of wide brown eyes. Mistrust tells me to be careful. This school is full of vipers camouflaged with smiles. I must always wear my armor. "Hi."

The girl is frail-looking with fine brown hair and small red lips. She's dressed in a pale pink top and jeans that seem a size too big. "You're, um...you're Alexis Hennessy. Lexie," she amends.

"I am." I wait for her to say more.

Her head bobs as she looks around the gymnasium. Forcing her gaze back to mine, the girl smiles. It looks like it's difficult. "I'm Anna. Anna Robertson."

I nod and look toward the center of the floor where the principal and other staff are forming. She slides closer, and I go still, wondering why she introduced herself, and why she's talking to me. What is she up to? Is this some trick of Melanie's? Did she tell Anna to harass me somehow?

I glare at the back of Melanie's silky brown head, loathing her like I've never loathed another. I didn't think it was possible to feel this way toward another human being. I want her to feel like I did. I want her hopeless, and tormented, and sobbing. I want her broken.

"M-my dad..."

My eyes snap to Anna and she goes quiet. She blinks and fiddles with her wavy hair, looking conflicted. Her gaze darts to mine and away, her mouth opening and closing. The whole thing is odd, and I instinctively know her interaction with me has nothing to do with Melanie. Anna is struggling to tell me something. You can't fake this kind of awkwardness.

"What about your dad?" I don't look from her.

When Anna seems like she's finally about to speak, the principal's voice overtakes the room with the help of a microphone. I stare at the girl, watching as she shrinks. She won't look at me. As the principal talks about stuff I have no interest in, curiosity pulls my gaze to her, again and again. Her lips are pressed together to keep her words locked inside, and she looks straight ahead.

"Is he into Cosplay or what?" I try to joke. "What's the big confession?"

Anna just shakes her head, obviously not finding me funny. Really, it wasn't all that funny of a comment.

I spend the next thirty minutes listening to puns equally as bad as mine, and well-intended encouragement from various adults who, outside of class, seem mostly indifferent to their students. My back and bottom are sore from the hard bleacher, and I just want to get out of here. There are too many kids, and only a few of them I can stand. I have my weekly appointment with Dr. Larson after school, and that means I get to see Nick, however briefly. A fluttering sensation takes over my stomach, and I hide a smile as I look at the teachers.

Standing near one of the teachers is the school guidance counselor. My jaw tautens. I went to her, this past winter. I told her what was happening. I told her about the kids picking on me, and the comments, and the drawing. She brushed it all aside like I made it up. I was the interloper, the outcast. The one who didn't belong. Why would she believe me over the kids she's known for years?

Maybe everyone in this school is so used to how messed up things are that they think it's normal. It's not normal to belittle others. It's not normal to think you're better than everyone else. It's not normal to think it's okay to put others down. It's not normal to want others to feel bad so you can feel good. Nothing about this place is normal.

Half-hearted applause breaks out as the last of the speeches ends, and then it's trampling feet and boisterous voices as the gym clears out. Kids bump into one another and push each other toward the gymnasium doors, anxious to leave the school and get to their lives.

Melanie stands with Casey and Jocelyn in the middle of the chaos, unmoving, like the world knows to move for them. It appears they're right. Everyone forms a path around them. Clothed in vibrant shades of fashionable garments, and with their pretty features, they stand out. They're chatting about something truly fascinating, I'm sure, like their favorite nail polish color, or the last boy they made out with.

"Nice jacket," I say to Melanie as I walk by.

I catch the way she glances down and unconsciously grabs the corners of the jean jacket before realizing what she's doing. I let out a soundless breath, ignoring the way my pulse jumps around like it has no idea if it should go fast or slow. Shame flashes through me, and I shove it back. I'm not doing anything to her she didn't already do to me.

For me, that was the worst part of the bullying; I was never sure if they were being nice, or making fun of me. I quickly learned it was the latter, every time. It made me doubt everything. It's a terrible feeling to lose your sense of self. When that's gone, what's left?

Anna is ahead of me in the hallway. It's strange that until today, I had no idea she existed.

I quicken my pace until it matches hers. "Hey."

She jumps at the sound of my voice. "You scared me," she mumbles, sweeping hair behind her ear.

"You had something to tell me—about your dad," I remind her.

She reaches a locker and fiddles with the combination, keeping her eyes hidden. "Um...no. Never—never mind."

"You sought me out, Anna." I pause as her hands still. "What is it?"

Grabbing a purple backpack, she closes the locker door and turns to face me. Kids bump and jostle us as they hurry from the school. I hold her gaze, refusing to break eye contact. Maybe what she wanted to tell me is completely insignificant, but then, maybe it isn't.

"I remember you," she says quietly. "From before."

I exhale deeply.

"What was it like?"

I frown, having no idea what she is talking about.

Her voice is soft and eerie as she finishes with, "To almost die."

Brown eyes stare into me, and it makes me uncomfortable.

"Horrible," I answer truthfully.

Anna blinks, looking down. "My dad is an EMT. He was...he was one of the responders. He was in the ambulance that took you to the hospital."

A flash of a hazy memory hits me. A man with glasses and brown hair in the ambulance, talking to me as he hooked me up to things.

Looking stricken. He said, "I have a daughter your age. Anna Robertson. Do you know her?"

I didn't know her.

I focus on Anna.

She looks back with her wide eyes, stamping herself into my consciousness.

"Are you picked on, Anna?"

Anna holds her backpack close to her chest. "Oh. I don't know." Her smile is nervous. "Maybe a little—but it doesn't bother me."

She's lying. I was invisible, and yet, she was too. Still is. I turn to go to my locker without another word.

Nine
NICK

SHE SMILES. SHYLY. SWEETLY.

Alexis smiles for me.

My nerves spark.

The room dims.

Alexis glows, holding all the light in the library.

I haven't seen her since last Saturday. Too many breaths and instances and lost chances to count.

Splayed out on the table are textbooks and notebooks—my independent studies. I've been self-educating since I came here. It's all just numbers and words I learn to pass the online tests. None of it really sticks. Not like Alexis. Her, I can't get out of my head or heart. I don't want to even try.

"I've never been to prom—or homecoming," she admits quietly as she traces the letters on the cover of the book she had in her hand when she showed up.

She brought me a book about a half-man, half-alien on a quest to save his kidnapped friend. Alexis went to a bookstore, she looked for a book, for me, and she picked one out, for me. Alexis gave me a gift. The book I'll sleep with, along with Rosie. Yes, I am aware how that sounds. Not really manly, maybe even slightly obsessed. I am completely uncaring.

"Why not?" I study her pale hand as it moves, noting the short, unpolished nails. She likes to chew on them when she's nervous.

She rolls her eyes. "I don't know; I guess because it works better when someone asks you."

I lean closer, bringing my face next to her neck. I see her pulse flutter. I watch her throat move as she swallows. "I would have asked you," I whisper. Now, this me, this person would have.

Alexis turns her head slightly, bringing our mouths inches from one another's. Her eyes seem a brighter blue at this proximity, but I catch flecks of silver and green in them too. "I would have said no."

I frown at her, and she laughs as I sit back. "What? Why?"

Shrugging, Alexis turns toward me in her chair, and our knees touch. She stares into my eyes, and I am centered. Everything I've been, anything that hurts; it all fades. "I can tell that if you and I were in school together, you would be in a different social setting than me."

"Only when I was stupider," I say fervently.

Alexis laughs once more. I love the sound of her laughter. It's light, and free. It sounds how I feel when I'm with her.

"Did you do those things?" Her knees are encased by mine, but her eyes are no longer set on me. They're on the book. "Go to prom and homecoming and whatever else?"

"Yes." My hands clench at my sides, and my body heats up.

Alexis glances up briefly. "Are you a junior like me?"

"Senior." My breaths come faster.

"When will you turn eighteen?"

The questions are harmless, but each one peels at a layer of the new me, leaving the old me behind. "July 1st."

"And then?" Alexis stills. "Will you be here until you can't?"

"I don't know," I reply tightly.

How do I integrate back into a world I no longer know? A world I dislike. How do I go back to that house, to parents who don't talk, and inescapable guilt and grief? How do I do that? My aunt would tell me slowly, and carefully, and without any expectations. Just thinking about it all makes my stomach sick.

"I'll make you a cake," she promises, giving me a sidelong look as she changes the subject. "What's your favorite kind?"

"Whatever kind you make."

With a smile on her face, she leans toward me. Alexis touches my hair. Tingles race down my scalp. "What if it tastes like dirt?"

My voice is hoarse when I tell her, "I'll eat it anyway."

"It could be a really gross dirt-tasting cake," she warns. "You don't know."

"Can you let me know beforehand? So I'm prepared."

Alexis drops her fingers, and I feel the absence of them like a void. "I'm not sure. We'll see. It's more fun if you don't know." She adds, "My mom never baked. All of our birthday cakes were ice cream ones, or store bought. I guess I should learn how to make a cake."

"If you ever want to get a husband, you should," I agree with an innocent look.

Alexis grins, shoving my shoulder. "Or I'll just find a husband who can cook."

"Good luck," I say solemnly.

Making a face, she tells me, "I have to go. My appointment is in about five minutes."

Alexis stands, holding out her hands to me. When I put mine in hers, she helps me to my feet. If she tips her head back, and I lower mine, our lips will meet. I want to tell her I'll take her to prom next year. And homecoming. And anything else she's never had a chance to do. But I keep the words unspoken, because I don't want to promise something I can't give her.

"There's a boy doing your kitchen duties now. He's a poor replacement for you." I'm stalling because I don't want her to go. I'm not ready.

"Oh?" Her eyes twinkle. "Why is that?"

"Well, for one thing, he smells like sausage. Always. No matter if sausage hasn't been on the menu in days. And he has gas, constantly, from both ends."

Alexis' lips twitch. "He sounds hideous."

I school my features to graveness. "I'm about to request a face mask from Manny."

"That wouldn't look odd at all."

"This is the place for oddities."

"True," she says.

As if on cue, a boy three tables over swears viciously and loudly as his chair topples over, taking him with it. He then proceeds to kick and punch the table, as if it's the table's fault that he fell. A man and woman show up, and he's gone. The usual. We look at each other as if nothing out of the ordinary occurred, because in this setting, it didn't.

"You have to admit that it's rarely dull at Live," I tell her. My pulse is faster than it should be, but I smile around the inward discord. Each time I see a breakdown, I think of how likely it is for me to have another.

"Again, true." She tries to smile too, but it falls flat. Maybe Alexis thinks the same for herself. We're all so close to breaking back open our wounds. Do they ever fully heal?

I step nearer, until we're toe to toe. I lower my voice as I tell her, "It helps to pretend it isn't real."

In a whisper, she replies, "I know."

"But it is real. It's always real. You can't forget that it's real." I sound manic, like a ghost from the world of the old me has invaded my tone and wants to force the truth of my words onto the earth. A ghost I see in my dreams, and behind my eyes when I close them. Every day I see him.

Alexis frowns, her eyes seeing more into me than I'm sure I like. She brushes fingers across my furrowed brow, and as if she has an enchanted touch, it instantly smooths. Her hands cup my jaw. "Stay with me, Nick."

A broken sound leaves me, small and close to inaudible. She knows. She knows I'm cracked. I try to hide it, but sometimes, it leaks out. If she knew…if she knew it all, she would hate me. All the bits and pieces of my broken mind.

"Nick."

"Yes." I nod, unable to look at her. I steal air into my lungs, and give it back. Until the library comes into focus, and I can look at Alexis.

With moves faster than I can gauge, she's holding me. Tightly. Fiercely. The side of her face is pressed to my chest, and I close my eyes and rest my chin on the crown of her head, wrapping my arms around her small form. She's tiny, but her soul is mighty. Holding her, having her hold me, brings me back to where I need to be. I inhale slowly, and exhale deeply.

"The past is behind you." The words sound nice, but they're false.

"The past is all around me," I counter softly.

"I hate the past," she says in a wobbly voice.

Without opening my eyes, I hold her closer. Peaches and warmth invade my senses, give me peace. "It brought you to me. It can't be entirely bad."

Alexis takes a deep pull of air, her body concaving as she does. "I'll be back next week," she vows, stepping back from me.

I remember when she came here. Her hair was short and uneven around her scalp. Her eyes were unseeing. Alexis was gaunt in appearance, and there were dark crescents beneath her eyes. For days, she was in a fog of her own making. I remember the charge when our eyes met for the first time, when she finally noticed me. I only had to run into her to get her to see me. I remember wanting to smile for the first time in a long time when she looked at me. I remember thinking everything would be different from that day on.

I want to protect her from whatever brought her here, but more than that, I want to protect her from me.

So I don't say all the things I want. I don't tell her I want to see her this weekend. I don't tell her how pretty she is. I don't tell her that she makes me want to be brave enough to step from this building and never return. I especially don't tell her I had another bad dream about her.

A tiny smile flutters across her lips. "Enjoy the book."

I'll worship that book.

Ten

Alexis

THERE IS A CHALKBOARD ON the wall in the kitchen. We've had it for years; through all the moves and other changes, it's remained. My mom got it from a decorative store. She was beaming when she came home with it. She'd leave messages on it for me, and once in a while, for my dad. Sometimes it would be encouraging words, a note, or a task she wanted one of us to complete.

I'm surprised my dad didn't get rid of it, like he did most of the possessions my mom didn't take with her. Like me. I swallow, and it hurts my throat. She forgot to take me with her.

More than that, I'm surprised he hung it up. It's blank. It's been blank for years. The last message placed on it with pink chalk, though erased, lingers faintly. Like ghost writing. It reads: *Don't forget your doctor appointment at 3:45 on Monday the 17th.* So mundane. It doesn't seem right that such a nonsensical reminder should be the only residual written proof that I ever had a mom. A message not even to me, but to my father.

I eat my cereal before school on Friday, staring at the black board. After washing the bowl and spoon and setting them in the strainer to dry, my attention goes back to the chalkboard. The one question prominent in my mind for months after my mom left comes back with a vengeance. It's been three years, and it feels like she left yesterday. I walk to the board, grabbing a broken piece of yellow chalk. It digs into my palm, and I lessen my grip. Breathing fast, my heart thundering out a forceful beat, I raise my shaking hand. If my eyes could, they would burn a hole right through the board and directly into my mom, wherever she is.

With scrawling, ungraceful movements, words form. A question. A demand directed at Peggy Hennessy. She'll never read it. She'll never answer it. But I ask it anyway.

How could you leave us?

I obliterate her pale words with my own, replacing pink with yellow. Tears burn my eyes, but still, I feel satisfaction in covering up her unimportant words with ones that matter. Anger. I feel that too. Even now. Always. I drop the chalk, brush hair from my forehead with fingers that yet tremble, and grab my backpack. It's time for school.

I walk the five blocks it takes to get to the stone building. The air is damp and chilly, sucking the heat from my body through the red sweatshirt and jeans covering me. At my old school, I dressed up once in a while. Nothing overly stylish, but sometimes I'd wear a skirt or a dress. I haven't felt like looking nice in too long.

My lips press together. Just one more piece of myself I haven't gotten back since I came here. I tell myself to get it back, vowing next week to wear the dressiest articles of clothing I can find in my closest. If anyone says anything, I'll punch them in the face. I smile. Okay, I probably won't do that.

At my old school, I had friends. I talk to them on the phone every so often, but it's not the same. I don't see them; they are in another state. They talk about people and events that no longer pertain to my life. I don't know what to talk about. I don't think my suicide attempt is really the way to go. Not exactly an icebreaker. We drift apart as time goes on, more and more.

My pulse picks up as the school comes into view, and my stomach flips. It's pale stone that is wide and long, and fairly unattractive in appearance. My reaction to seeing the building hasn't changed. This place is the epitome of my definition of perdition. No one likes to step inside the walls of their inevitable suffering, whether present or past. *Just a little over two more weeks*, I tell myself. Less than fifteen days, and then I don't know what will happen. But I won't be coming back to this school next year. I refuse.

It used to bother me, walking into this building, and not having a single place where I belonged.

Now, I roll back my shoulders and deal with it. Life isn't soft. It isn't sweet. It's hard, and in order to survive it, you have to be hard too. It's sad, and it sucks, and I guess I should be grateful that I learned it by the age of sixteen.

When I think of how Nick would react to everything going on with Melanie and her friends, I almost end it. Almost. He would never stoop to their level, or the one where I currently reside, which is just a shade above them. To get back at my bullies, I have to think like them. Treat them as they treat others.

Retribution is a black taint on my world, something I am not proud of, but consider necessary. I am split in two. There is the me when I'm not at school, and there is the other me—the hard, unrelenting, vengeful one. The spiteful one.

I don't think of Nick when I'm at school. Or, at least, I try not to. He's separate from this. He's my hope, and what I look forward to day after day. This school is my crux, the thing I endure until I am released from its talons. Until I can release myself from this pit I have to learn to scale.

I also think Nick might be able to understand. He had to have gone through something similar to be at the facility, right? Something inside his head couldn't deal with something in his life, and I wonder what it was. I want him to tell me, but I haven't told him my story either.

Of course, immediately upon entering the school, I see one of Melanie's friends. Jocelyn Rodriguez. What can I say about Jocelyn? 'Beauty is only skin deep' is a statement that explains her perfectly. She smiles evilly, and her eyes show the darkness of her soul. She's the kind of person who would watch a kitten die, and not feel anguished, or even the smallest amount of sadness. She'd probably be indifferent, above all. She's the silent spectator who enjoys the outpour of decay from others' minds.

Jocelyn looks at me, but she doesn't really see me. I am one of many unimportant masses who happen to rotate around her world. She is blind to that which does not interest her. I would have been glad, months ago, but not now. One day in the hallway, she told me the lunch I brought from home looked like shit. I didn't say anything. I gathered up my things and got away from her as fast as I could. I ran. My body temperature rises at the recollection. *No more running.*

As I watch, she dabs her index finger at the corner of her red mouth, like a vampire removing a drop of blood, and winks at Jeff Oliver as he walks by. Soul sucker. That's what she is. How can she not feel my eyes glaring into her? I clench my hands, the urge to grab her long hair and swing her around by it, extremely hard to resist.

Jeff pauses beside her, and with a faint smile on his face, he keeps walking.

"See you later, Jeff," she calls after him.

Without looking back, he lifts a hand.

When I first came to Enid High School, Jeff talked to me every day. It wasn't anything major, usually just a hello. I thought it was sweet, but all it was, was him testing me out before determining whether or not I was worth his time. A game. When it was apparent that I wasn't into sports, and was quiet, it stopped. I wasn't anyone notable. No one that someone like him would want to know. It's astonishing how quickly he turned from friendly to unresponsive. My fingers tighten on the straps of my backpack. I swear this school has been bathed in idiocy—not to mention all the regrettable aromas currently infiltrating the air.

I am mere feet from Jocelyn when Lucas Haskins becomes the object of her attention. Like a predator on the prowl, Jocelyn smells someone weaker than her. I only know who Lucas is because he's in my gym class. He's even more athletically challenged than I am. With messy blond hair that counterbalances his impeccable clothes, Lucas is the classic intelligent boy who is socially clueless.

Jocelyn smooths her hands down the tight pink top hugging her upper body, and approaches her prey. My nerves stiffen, and I stop where I am near the lockers. I can't walk away; I can't even quit watching. I am riveted. It is last fall all over again, except I'm observing the upcoming humiliation instead of living it.

"Lucas, nice shirt." Jocelyn circles him, picking at the lavender fabric of his collared shirt.

His face turns pink, and Lucas fumbles with a book under his arm. "T-thank you."

"Where did you buy it?" Half of her full mouth hitches. "Walmart?"

"Uh...I don't know. My—my mom got it for me." It's clear from the confusion on his face that Lucas can't figure out why Jocelyn is talking to him.

Her laughter is tinkling in the way I imagine death bells to be.

The hallway is crowded, boisterous, and no one sees what's happening right before them. No one but me. I look around. Kids push at one another, tease, and laugh, but no one looks our way. Why doesn't anyone care? Why am I the only one paying attention to this?

"Your mom shops for you?"

Sensing someone as engrossed in the exchange as me, I look up and meet Casey's worried eyes. She's standing two lockers down from Lucas, as if she was in the process of approaching him. Suddenly, it all makes sense. Jocelyn knew her friend was nearby. She's doing this to her, not Lucas. Her friend. Lucas is simply a casualty. What kind of domain do they live in—where friends are enemies, and enemies are anyone else? I don't want to be in their atmosphere. But I am. Just for now.

"Um, well..." Lucas rubs the back of his neck, his knuckles white on the hand gripping his textbook. "Sometimes, yeah."

Jocelyn crosses her arms and gives him a disappointed look. "Your shirt is purple, Lucas, and not a bold, strong purple, but a pathetic, girly purple."

Dismay enters his expression. "Oh. I..."

I'm not trying to be a hero. I'm not going after my bullies for anyone but me. And knowing this, I still can't continue to watch the two and not do something. I can't be a Casey. Casey, who even now stares at Lucas and Jocelyn. I've seen her talking to Lucas. I've seen the way her cheeks flood with color when their eyes meet. She likes him. I can tell Jocelyn's treatment of him bothers her, and she does nothing.

Striding toward the pair, I purposely ram my shoulder into Jocelyn as I come to a halt. She staggers to the side, banging her elbow against a locker. I hope it hurt. Daggers shoot from her eyes to me when I glance at her. Like I care. I've had my own eyes looking back at me through a mirror, and I've not recognized them. What could be worse than that?

"Hi." I smile at Lucas as Jocelyn's arm burns mine. I want to step back from her, but I won't. She can retreat. "Don't listen to Jocelyn. Her fashion style stinks. I mean, who wears a shirt three sizes too small? Hello, we're juniors, not toddlers."

She stiffens beside me.

I continue, my attention firmly locked on Lucas. "I happen to like your shirt, Lucas."

"It's effeminate," Jocelyn says scornfully.

"Do you even know what that means?"

"Do you?"

"Maybe your face is effeminate." My eyes don't leave Lucas. His go back and forth between Jocelyn and me.

A sound of fury leaves Jocelyn, like a low growl. I hit a nerve that time. My arm is grabbed, and I am jerked around to find myself looking into dark, scary, fathomless eyes that make me think of black pits with pythons at the bottoms of them. I have to tip my head back to fully see her face. It's ugly, but in an exquisite way. Carved with perfect, deadly care, her facial bones are slim and elegant. If only her soul could be on the outside. If only we all could see with our eyes how truly hideous she is.

"Get your claws off me." I wrench my arm from her grasp, feeling the sting of her sharp nails in my skin as the limb is released from her clutches.

Vileness glows in her eyes, and I imagine it crawling out of her eye sockets to enter my brain. Annihilating me. My breathing quickens, and I steel myself against her wrath. I crossed a line I was not allowed. The best way to insult someone who is vain is by criticizing their looks, naturally They can't handle that. They live on the high of knowing their beauty. Take away the perception of it, and what are they left with?

Me. They're left with me.

Stripped bare. Small. Fractured. Unable to hide. And with no one to protect them from the horror of reality. Most days I wish I could close my eyes to it.

"I am prettier than you'll ever be." Jocelyn's voice is harsh. It reminds me of dead leaves crackling as they fall apart. I decide she's scarier than Melanie. Melanie is selfish and petty, but Jocelyn is wicked.

"On the outside. The inside is a different matter," I reply evenly.

"Insult my looks again, and I'll rip your tongue from your mouth." A deadly spoken promise.

I narrow my eyes, my head spinning with trepidation even as I glare at the taller, olive-toned girl. "That's going to be hard, since you constantly give me new material."

She steps closer.

I swallow, thinking she means to get physical.

"Jocelyn. Jocelyn, let's go. The first bell rang," Casey pleads, finally breaking her silence.

Coward, I think as I shift my gaze to the blond-haired girl with her doll-like attractiveness. She's as fake as a Barbie doll too. Guilt bleaches the color from Casey's face, and she quickly averts her eyes. She sees what I think of her. Casey is powerless, and do you know why? Because she made herself that way.

I once felt powerless. I floated in it for a time, and then I sank, and I drowned. I will never allow myself to feel that way again. I will fight, even if I'm fighting myself.

"Hi, Casey," Lucas greets.

Sliding her eyes to Lucas, Casey looks like she's going to say something. Instead, her face goes blank, and she turns to her friend. I feel the dejection from Lucas. It's thick, and heavy. "Jocelyn. Please."

With a tiny smile, Jocelyn taps me on the nose once, and spins on her heel. "All right, all right. Let's go, Case. We wouldn't want to be late for English class because of a couple losers."

Sucking air into my lungs as soon as she vanishes around the corner, I place a hand to the cool metal of a locker. I briefly close my eyes. I feel dizzy. Sweaty. Sick. Like I just ran ten miles on the tracks of a rollercoaster. Underneath it all, niggling at the base of my neck,

I feel something else. Something great. Something heady, and addictive. Power. And I want more.

"I'm not all that certain I know what just happened," Lucas says quietly from my right side. "But I think I need to thank you. So...thank you."

Without looking at him, I nod. I slowly lift my head, step back from the row of lockers, and head to English class. Lucky for me, I get to spend it with some of my favorite people. I make it through the door as the last bell sounds. Jocelyn looks up as I walk by her desk, smiling haughtily. She thinks she's won. She thinks she put me in my place, and all is right once more in the pecking order.

She's wrong.

I've learned their game, and I'm going to crush it.

THE THING ABOUT THE BULLIES in this school is that, usually, they're not obvious about their attacks. They're subtle. I think that's more vicious than if they were blatantly cruel. Maybe in the Enid School District, there's a class on it in eighth grade—a prerequisite to entering high school. 'How to be a Proper Bully – 101'. Once a target of them, you're always unsure; you're always second guessing the situation. It makes you helpless, and it's lethal to your self-value, like a tiny chisel chipping away at what makes you, you.

You begin to doubt everything. Even actual kindness.

Anna Robertson waits by my locker at the end of the school day. My first instinct is to be suspicious. Why is she here? What does she want? Is she really as nice as she seems? Is Anna an actor like all the rest in this morbid play centered on a high school and the rude-ass kids within its walls? I don't believe all that, but I can't say for certain it isn't true. And I hate that I can't.

This school broke a part of me.

"Hello," she says in her soft voice, giving me a faint smile.

I reach for the lock and Anna moves to the side. I think of her dad, and his role in saving me. It makes me feel embarrassed—that he witnessed my weakest moment. That his daughter, knowing about it, is standing near me and talking to me. Mental breakdowns aren't usually something people want everyone to know about. I made it impossible for them to not know. Lucky for me, most of the people in this school can't see past themselves. Handy.

Quickly working the combination, I have it open and my backpack in hand within the span of a minute. Kids are practically running for the door, excited for the weekend and all their plans. I remember having that in my old school, with my old friends. The weekends were spent together, doing nothing and everything. We didn't know what we were doing, or where we were going, but we knew we'd be together. It was easy, the simplicity and sureness of knowing where you fit.

My eardrums sting at the volume of stomping feet and shouting voices. I glance at Anna as I sling the backpack over one shoulder and enter the mob aimed for freedom from the school. "Hey. What's up?" I ask.

Looking small and unsure, Anna keeps to my side. Her brown eyes dart to me and the kids around us, but she remains quiet. I give her a sidelong look as we step outside to sunshine and a cool breeze. If she's been in this town her whole life, what has it been like for her at this school? She's the perfect candidate to be picked on. Silent and meek. Like I was. But I was like that because I suddenly found myself surrounded by strangers. I was vulnerable. Naïve.

"I wondered if, I don't know..." Anna angles her head toward the sidewalk. "Maybe you'd want to do something sometime. Or...tonight."

Shocked by the invitation—my first since I moved to Enid—it takes longer than it should for me to respond.

"Or—not," she says hurriedly, lengthening the space from her to me. "That's fine too."

I open my mouth to tell her that it sounds like fun, and yes.

"Watch out, it's the leader of the Dork Patrol. Accidentally touch her and you become a lifetime member."

My shoulders shoot up at the familiar voice and I glance over my shoulder. Clint Burns looks at Anna with a smile on his face, like his words are said in harmless fun. He wore a similar smile on his face when he made fun of me during the first part of the school year. He's ugly. Ugly personality, ugly face. All of him—ugly. He's flanked on either side by a grinning goon. Frown in place, I look at Anna as well. She almost looks apologetic as our eyes clash, like it's her fault Clint is a jerk.

"Who would want to touch that?" Cruel brown eyes look Anna up and down, the gleam in them degrading and wrong.

Although she doesn't move, I swear Anna escapes into herself. She becomes translucent, almost unnoticeable. I want to tell her to stick up for herself, but then, did I?

My hands clench as fire explodes in my veins. I unconsciously take a step closer to the boy who spoke. I don't know who he is, but I know he deserves a fist to his face. As if powered by my anger, by this present injustice to an undeserving girl, the breeze grows stronger. "I'm sorry, are you talking about yourself? Because you're one person I would never touch, personally."

His face goes red, and he looks around to see who's watching us. "As if I'd want you to."

"As if I ever would." My face is hard; my voice is hard. I am wrapped in a granite shield that cannot be weakened.

The other unknown boy grins. "You can touch me if you want. I bet your sassy mouth knows all kinds of tricks."

My stomach lurches. The sexual comment—that's new, and somehow fouler than the simple putdowns. "Leave her alone," I tell Clint. "Leave everyone alone."

"Or what?" Clint taunts, crossing his arms over the forest green shirt he wears. He's skinny with toothpick arms and legs, knobby and gangly.

I lean down and pick up a rock, studying the sharp points aligned with smooth edges. I think of Nick, and how he'd say something earthshattering about this small gray rock, see it in some way I never would. How he makes everything better. How he isn't here. How he can't make this better. But I can. I look up, the rock locked tightly inside my hand.

"Lexie, it's okay," Anna whispers in a voice without hope.

"Actually, it's not." I don't look away from the three boys. I want to smite them with my eyes; I want to send them to a place where they feel how wretched they make others feel.

Recognition lightens Clint's eyes. "You're in my English class."

Except for my stay at Live, I've been in your English class all year, you unobservant prick.

"Talking back only makes it worse," Anna beseeches.

The pleading is what does it. She's begging me to let them get away with their mistreatment of her. They're the wrong ones, and everyone thinks it's okay. It's not okay. It's not okay to treat other people like crap. My face turns to fire, and I snap. The rock goes flying from my hand before I am fully aware I threw it.

"Ow! You just hit me in the head, you crazy bitch," Clint shouts as he claps a hand to his face, his voice a shade higher than normal. Good.

"That's right." I take a step closer to him.

I am not me. I am a better me. Stronger. Unforgiving. I will not pardon his insensitive and cruel actions. No one should. I can smell his sweat, and it stings my nostrils. But I like that he's scared of me.

He careens back. Wariness covers his face.

I smile faintly, and I know it's twisted into something fearsome. "I am crazy. Remember that."

"Let's go," he commands to his thug friends. I keep my eyes on Clint as he walks backward, his attention trained on me in case I decide to throw another rock at him.

My smile widens as my pulse thrums, and my heart pounds. I watch a bully who was temporarily conquered by a bullied scurry away. As soon as they're gone from the school grounds, the smile drops from my face. The words aren't enough anymore. I can fight back with them, but what are they accomplishing? Nothing. They have no lasting mark, not on these kids.

I look at Anna. She's wide-eyed and pale. "Is it just the junior class, or is the whole school made up of imbeciles?"

"Mainly the junior class."

"Maybe their parents were all on some heavy drugs when they were conceived."

She doesn't say anything.

"Not yours," I add.

Anna steps in front of me as I begin to walk. "You didn't need to do that."

"I know."

She swallows. "I didn't want you to do that."

I blink. "What?"

"If you ignore them, they go away. You should have ignored them."

I can't believe what I'm hearing. The first part of the school year, all I wanted was to be brave. Now I am, and I'm being told it's better to not be. That it's better to let bullies get away with their unkindness. I just stood up for her, and she's upset about it.

"How long have you lived in Enid?" I ask her.

She shifts her feet, keeping her eyes from mine. "I was born here."

"You've gone to the same school, with the same kids, the whole time, right?"

"Yes."

"Has it ever stopped, or even gotten better?" My voice is sharp.

Anna swallows, but doesn't answer.

I shake my head and step around her. "You don't ignore bullies, Anna. That doesn't do you any good. You get back at them."

"How?" she demands in a wavering voice.

I meet her brown eyes that are dark and troubled. They lack the warmth that was earlier there. "You make them pay. You do to them what they did to you."

Her expression falls, like she's disappointed in me. It makes my jaw stiffen. "How does that make you any better than them?"

It takes me a moment to respond. "I guess it doesn't."

And I can't even pretend that I care.

As if the afternoon needs to get any more exciting, I see the Trio from Hell lingering near Melanie's sleek blue car. They don't see me, and I step to the side to ensure it stays that way.

"Of course I said yes." Melanie fluffs her shiny brown hair and looks at Casey. "It's *Jeff Oliver*."

Jocelyn turns her head and rolls her eyes where Melanie can't see. Her voice is pleasant enough when she asks, "What movie are you seeing?"

"I don't know, and I don't care. I doubt we'll watch much of the movie anyway."

Casey laughs along with Melanie, but Jocelyn seethes beneath her smile.

"Maybe we should take a vote," Jocelyn says, crossing her arms. "We voted down Casey dating the dweeb. I think it's only fair that we do the same for you."

Melanie's face reddens. "We've never done it for any of the thousands of boyfriends you've—oh wait, you didn't date most of them, did you?"

Jocelyn's smile drips venom. "Maybe I'll add Jeff to the list of boys I didn't date."

The color drains from Melanie's face and her lips press tightly together, making it appear as if she has no mouth.

They're so preoccupied with themselves that they don't really know each other. I don't think they even like one another. I pause near a tree. Casey is afraid to show her true self. Jocelyn is tenacious; nothing is ever enough. Melanie needs attention to feel important. They're such a joke. And they don't realize that I'm observing everything, taking notes. Forming ideas. Figuring out their ticks to better exploit them.

Thank you for being so self-centered and clueless, ladies, I inwardly mock as I quicken my pace.

I forget about Anna as I turn for home, left behind without a goodbye. I forget about her asking me to do something tonight. I forget about everything but how I can make Melanie's date at the movies a complete disaster. Hunger burns through me, and it is righteous.

Eleven

Melanie

MY CHEST IS TIGHT. I'VE never felt like this before. I don't understand what it means. What is happening to me? My skin is hot, yet clammy. I place a palm to my unbearably fast heartrate and wonder if I'm having a heart attack. Impossible. I'm too young, too everything that should guarantee things like this do not happen.

"Melanie? Are you okay?"

I blink at Jeff, dropping my hand. I smile around the unwanted sensation of my heart being torn from my chest. "Yeah. Of course I'm okay." I laugh, but It sounds fake. "Why wouldn't I be okay?"

His midnight blue eyes move across my features. "I asked if you wanted anything from the concession stand. You didn't say anything."

It's our first date, and I'm messing it up. My hair has been perfectly straightened with an iron and sways becomingly when I move. My eyeshadow, eyeliner, and mascara have never looked quite this dazzling. My mouth is covered in cotton candy pink lip gloss that smells and tastes like it—exactly made up for kissing. My dress, an emerald green that is somewhere between casual and daring, complements my frame. Which...is also enviable.

Jeff's personality is interesting enough, and when he focuses his deep blue eyes on me, it sends a charge through my body. His body is honed with defined muscles, and the thought of his hands on me, and his body over mine, makes my breath catch. I'm definitely attracted to him, and the way he always sneaks looks at me, and finds reasons to touch me, tells me he wants me too. Everything should be going smoothly. He likes me; I like him.

But there is a single, large, dark blemish on the evening.

Fire sparks across my flesh, and my gaze moves to Lexie Hennessy sitting three rows back. Why won't she just go away? She's been everywhere the past two weeks. Even here, at the movie theater, on a Friday night, I can't forget about her. I don't know her. I don't know where she came from, and I don't know why she hates me so much. She just appeared one day and decided to torment me. That is seriously screwed up. Who does that?

At least she's alone, which tells everyone how many friends she has. Loser.

She looks up, meeting my eyes. Heat, dark and fearsome, floods my body and face. Lexie shifts her attention to Jeff, and I stiffen. With a calculating expression on her face, she gets to her feet and heads in our direction. *Don't even*, I think. But she is. She is even-ing. With a small tub of popcorn in one hand, and a soda cup in the other, Lexie plops down in the seat beside me.

"Hey, Melanie. Hey, Jeff," she says airily and tosses a handful of popcorn in her mouth. She chomps away at it, the sound unusually loud in my ear closest to her.

My jaw sets.

Jeff looks around me to get a view of Lexie. "Hey." Confusion lowers his eyebrows as he brings his gaze back to me. He mouths, "Who is that?"

"Oh, Melanie didn't tell you?" Lexie leans toward me, and I lean back. She smells like butter and popcorn. "I'm Lexie Hennessy. We're best friends. Like this." She holds up a hand and crosses two fingers.

"No—" I begin, horrified at the thought of Jeff thinking we're associated in any manner. It would cripple my popularity, with little hope of a rebound. Lexie doesn't dress right, and she has an unlikeable personality. I mean, obviously. I wouldn't be caught dead hanging out with her.

Lexie shoves my shoulder. "Yes. We are. Don't try to deny it. We totally hung out last week." Cupping her mouth, in a loud whisper, she says to Jeff, "She just doesn't want people to know we're so close, since I'm way smarter than her."

I choke on air.

Jeff laughs faintly. "What?"

I twist in my chair, bringing our faces close. Her skin is pasty, and her eyes look too big in her small-framed face. Big and shadowed, hiding things. I would never be her friend. I hope Jeff realizes that. "How did you know I was going to be here?"

Lexie grins. "What, you think I'm stalking you or something? I was just sitting over there by myself and saw my good friend Melanie Mathews, and thought I should come over and say hi. Any decent person would."

"You said hi," I say around gritted teeth. "Now go."

"But the movie's going to start."

"Exactly." I arch my eyebrows. "Leave."

"I'm going to get popcorn. Do you want anything?" Jeff asks, sounding annoyed.

Without looking at him, I answer, "Yeah. Sure."

"What do you want?"

"Whatever."

Jeff mutters, "Typical."

The chair creaks as it flips up, and the lights dim in preparation of ads and movie previews.

Lexie smiles and sips her drink through the straw. I narrow my eyes, noticing the slight tremble of her hand, and how tightly she clutches the cup. I want to dump the cup of soda over her head and have it rain down popcorn on her tiny-brained skull.

"He's cute." She pauses. "I see him with Jocelyn a lot."

Those were the wrong words to say. "He likes me, not her."

"Sure." Lexie winks, her smile tightening as her eyes meet mine. "Whatever you have to tell yourself."

My tone is louder than I like when I state, "He's here with me, not her."

"This time."

"You don't know anything." I sound weak, like even I don't believe my words.

"I know I saw him and Jocelyn eyeing each other up this morning."

I take a breath around the sharp jolt that hits my chest. Friend or not, I will mess Jocelyn up if she steals Jeff away from me. And Lexie—my eyes fixate on her. She acts tough, but something's not right. Not that it matters, because if she keeps this up, it won't be good for her. I am not being dethroned because of some weirdo who has nothing better to do than screw around with people's lives.

"Mind your own business."

Her smile widens to a grin. "It is my business if it concerns you. You're my friend, remember?"

"I don't even know you," I retort.

Something crawls across her face. A black shadow. "We should change that, don't you think? We can start here, now, on your date with Jeff. It'll be fun."

"If you ruin my date, I will ruin you," I vow to Lexie through lips that don't move.

Even with the faded lighting, I see the blaze of anger in her eyes. "Didn't you already do that?"

Not understanding what she means, and not caring, I lean toward her until our noses bump. "I haven't even started on you yet."

The first preview begins, blocking our voices from the people in the movie theater.

Lexie thumps her forehead to mine, and I cry out in pain and shock. I rear back, wincing as the armrest sharply digs into my back. She puts a hand on the armrest behind me and rises over me, until all I see is black rage and scorn. I choke on air as I try to inhale. I can't breathe. She's insane, and I can't breathe.

"No, Melanie," Lexie purrs in an alarmingly pleasant voice. "I haven't even started on *you* yet."

She goes back to her seat after that, leaving me shaken. My chest does that painful squeezing thing again, and I stare at the screen, not really seeing anything. Jeff comes back with popcorn and drinks, but I can't drink or eat anything. He grumbles about buying things just to be wasted, but I barely hear him. In fact, the whole movie is a blur. Jeff. Everything is, except for Lexie, sitting behind us.

Her eyes sear me where they bore into my back. My date is ruined, and my nerves are scattered.

She in unhinged, and I am past being annoyed and angry.

I am afraid.

Twelve
NICK

I SHOW UP AT ALEXIS' house Saturday morning at a little after nine, half-mad and full-on tense. I wanted to surprise her, but more than that, I just wanted to see her. Desperately. It took hours for me to talk myself into leaving the center, even though I already discussed my plan with Dr. Larson earlier in the week. I didn't want to leave Live, but more than that, I didn't want to go another day without seeing Alexis. So, here I am, freezing in the cold rain and wind, waiting to see if I have enough guts to ring the damn doorbell.

I don't know that she'll be here. And if she is, that doesn't mean she'll want to see me. But for me, I wake each morning longing to see Alexis, and I have to think, that I can't be the only one unable to look away when our eyes meet.

Fidgeting, I lift my hand to ring the doorbell, and then I can't move. I'm frozen. I step back and drop my hand. Swallow. I stare at the doorbell before forcing myself back to it. Closing my eyes, I take a deep breath, and slowly release it. Before I can change my mind, I point a shaking finger at the button, and jab it.

I shake my head and water drops from my hair to my face. I tell myself I should stay away, and yet, I'm the one who pursues Alexis. Stupid. I'm stupid. I halfway turn to go, but my feet won't move.

The sound of the lock flipping has me turning to the door. It opens. There she is—with her light brown hair choppy around her head, she is clad in a thin blue shirt and white lounge pants. Warmth rushes through me at the sight of her. Blue eyes swollen with sleep, Alexis blinks at me like I'm a mirage. A shivering, wet, cold mirage whose courage is quickly disappearing the longer she stares at me without saying anything.

This was a bad idea.

Deciding to end the torture I brought upon myself, I start to face the street. "I should go."

"No! No." A hand clutches my sleeve, and then she tugs me into the house. It's cool in the kitchen, and smells like coffee. The door shuts, and Alexis goes back to examining me. "I just...I thought I was still dreaming."

A smile tugs at my mouth. "You dream about me?"

"I...um..." Alexis opens her mouth, and then shrugs. "Yes. I do. So far, none where you die." She watches me closely as she says this.

The water thickens on me, leeches through my skin. It takes form, entering my throat to choke me. Numb. I'm numb. I look at Alexis, and all the color fades from the room.

"I'm sorry." Her eyes dim. "I don't know why I said that."

I take a breath, and it rasps in the uneasy quiet. "It's—it's okay."

"It's not okay." Alexis moves closer, the proximity of her body warming the air between us. "It isn't like you want to have dreams like that." I hear the question in her tone. *Do you?* she asks. *Do you want to have dreams like that?*

I lurch to the side, banging my shoulder against the closed door. If it was open, I would already be through it. Back into the rain, being soaked by it instead of cold by her statement. I want to escape the doubt I feel pulsating off her. She wonders about me. She wonders if I am as harmless as she initially thought. I haven't given her many details of my life, but shouldn't she just know the kind of person I am, instinctively? *No,* I answer myself. *No, she shouldn't.*

"No," I choke. "Of course I don't."

Alexis looks like she wants to say something, but she instead presses her lips in a thin line, keeping the words inside. Her gaze trips over my straggly hair that is partially covering my eyes, moves over my black long-sleeved shirt clinging to me, and ends on my jeans heavy from rain. Pulled by some undetectable force, her eyes rise to mine, and there they stay. Light comes back to the room, fiery and brilliant. I can't breathe when she looks at me like that.

"How did you get here?"

"I walked."

Alexis' eyebrows lower. "It's raining."

"No way," I softly mock.

A water droplet slides down the side of my face, and Alexis wipes it away, her fingers lingering on my skin that is blazing where it was chilled a moment ago. My hands move before I can stop them, and I slowly pull her to me. Our eyes never leave each other's. She's warm, and soft, smelling of mint and something fruity, and for a moment, she is mine. I drop my forehead to hers, need pulsing through me. My fingers tighten on her hips. I close my eyes.

"Do you have plans today?" I ask hoarsely.

"Did you walk two miles, in the rain, to ask me if I have plans?" Alexis whispers, her hands moving to my biceps and stopping there. "Wouldn't it have been more practical to call?"

"More practical, yes, but it would have had a substantially less dramatic effect than showing up on your doorstep, looking partially drowned." I keep my eyes closed.

Laughing quietly, Alexis locks her fingers behind my neck and presses her body to mine, shivering at either the wet or cold, or maybe the shock that goes through me, and I have to believe, her as well. My whole body is sparks and nerves and electricity. It thrums in place of my veins. I wonder, if we kiss, will it produce lightning.

She tilts her face to mine, her breath tickling my jaw as she talks. "You left the center. For me. That's a big deal, Nick."

I swallow around a tight throat, opening my eyes to find hers riveted to me. They zap me with heat, and my arms harden, wanting all of her touching me. Without barriers, without secrets. Without clothes. This is dangerous to think, and I can't stop. My heart pounds an impossible beat, and hers is the match to it.

"My only plans are whatever you want them to be," Alexis tells me, smiling.

"Is your dad here?"

She shakes her head, and her smile falls.

"Good."

I kiss her.

Not softly, not sweetly, but with unbridled intensity. It doesn't create lightning, but fire. It engulfs us. I'm burning, and I want her to feel the burn with me. She tastes good, like mint-covered redemption. I slant my mouth, deepening the kiss. It's a hard kiss, demanding. It takes, but only because I want Alexis to give. *Show me you feel what I feel. And* she does. She gasps into my mouth, her fingers digging into my shoulders, her body taut. She moves against me, and firecrackers flare to life behind my eyelids.

My hands move from her hips to her back, wrapping completely around her, bringing her fully to me. With fingers that shake, I slide them up the sides of her torso, and a sound of pleasure leaves her when I palm her sides through her shirt. Alexis' skin is hot, and soft, and touching her bare skin makes me feel drunk. It makes me tremble. It makes me unsteady—with my actions, with my thoughts.

It makes me want to reveal all my secrets. It tricks me into thinking she'd take them and still want me.

I've kissed plenty of girls, but none have made me feverish, not like this. I even had sex a couple times with my most serious girlfriend, before we broke up. But that's all it was: sex. I don't just want Alexis; I need her. The way she makes me feel, the thoughts I have of her, because of her. How I never feel completely whole until I see her. There is lust, and desire, and then, there is this. Something inexplicable, something that takes a sliver of your soul, promising to never give it back. I don't want it back. It's hers.

I would say that I love Alexis Hennessy. I would say that, if I was allowed.

THROUGH THE FOG OF MY brain, I feel her shaking, and the tiny bumps on her flesh. My wet clothes have iced her skin and dampened her pajamas. I tear my mouth from hers, and drop my hands, taking a moment to get my breathing and body under control. I want to strip her clothes from her body, and feel her around me— and that is the last thing I should do.

"You're freezing," I say stupidly.

"So are you." Alexis unlocks her arms from around my neck, putting space between us as she shows me her back. "I probably

113

have some bigger clothes that will fit you, if you want me to put yours in the dry—"

Her words drop to oblivion, like they found an unknown cliff and took a dive. I kick off my sodden shoes and cross the room to her. "Alexis? Is something wrong?"

She stares at the wall near the doorway to the hallway, still as stone. It doesn't even look like she breathes. I follow her gaze, seeing the chalkboard, reading words I don't understand.

How could you leave without telling Lexie goodbye?

That is what's written in yellow chalk on the black board. The handwriting is bold, straight, all capital letters. I look from it to her, and I touch her arm. She jumps, takes a shuddering inhalation of air, and slowly looks at me. Tears hang from her eyelashes. Alexis looks shattered. She looks like I haven't seen her look in a long time.

"What does it mean?" I ask quietly, brushing a tear from her cheek as it falls.

She shakes her head. "I can't—I can't talk about it right now."

"Okay." My eyes drill into hers. Why can't she tell me? *Why can't you tell her?* "But when you're ready, I'll be waiting."

Wiping at her face, she hides the brokenness like it was never a part of her. "You better be." She focuses on me. Her eyes twinkle with mischief. "Take off your clothes."

My body twitches. "What?"

Alexis smiles. "There's a bathroom around the corner in the hallway. You can get undressed in there. I'll bring down some clothes I think will fit."

I somehow tangle one leg with the other as I stumble for the bathroom in a supremely suave way. Looking at Alexis instead of

114

where I'm going, I thump the side of my head against the doorframe. She's oblivious, which is good for me. I pause by the door. Alexis lingers in the kitchen, her eyes back on the chalkboard. The sadness, and something else, has taken residence on her face once more.

I slowly close the door on her solitary sorrow.

Inside the cream room with the pink and yellow fish shower curtain and bathroom accessories, I peel off my wet clothes, leaving on my boxers. The washer and dryer are near the door. Hesitating briefly, I open the dryer door, shove them inside, and turn it on. When minutes go by, and there is no word from Alexis, I open the door, and there she stands. Her hair is tamer than when I first got here, and she's dressed in jeans and a yellow shirt. With clothes in her arms as she heads toward me, she pulls up abruptly when her brain realizes what her eyes are seeing.

I give a weak wave.

"You're naked," she blurts.

"I'm not—" The clothes are thrown at me, landing on my head. I yank them down. "You told me—"

"Put those on. Now." She won't look at me.

Frowning, I observe her creamy skin as it turns a startling shade of red. I used to lift weights, and was active with sports. It gave me a physical form I took for granted. When I look in the mirror, I don't see the muscles and definition I used to have, even if some of that remains. Alexis appears to see it, and like it.

"Why?" I ask faintly, my voice or words pulling her eyes to me.

"W-what?"

"Afraid you won't be able to keep your hands to yourself?"

I wink, and it's like I'm back there, in that other dimension, being that other guy. I can argue that that other guy *is* me, and I'm probably right, but he's dangerous. I try to keep him concealed. Bad things happened when he was out.

But Alexis shakes her head, and I exhale with relief. She's not interested in him. She wants *me*, the real me. The guy who doesn't play games. "Get dressed. We can attempt to make some food. I'm hungry, and you're a guy, so it's pretty much a given you're hungry too."

I lift an eyebrow. "Attempt to make food?"

She pushes against my arm, turning me around, and then closes the door once I'm inside the bathroom.

"We eat out a lot, or I make easy stuff where you just put the food in the microwave or oven. I can't bake—or cook," Alexis explains through the wood of the door.

"That makes two of us." I look at the gray tee shirt and jogging pants.

"I can boil water," she says cheerfully.

"This should be interesting," I mumble, thinking of the too-small clothes I'm about to attempt to put on, and not about our future cooking endeavor.

Alexis laughs when I come out. It makes her face light up. She stands near the stove, using a turner to stir something in a pan. It smells like burnt butter. "Do you like pancakes? I have a boxed mix. I figured it can't be too hard, right? Just add water."

I tug at the constricting clothes and walk to her. The tee shirt is skin tight, and the jogging pants are too short, ending inches above my ankles. I turn my gaze to the stove. Inside the pan is some kind of white powdery substance with pools of water intermeshing with butter surrounding it. "You're supposed to mix it before you put it in the pan."

"Oh! *Shit*."

My lips tug upward as our eyes meet. Curiosity has me asking, "What were you thinking?"

"I don't know." She shrugs. "Just dump and go, I guess. I should have known it wouldn't be that easy."

The smile grows when I note the smear of pancake batter on her forehead. "I know how to make somewhat edible scrambled eggs. Do you like those?"

"Yeah," Alexis says with a sigh, grabbing the handle of the pan and dumping its contents in the wastebasket. "But I like pancakes better."

I make us eggs, neither of us commenting on the crispy, brown edges, and we eat.

"Where is your dad today?"

Alexis pauses with her fork mid-raised, her eyes darting to the words on the wall.

Knowing she might close the topic before it really begins, I plow ahead. "He wasn't around last Saturday either. Is he usually gone on weekends?"

She lowers her fork, the food on it untouched. "He's gone as often as possible."

I set down my own fork. "Because of work?"

"Because of me." Alexis blinks, looking uncertain of her words.

Not knowing what to say to that, I say nothing. I wait, examining her lips as they tremble. I know Alexis is gathering words. Whether she speaks them or not, I can't say.

When it's apparent she won't say more, I lean forward and whisper, "Tell me something wonderful."

She turns to me, absently wiping at the pancake mix on her forehead. With her pursed lips, it gives her a quizzical look. Her eyes move over my features, landing on my eyes and staying there. She takes a deep breath, and says just as quietly as I did, "I like looking at your eyes. They make me think of the ocean, deep and never-ending. Full of undiscovered wonders."

And hidden passages that hide monsters.

I swallow thickly. "Tell me something wonderful about you."

Alexis answers promptly, as if the words were waiting to be said. "I am grateful to be alive."

I straighten, my back pressing to the chair. I open my mouth to ask what she means. *Careful*, a voice inside tells me.

Alexis pushes her plate to the side. She closes her eyes. "I tried to kill myself." Her eyes fly open like she doesn't understand how those words came from her mouth.

My throat tightens, darkness hovering on the edges of my vision.

"That's why I was sent to Live."

Her voice is faint, like she's cried so many tears that it altered her vocal chords. I swallow, and it burns. The eggs feel like rot in my stomach. The scent of them makes me nauseous. Words. Stupid, senseless words. That's all I have. I choke them down, knowing the futility of voicing them. Alexis doesn't need to hear what I have to say; she needs me to listen to what she has to say.

"I, um, my dad and I...because of his job, we moved here last August. I'd only been to one school since I was four, and then my junior year, I was in a new one." Her knee bounces, knocking into mine. I let it. Alexis' hands are splayed on the tabletop, her gaze riveted to them.

"The kids—" she breaks off.

I close my eyes. Dread cascades down my spine.

"I got picked on. A lot. Every day. I wasn't used to it. I didn't know how to respond."

My nails dig into my thighs. I don't want to hear this. I don't want to know. Not this story, not this kind. No. At the same time, I feel I owe it to her to listen. I do, in quiet pain. My own pain. Her pain. And the boy from my dreams. His pain is here too.

"I was hurt by the way I was treated. I felt...hopeless."

She stops talking, and I finally look at her. I force myself to observe the memory of her tragedy. Alexis stares back, her eyes large and turbulent, her nostrils slightly flared. Her eyes go unfocused as she inhales. She sounds scratchy when she next talks.

"I remember trying to talk to my dad about it. He told me to make more of an effort, to not let it get to me. He made it seem like I was exaggerating, and worse yet, that their cruelty was my fault."

Her dad is a jerk.

"I lost weight." She picks at her shirt. "I looked horrible, like I was sick, and a lot of the time, I did feel sick. My nerves were a mess. I stayed home from school as much as I could, but my dad only let that go on for so long."

Breathing seems irrelevant at this point. Shallowly, hardly, barely, just enough to survive, I breathe.

"One night, I went into his bedroom. It was late. I was crying. I told him—I told him I wanted to die." Alexis smiles, and it guts me. That's the kind of smile I never want to see on her lips. It's full of grief. "He told me that I didn't mean that, and to go back to bed."

A single tear makes its way down her face. I feel like crying myself.

"The next day, after he left for work, I grabbed scissors and cut off my hair. I stared at myself in the mirror. I didn't know who I was looking at, but she wasn't me. She was someone I didn't like, and I wanted her gone. I wanted it all over. I couldn't stand feeling like I did, not for one more day. I took a bunch of the painkillers my dad has for back problems.

"The pills were large and white and hurt my throat. I took them until I couldn't take any more. The room...the room started to turn gray, to fade, and I couldn't hear right. Everything was distorted. I was dizzy. I became scared.

"I called my dad, told him what I did, and an ambulance came. I was taken to the hospital. I had a tube with charcoal shoved down my throat to make me vomit the pills I took."

She curls her fingers, and hides her hands beneath the table. "Since the day I almost died, I've wanted nothing more than to live. I'm lucky I got a second chance." Alexis gives me a sidelong look, gauging my reaction to her confession. "You know the rest. Enough of it anyway."

I try to catch my breath, to appear normal. I almost laugh. Normal isn't close to what I am these days. My head pounds, and it tastes like the fire burning my throat turned to ash in my mouth. The story she told me could have been from any terrorized kid, but it wasn't. It was from her. From Alexis. She was bullied. I drop my head, digging the heels of my hands into my eyes. Needing the sting, deserving it.

My voice is rough when I finally speak. "How did it get to that point? To the point of giving up?"

I'm asking for selfish reasons. What was the final act that tipped her over the edge? Maybe if I understand her, I can understand my own demons.

"I forgot who I was, Nick."

Such a simple, unhelpful response. I've never known who I am, but there are times, generally when I'm with Alexis, that I think I know. I know who I want to be, if that counts for anything.

"I still don't feel like I know. I've changed. I'm different." Her eyes capture mine as I look up. "I feel split in two. Divided. There is who I am when I'm with you, and who I am when I'm not."

"Which one do you like better?"

Alexis drops her eyes quickly, and still, not fast enough. I saw the ache pulsing in the blue depths. The glimpse of something deadly beneath that, like the foreseen annihilation of hope. It makes my insides cold. She's told me part of it, but she hasn't told me it all. I sense that. I know that. I would do the same, if I had something to hide. And I do.

"I just want to live in a world where there is no one but you, and me," she whispers with a catch in her voice.

I reach across the table, needing to touch her. But she's out of range, and it's just as well. My fingers move through air, and I let them fall to my side. My words feel like lies, no matter how true I want them to be. I am a fraud. Still, I say them anyway.

"Doesn't it feel like that when we're together?"

I want this to be real. I want this to be me.

Her eyes fly to mine, surprise and hope shining in them. Turning them from blue to every shade of loveliness. Making it seem like I can have happiness. My own. Ours. Not borrowed. Not something I have to give back, or that can be taken away.

Lies. It's all hopeful, naïve lies.

"Yes," she breathes. "It does."

I think maybe Alexis lies too, and worse than that, I think she lies to herself.

Thirteen

Alexis

FOR SUPPER SATURDAY NIGHT, DAD brings home fried chicken and mashed potatoes from the grocery store deli. We eat in silence, my eyes finding the question on the wall again and again. He asked that for me. And yet, he says nothing while in my presence. When I look at him, his eyes are down, his attention solely on the food before him, and it's hard to imagine that he cared enough to write that on the chalkboard. He doesn't seem to remember writing it, or now even see it.

In person, he is forever indifferent.

But, what if, underneath it all, he mourns as much as I do?

"How are things going at the factory?" I ask to fill the uncomfortable quiet.

A grunt is his reply.

I try again. "Will you be home tomorrow?"

He nods.

"Nick came over today." I pop a forkful of mashed potatoes in my mouth as I wait for him to respond. I add more pepper from the shaker on the table, and take another bite. I'm not telling him to cause conflict. If anything, I want to talk to him about something, someone, who is important to me. He's my dad; this should matter to him. Some reaction would be nice.

His shoulders stiffen. "The boy from the center?"

"Yes." I pull off a piece of crispy chicken skin and chew on it, an explosion of flavors erupting in my mouth. Hesitating, I tell him, "He's really nice. You'd like him."

The sound of his fork clanging against the plate is his only answer.

"I like spending time with him," I add softly. I don't feel splintered when I'm with him. I can forget about the school, and the kids, and every bad thing I've done, past or present. Nick becomes the pinnacle of all that is relevant.

He sits back, folding his arms over his substantial gut, and scrutinizes me. My father's unresponsiveness is gone, and beneath the intensity of his ice blue gaze, I desperately want it back. "Why is this Nick person at the center?"

A torrent of energy zips through my nerves at the "Nick person" reference. "He flipped out one day and went on a killing spree at the local library. They didn't have the sequel to a book he really, really wanted to read."

Silence greets my words.

I sigh. "I don't know. I didn't ask. The kids there—we don't really talk about why we're there."

"He could be dangerous."

"I could be dangerous." I mean to sound casual, but I pause and blink. I think of the rock I threw at Clint. I think of the movie theater with Melanie. In the hallway with Jocelyn. I think of how the more I antagonize those who traumatized me, the more I like it. I feel vindicated, like they are owed, and I am providing what is due. It becomes easier to ignore the other voice in my head, the one that cautions.

But me? Dangerous?

I'm not dangerous. The person I am at school isn't real. She's a character. I just play her well. Really well. I shift on the seat and shove more chicken in my mouth. The look my dad gives me as I chew tells me he thinks I am as dangerous as a hangnail. Maybe I am—those suckers hurt. I can fester and annoy.

From the way Melanie acts, I must be doing a pretty good job in my role as antagonist. I'm finally getting to her. I see the cracks in her bulletproof beauty. What's more, I've overtaken the writing project. The three of them don't seem to mind. If they were smart, they would. They don't know I'm telling my own story, and theirs. They don't know they'll be the ones reading it, because, unfortunately, I'm going to be sick on the day the assignments are to be read in front of the classroom.

I almost hate that I have to miss it.

"You have an odd look on your face," my dad comments, wiping his fingers on a napkin before reaching for another piece of chicken.

I change the subject, possibly saying the one thing that is sure to make my dad leave the room. But my eyes are back on that board, and if I don't voice the thought, it'll eat away at my throat until I do. "Do you think she ever thinks of us, or are we like some part of her past she doesn't want to remember?"

The room goes cold.

"You have to wonder. You wrote that," I say into the glacial setting, nodding toward the chalkboard. I don't know why I say it. He knows he wrote it.

"There's no point in discussing it," is his rigid response.

"Why can't we?" Old anger surfaces, anger that never truly goes away. She left me, but he's still here, and he might as well not be. Appetite snuffed out, I shove my plate away and glare at my dad.

"It doesn't change what is."

"Right." I cross my arms, my facial muscles stiff. "We probably shouldn't talk about the fact that you've barely spoken to me in the three years since she left. That doesn't change anything either."

He flinches, as if I've stolen all his food and told him he doesn't get another scrap.

Getting to my feet, I pick up my plate, fork, and glass, being sure to clang them together in a choir of dishware injustice for my father's ears to enjoy. Something hot and red sweeps through me, something I don't want to push back.

"We probably shouldn't talk about the fact that when I tried to talk to you about how mean the kids are here, about how…" I set down the dishes near the sink and grip the counter ledge between my fingers. I watch a raindrop slither down the windowpane, and turn my eyes to the grayness beyond. "…how hopeless I felt here, you told me to try harder. Like it was my fault the school is full of malicious pricks."

"Lexie—"

"You haven't even asked me how things are going. Two weeks I've been back in that hellhole, and you haven't asked me a single question about it."

"Hellhole? I assumed—"

"Assumed." I laugh darkly. People assume things so that they feel better about not asking.

"I thought you wanted to go back."

Oh, I did.

"I know things were bad, but it seems like they're better now."

Assume.

Seem.

Stupid words that shouldn't be allowed in existence.

I whirl around, something in my face halting whatever words he is about to say. "Do you even know how I felt, what I went through? I was bullied for months. That doesn't just *get better*."

He looks at me like he doesn't recognize me. "I don't understand."

"Maybe I was too sensitive, maybe I should have been stronger, maybe I should have fought back, but you—" Tears trail down my face, much like the ones on the other side of the window. I'm crying, and the world is too. "—you should have been there for me."

Like a punishing gift from a time I wish didn't exist, I remember how I used to think, what thoughts steered me through each day.

There's a voice in my head, and it says: Why don't you give up?
It's cruel, and dominant, and forceful.
And I want to listen to it.
Every day I hear that voice, and I hear those words.
I wonder why I don't give up.

"I wanted to give up. I did give up. And you didn't even know."

Fresh crevices line his face, making him appear older.

I choke on my next words. They're shameful, the kind of words no one wants to speak. "I almost died—yes, by my own hand, but you act like it never happened."

He stands, looking shrunken. Looking like he can't bear what I have said. Well, he has to. I do. I live every day with the choices I made. I live every day knowing I gave up on myself.

It happened.

It was real.

I almost died.

I tried to kill myself.

I say the words out loud, his skin turning grayer as I do.

"I almost died."

I swipe tears from my face.

"I tried to kill myself."

My dad swallows. "Stop."

I shake my head. No. I can't stop. Not this time. "I feel like I've been dead to you for a long time now, Dad. I even wondered if it'd really make all that much of a difference if I was dead. Maybe you'd be happier even. You haven't been there for me since Mom walked out on us. Didn't you think I might need you more with her gone? How could you shut me out?"

Pain lances his blue eyes; broken pieces of anguish fill them and recede. It's gone as quickly as it appeared, but I saw it. I won't forget that I did.

"Is it because I remind you of her?" My voice is a fragmented whisper, thick with the agony of my heart. "Is that why you stopped talking to me, stopped caring? Because I look like her?"

I'm standing alone in the center of the kitchen, and all the emptiness in the air gathers around me, suffocating and treacherous. Talking about my suicide attempt earlier with Nick opened up something inside me, and I don't know how to close it. I don't want to. I'm tired of feeling invisible, of games. I'm tired of shoving emotions back that aren't acceptable, that aren't supposed to be felt. I think of the kids at school, and I just want that over with. I think of the mystery surrounding Nick. I'm tired of his secrets.

I think of my own.

I'm even tired of me.

Thunder rumbles across the outside sky, but inside, it's quiet.

I stare into a pair of blue eyes similar to mine, but colder, darker.

"Say something," I demand hollowly.

He looks at me.

"Tell me why you don't want me!" I sound volatile. I sound like I feel. I impulsively grab a plate, my fingers gripping it hard enough to hurt. I want to fling it at my dad, at the chalkboard, at the memory of my mom—and I want to destroy it all. The wall, the world, but especially, her. I want to forget her.

Most pathetically of all, I want her to remember me.

I think of the rock, and how I threw it, and I hurl the plate at the wall. It shatters, resembling my life, and my dad flinches. I stare at him, chest heaving, hands knotted tightly enough to make my knuckles hurt, and I will him to say something. Yell at me, kick the wall. Show emotion of some kind. I belong locked up. God, I'm a mess. Still...such a mess. My mouth quivers, and I fight back another round of tears.

"Tell me I matter to you at all."

He opens his mouth, but no sound comes out.

As suddenly as the rage enters me, it leaves. With slumped shoulders, I clear off the table, careful to keep my distance from my spineless, wordless, uncaring father. I even take his plate with food still on it, immaturely glad that he isn't able to eat either. Dishes clatter as they collide, and I reach to turn on the hot water.

"I—" he begins, and falters.

I stiffen, and slowly turn.

The ceiling light glints off the baldness of his head, like a twisted halo on an undeserving man. Some inner struggle abounds within him. I see hints of it in the muscle spasm under his right eye, and his lips become a thin slash of pink across his face. I wonder if his heart pounds as strongly as mine, if he fights to say words, or fights to not say them. The rest of our relationship rides on what my dad says, or doesn't. I know it. I think he does too.

He sounds frail when he finally speaks, a partial man where usually there is a whole. Cracked into halves. It's disconcerting. "The truth is...it's because it's my fault, Lexie. It's my fault that she left."

I don't say anything. My eyebrows lower, my mouth shifts, but I don't say anything.

"How can I look at you, talk to you, knowing that I am responsible for the hole in your life?" He lifts his hands, his features stiff in denial of his words, even as his eyes burn with truth. He's good at hiding what he feels. What this must cost his pride to voice his thoughts.

I want to cry. I want to run to my dad and hug him, even if he doesn't hug me back. But I stay where I am. I harden myself to him, like he has to me.

"I don't know, Dad, I guess you just try, right?" His excuses don't cut it. I brush hair from my temple. Looking at him in this vulnerable state, it's easy to imagine I am the parent and he is the child. "Why do you think it's your fault? You didn't make her walk out on us. She did that."

"I wasn't there for her." His eyes shift around the room, touching on the shards of porcelain littering the floor. They pause on the chalkboard before returning to me. "I worked too much. I focused on providing for us. To me, that was how I showed that I cared, by making sure we all had things."

I narrow my eyes. "If what you're saying is true, and that is what pushed Mom away, why would doing the same thing with me somehow be okay? You don't make sense."

His blue eyes turn pleading. He, who carefully guards what he doesn't want those around him, to know he feels. "I don't know anything else. It guts me. Every time I look at you, it guts me. I'm failing as a father, and I know it. I don't—I'm not good with showing my emotions. You're right—I wasn't there for you. I haven't been there for you in a really long time, and I'm sorry. I thought it was better, if I kept my distance. I didn't know how to help you."

My lips tremble. "I just want you to be my dad. That's it. I just want one parent to care."

"I do care." He hesitantly walks toward me, his shoes colliding with broken plate pieces as he moves. "I do care, Lexie." He wraps me in his arms, and I'm cocooned by warmth and his peppery cologne. "I don't blame you for anything. I blame myself. I'll do better, I promise." His calloused hand smooths my hair. "I love you, Lexie."

I choke, my ears stinging at the wanted, and needed, words. I don't remember the last time my dad told me he loves me. "You didn't make her leave. You didn't make her decide to forget we exist. That's on her."

My dad holds me tighter, and he presses a rough kiss to my temple, the scruff on his face scraping my skin.

"I'm not going back to that school next year," I tell him in a voice that doesn't shake. The rest of me, though, is shaking. He can make me go, if he decides. I don't know if I can continue the façade for another year. Even the thought of the next two weeks at Enid High School wears on me.

He drops his arms and steps back, peering down at me. His expression is back to its neutrality, and I'm kind of relieved to see it. "Why did you go back now?"

"I wanted to finish the school year. I wanted them to know they didn't break me." True enough. I can't exactly tell him about my nefarious plans of revenge. He might send me back to Live.

His eyebrows lower. "And next year?"

I shrug and look at my pink socks. "I can be homeschooled. I'll do all the work on my own. You don't have to worry about me slacking off."

"I'm not worried about that."

I look up. His tone implied he's worried about something else. I guess that's smart. It's smart to be worried about me.

"Don't you want to graduate with your class?"

I do, but not this one. I want to graduate with my old classmates, in my old school. That was my school; that was my class. I shrug, knowing it's futile to want that. The only way I'd be able to do that is if my dad let us move back to Iowa. And he won't. His work is here.

"We have time to discuss it," my dad finishes.

It's better than an outright no. I'll take it.

"I'm going to work on the dishes," I say into the quiet.

"I can help."

"No, that's okay." I want to be alone right now. I need to think. I need to let go of a mother who is no longer mine, and I can't do that with my father nearby.

"I have some paperwork to go over for work," he supplies.

We stand before one another, the atmosphere awkward in the wake of the revelation. I am drained, but also lighter. Our eyes briefly meet, and in his, I see something I haven't before. Regret. Understanding. Love. It makes my chest squeeze. I exhale carefully. We turn at the same time to go about our chores.

"Lexie."

I face him.

My dad lingers near the doorway, and the chalkboard. "I've never been disappointed in you, or the person you are. I want you to know that. And—I should have shown you...told you."

Eyes stinging, I swallow and nod.

His gaze drops to the floor. "You owe us a new plate."

I laugh shakily.

He leaves the room, and I start to wash the dishes, but the whole time, I'm plagued by my thoughts. I think of my mother, remembering her laughter and her dancing eyes, and I push the memories of her into a box in the darkness, locking it. I can't hurt for her anymore. I think of Nick, and how I can't put a name to what I feel for him, but that it's strong, and terrifying. I think of my dad, and realize that it's never too late.

But then I think of school, and the kids within it, and everything good I feel, is snuffed out. *I have to do this*, I remind myself. I have to keep at it. They deserve this. I'm not proud of my actions, but it doesn't matter. Sometimes, you do things that you don't like, but feel are necessary. *And sometimes you like them*, a voice whispers. I shake it away, and focus on cleaning up the kitchen.

I write on the chalkboard before I go to bed.

Fourteen

Melanie

I CRY BEFORE SCHOOL ON Monday. I don't understand why I'm crying. I just know that it feels like there's crushing weight on my chest, and everything around me is duller. I'm not happy; I want to be happy. I want it to be two weeks in the past, before Lexie appeared in my life, and everything went wrong. Instead, I am in my bedroom with its mauve-colored walls and matching bedding, quietly sobbing.

School will start soon, and for the first time that I can recall, going there is something I want to avoid.

What has happened to me? I sit in the middle of my bed and clutch a pillow to my chest, feeling like my life might as well be over. The sounds are pitiful, and I know my makeup is ruined. My throat hurts, and my eyes burn, and I hate feeling this way. I haven't cried since I was thirteen and got a bad haircut. As devastating as that was, this is worse.

I think of Lexie waiting for me at school with her unfair animosity. I think of Jocelyn with her predator eyes on Jeff. My blood heats; my fingers dig into the soft pillow. And Jeff—after our disastrous date, I might as well kiss goodbye any hope of him being my boyfriend. After my encounter with crazy Lexie, I was so spooked for the rest of the movie Friday night, that whenever he tried to touch me, I recoiled. After the movie, he left me on my doorstep without a goodbye.

My life is coming undone, and I can't seem to stop it.

"Melanie! You're going to be late for school," my mom calls up the stairs.

"Coming," I call back in a voice that cracks.

Irritation clings to my mom's words as she starts, "If you don't leave in—"

I throw a pillow at the door and scream, "I said I'm coming!"

"Be late then," are her parting words.

Glaring at the door, I jump down from the high bed and stomp to the full-length mirror. A sound of disgust leaves me at the sight of my runny eyes and red face. I tell myself I still look better than ninety-five percent of the girls in the school, but it doesn't boost my spirits like it normally would. I push a wayward lock of chestnut hair from my eyes and examine my ripped skinny jeans and flowy black tunic top with black calf-high boots. *At least my hair and clothes look good*, I think as I turn from the mirror.

I take my backpack from the carpet near the door and make my way down the stairs. It smells like coffee and syrup in the hallway leading to the kitchen, and I make a face. The thought of drinking or eating anything this early in the day makes me queasy. Plus, I don't want to get fat. I shoot a grimace in my overweight mom's direction where she stands before the stove. Her grossly large frame barely fits in the gray dress pants and pink top, and there are bulges everywhere. Her face is twice the size of mine, and her fingers remind me of sausages. When she moves, her fat moves with her.

She's embarrassing. Like, take some pride in the way you look and go on a diet.

After the divorce, my mom had the entire house redecorated, using the best quality wood and tiles and carpet to create a home that shouts her monetary worth. Other than in my room where she let me pick the paint and accent colors, the color theme of the house is gray, white, emerald green, and turquoise. She went all out in the kitchen. It looks like the sea vomited in here.

"You won't have time to eat now." She faces me, exasperation clear in Veronica Mathews' gray eyes. She used to be slim and pretty. She even won pageants, but after having two kids, she completely let herself go. She doesn't dye her hair anymore, and there are gray hairs streaked through the unflattering brown bob. It's no wonder Dad divorced her and married the receptionist from his veterinary clinic.

"That's really sad. I'd hate to not be able to eat." *Unlike you.* I swear she's trying to make me fat. She's always pushing food on me. I look at the plate of pancakes on the counter near her elbow. "And pancakes? Could you have picked anything unhealthier to make?"

"I wanted to try a new recipe. They're gluten free."

"Are they fat free?" I mutter beneath my breath. I grab an apple from the bowl on the table, catching the flash of hurt in her eyes before turning in the direction of the front door.

"Your bad attitude is getting old," she says sharply, and I turn back. She takes the plate of pancakes from the counter and drops it on the table. The porcelain clatters on the wood. Hands on her ample hips, she looks at me with a flushed face and glittering gaze.

I meet her angry eyes with my own, ready for a fight. A fight is better than feeling like bawling and hiding away. "Maybe you should have let me live with Dad then, like I wanted."

Her index finger stabs the air that leads to the door. "No one's stopping you."

We both know that isn't true. My dad doesn't want me in his new life, and neither does Pam, his wife who is only eight years older than me. I'm stuck here. I don't think my mom really wants me with her either, but what choice does she have? I press my lips together, for once not having a comeback.

My mom sighs, the ire melting away as she takes in my silence. "I won't be home from the office until after seven. We have a mandatory meeting—"

Blah, blah, blah, don't care. "Whatever. I'm going to be late for school."

I wave dismissively and leave the house, forcefully shutting the front door behind me. I peer at the houses around us, none of them as grand as ours, but they try. Ours is multi-colored brick in pale browns and grays with a pebbled walkway and flowering shrubs. Mom got a lot of money out of the divorce, and I can forgive some of her faults because of that, but not the fact that she let Pam win. She let her steal her husband, and my father, and left us with what? My brother Jamie is away at college, studying to become an architect. It's just me and my mom.

We argue more than we get along. I can't remember if we do get along. I hate her for her weakness. I blame her for the divorce, for everything. It's her fault my dad left. A horn honks and I look up. Jocelyn and Casey are waiting across the street in Jocelyn's white Prius. Usually, I would smile and skip over. Usually, I would be glad to see my friends. Usually, my stomach wouldn't twist in knots to the point that I have to stop for a minute, close my eyes, and just breathe.

"Let's roll, you crazy bitch," Jocelyn greets with her feline grin.

Usually, I would laugh off the insult, and toss one back.

Today, I don't say anything.

Usually, I would make Casey leave the passenger seat and get in the back.

Today, I silently open the back door and climb inside.

"Do you want to sit up front?" Casey is already reaching for the door handle.

"I'm good." I close my door and wait for the car to move. It doesn't.

Jocelyn cranes her neck around to eye me in the backseat. Her glossy black hair is styled in waves; her eyes are highlighted in lime green. A plum-toned top hugs her perfect curves and the scent of her perfume is all I smell. She looks beautiful, and determined. She looks like she won a game where I didn't know the rules.

Jeff is already hers, I intuitively know.

"What's up with you? Did you get in another fight with your mom?" she questions, looking like she cares.

Casey turns her hazel eyes to me as well, just as concerned.

Fake. They're both fake. Do they even like me? Do I like them? I shake my head and look out the window. I feel the two of them exchanging looks without having to see it. They're wondering what my problem is, and they're calling me names in their head. Was I ever as well-liked as I thought I was? Have all these years been spent with me really having no clue? Maybe Lexie is the only one acting like everyone else feels.

"Are we still on for the party at your dad's next weekend?" Jocelyn wonders, zipping along the road without any concern for how fast she's going, or pedestrians.

"Yeah," I answer, feeling a little better as I think about the party. My dad and his wife will be out of town for the weekend, and he okayed having a few friends over for a sleepover at his cabin near Murphy's Lake. I invited a handful of people, but that's all that is needed to ensure a full house. You invite one person, and they invite another, and that person invites someone else, and on and on it goes. As long as everything goes smoothly, he'll never know.

"I'll bring the popcorn," Casey supplies in a light tone.

Jocelyn snorts. "I don't think popcorn is going to be on anyone's mind."

Casey looks to the side, her profile showing her pinched expression. "I like popcorn."

"I like beer," is Jocelyn's comeback.

Shifting in her seat, Casey lowers her head. "You know I don't like to drink."

"I do, yes. More for me and Melanie. Right, Mel?"

We're almost to the school, and my throat tightens as it comes into view.

"Right," I answer hollowly, my eyes dropping to the apple in my hand.

"How did your date go with Jeff?" My dark-haired friend's voice is innocent enough, and yet, too interested.

I tense, and then force myself to relax. "Are you saying you don't already know?"

Her eyes fly to mine in the rearview mirror. Smugness swirls in the dark depths. The car jerks to a stop as she parks along the curb, and Jocelyn releases my gaze as she takes the keys from the ignition. She doesn't reply until we're on the sidewalk. "I'm asking, aren't I?"

"It went really good," I lie. "So good that he asked me out again."

Half of Jocelyn's mouth lifts. "Oh?"

Cool wind streams through my clothes, chilling my body.

"Are you sure?"

My skin prickles as our gazes clash. She knows exactly how the date went, and that means she was either with Jeff over the weekend, or at least talked to him. Jocelyn never looked at Jeff until I did. It seems to be a recurring occurrence with us and boyfriends.

I'm surprised by how even my voice is when I say, "Don't act like you don't know exactly how the date went."

"Guys, we should really get going before we're late." Casey looks from us to the school.

With a smile, Jocelyn breaks eye contact. "You're being paranoid," she tells me, putting an arm around me. She's like an inferno, scalding me where we touch.

"Guys."

Jocelyn's gaze flickers to Casey. "So go."

With a sigh, Casey shrugs and leaves us.

Her one-armed hug becomes uncomfortably hard. "I'm your friend, Mel. If you tell me to not go after Jeff, I won't."

Liar.

"Actually," I begin, pulling away from her. I breathe easier with space between us. "I decided I don't like Jeff all that much. He's too muscled for me. You're welcome to him."

I am a liar too.

Jocelyn's smile grows, becomes ferocious as she steals my apple and takes a bite. The crunch of it sounds like bones cracking. I imagine her teeth tearing through my jugular. "Great. I'll see if he wants to come with me to your party."

She will too.

My friend hands back the apple, her teeth marks and lipstick on the green and red fruit. I look at it in bemusement, thinking it is symbolic of our friendship. Jocelyn takes from me, and then she gives back whatever she took, but it is no longer in one piece. It is no longer mine. I don't want her leftovers. I didn't know I was her competition before, but I do now. I chuck the apple at the nearest wastebasket.

A boy who doesn't matter enough to know his name glances at me, and I sneer. "Did I say you had permission to breathe my air?"

Like a startled deer, he zips past Jocelyn, and I watch her saunter toward the school, most of the guys around watching her as well. Even Mr. Loomis, the Phy. Ed. teacher, ogles Jocelyn, and I know she likes it. She feeds on it. Jocelyn wants everyone to want her. Disgust slides down my throat like dirty water. Things were better when I didn't notice her as much as I have been lately. Why didn't I? Because things were good in my life, and I didn't pay attention to anything around me until they started to go bad.

With apprehension coating my frame, I pause outside the building, standing still as the last of the students make their way through the doors. Lexie's in there. Jeff's in there. Jocelyn's in there. They're all in there, and I finally realize, whether I am or not, doesn't matter to any of them.

School is almost done for the year, and then I'll have the summer to get myself put back together, and my party can be the start of my comeback. I'll start my senior year better and more spectacular than this school has ever seen me.

I am Melanie Mathews.

I am pretty, rich, and popular.

Boys want me; girls want to be me.

I own this school.

I'm not scared of anyone.

Shoulders back, I make my way to the double doors, recoiling when someone shoots past me in an attempt to make it inside before the bells ring. I set a hand to my pounding heart and walk into Enid High School, smiling like I am oblivious to anyone but myself. I wish I could go back to being that way.

I HEAR THE GIGGLES AND whispered words before I know what's going on. I got through Monday without any incidents, but something told me today wouldn't be as easy. I don't know what it is, but a black cloud hovers over me. Everything is wrong.

There's a cluster of five girls near the cafeteria, and the scent of whatever they're passing off as food for our lunch today, makes my stomach turn. They're freshmen and sophomores; kids I don't generally associate with, or even notice. The circle of bodies divides as a couple of the girls become aware of my presence. Whatever they're laughing and talking about, I know it involves me.

They go silent, cautiously watching me approach.

"Melanie, I had no idea, but I have to say, I like it. If it doesn't work out with Jocelyn, I'm always available. If you still go that way." Clint Burns eyes me as he saunters through the doorway to the lunchroom, a leer on his unpleasant face. When he wiggles his eyebrows, I want to throw something at him.

"What are you talking about?" I demand, but he's gone. I turn to the girls, narrowing my eyes. "What's going on?"

One of them moves a hand behind her back, and I dart for her as she squeaks, tearing the photograph from her hand. It's clearly been altered with Photoshop, but still, it's shocking to see Jocelyn and my faces on the barely dressed bodies of two women in bed together. My neck tightens as blood boils beneath the surface of my skin.

I speak slowly, with only a faint tremble noticeable in my voice. "Who gave you this?"

"They're all around school," one of the braver, or stupider, girls tells me.

"All...around...school." I arch an eyebrow and meet each set of eyes.

Nods proceed, and the underclassmen look like a bunch of bobble heads.

I tear up the printed off photograph, the sound of the destroyed paper not even near as satisfying as finding the culprit of this will be. I crumple the pieces into balls and clench them between my hands. "You see one of these, you throw it away."

Another round of nods.

I jerk my head to the side. "Get out of here, and find them."

"But, it's lu—"

I close my eyes. "I don't care. Find them!"

The girls scatter.

My legs carry me into the cafeteria, all the sounds muted in my rage. The kids turn into blurs, and even the few who call out to me are immaterial. I zero in on Lexie. She sits alone, reading a book. She sits alone, and yet, she doesn't look uncomfortable. She looks like she wants to be alone. Even that feeds the fury inside me. No one *wants* to be alone. She has no right to look happy about being a loner, and a loser.

I stomp toward her, seeing her outlined in red, like the haze of my anger has seeped into my eyeballs. "You," I seethe, my voice unfamiliar to my ears.

Lexie sets down the book, takes a sip from her can of pop, and looks at me. Her blue eyes are startling bright, and her brown hair is styled in soft waves around her face. I give her midnight blue dress an absent look, vaguely surprised to see her dressed so nicely. "Yes, this is me. Are you going anywhere with this?"

"Find someone else to make as miserable as you apparently are."

"But I already did," she says innocently. A smile wants to take over her lips, and I want to smash my fisted hand into her mouth.

"You can't do this to me!" I lean toward her, my body coiled and ready to pounce.

A small frown captures her mouth. "Do what?"

The breaths that leave me are ragged, and too fast, and I place a hand to my pounding chest. Am I having a heart attack, for real, this time? "You won't win at these sick games."

"All I'm doing is reading a book," she says with a sigh. "What exactly do you think I've done this time?"

"The picture..." I break off as I look around the room. It's too quiet. Everyone is watching us.

The principal makes his way toward Lexie and me, looking like a pig stuck in a penguin's body as he waddles over.

"The picture?" Lexie prompts, a touch of wariness in her tone.

There's a chance some people haven't seen it yet. I don't want to bring more attention to it, or us, in case I'm right. I back away, my gaze flitting from person to person, wondering who's seen it. Wondering who's laughing about it. My skin crawls. I swear they all know, and they're all laughing at me.

They hate you.

I flinch from the thought.

"What picture?" she asks again.

I backtrack from her, bumping into a chair leg. The occupant of it hastily propels the chair from me, the legs screeching along the floor as it moves. Other than someone coughing, it's the only sound in the spacious room.

"Stay away from me," I tell Lexie.

One shoulder lifts and lowers, and Lexie goes back to her book.

As I hurry from the room before Principal Stenner can catch me, I feel like I'm in the middle of some onstage play where I've lost my mind, or everyone else has, and they're all trying to make me think I'm the one who has. This whole school is warped. Or I am. I don't know anymore. I just know that it feels like my heart is going to jump out of my chest, and I'm afraid.

Jeff and Jocelyn enter the cafeteria together, and all the sounds and smells hit me with overpowering clarity as I watch them together. Perfectly paired, their good looks complement one another. Jeff at least looks guilty when our gazes collide. Jocelyn's eyes light up, and she grabs me before I can move away, smacking me loudly and firmly on the lips with hers. I wrench from her grasp as gasps and catcalls ring out.

"Take off your clothes!" a male voice that sounds a lot like Clint's calls from some dark corner he belongs in.

"Are you crazy?" I screech, savagely rubbing at my mouth with my hand. I can taste her cherry lip balm on my lips, and it makes me gag.

She laughs. "Oh, come on, don't be such a prude. Everyone's talking about. We might as well play along." Jocelyn leans close, her thick hair sweeping across my check. "Jeff liked it."

I jerk back, looking at Jeff before I can help it. He stares back, interest dilating his eyes. "Pig," I mutter, shoving past my friend.

I stalk up and down the halls, ripping up and tossing each digitally enhanced photograph I can find. Skin on fire, pulse careening, I work at removing the photographs from the school. They're endless. On lockers, in the bathroom; I even find one on the window of the main office. Hot tears splash against my cheeks as I become a tornado of purpose, and a sob of dismay leaves me as I enter the girls' locker room.

The door slams shut behind me, the thundering noise echoing in the pink-painted room. It's final—the sound of my role as queen of Enid High School falling away. The pictures are on every locker, with more on the walls. One person could not have done all this. I don't just have Lexie after me—I have a legion. Even Jocelyn seems to be in on it. There's no point in taking down the photos. Everyone has either seen them, or at least knows about them.

Sliding down the wall, I crumple to the dirty floor. I pull up my knees to my chin, and stare at the closest picture, literally feeling the moment I become unpopular.

Fifteen

Alexis

I SHOULDN'T BE AT THE center on a Tuesday. I have no reason to be, other than the intense need to see Nick. The unbreakable veneer that separates Melanie from the rest of the student body cracked today, and it didn't make me feel good, like I thought it would. It made me feel dirty. I want to feel clean.

It doesn't matter that I wasn't responsible this time. For the rest of the school day, I just kept seeing her devastated eyes, and I know I helped bring her to the place where she now suffers. I raced from the school to here, needing to be reminded of who I am.

Wanting to pace the room as I wait, I instead force myself to sit at one of the tables near the back of the visitation area. The room has mocha-colored walls, some abstract paintings in black and white, and round tables with chairs. A Live employee oversees the room from a desk near the doorway, presently looking at a magazine. It's odd to be on the other side of this. I was the patient, not the one coming to see the patient. To be honest, part of me feels like I should still be here. I mean, undoubtedly, I have some issues I'm struggling with.

Do I have to keep doing this? My dad and I are headed in a good direction, and in my heart, I said goodbye to my mom. There's no point in caring for a woman who doesn't care for me. I have Nick. I have my future. Why focus on the past? The black taint on my soul rears up, hissing that it isn't enough. I haven't gotten them back enough. But when is it enough? How far do I go? When do I stop? And what if I can't?

I chew on an uneven thumbnail as a shudder runs along my spine, my gaze shooting to a red-haired girl as she hugs a guy I am assuming is her boyfriend. A black tattoo crawls up the side of his neck, and the scent of cigarettes emanates from their corner. She's crying, and his face is streaked with tears too. At another table, a middle-aged woman watches her son with wretchedness lining her face. The boy stares back, mute and unmoving. This place is sad, more than anything. Everyone here fights demons, and too often, they lose. My eyes on the doorway, I wait for a boy who makes me feel everything I don't think I am.

I forget to breathe when he appears in the doorway, his brown and blond hair disheveled, fear creasing the sides of his mouth. I almost smile at the dark blue fleece pants. His eyes dart around the room, and as soon as they find me, they stop. The room warms, and my heart beats harder. I feel his gaze all the way to my center; I bloom beneath it. I sit up straighter, and then I'm to my feet, moving for him.

Nick meets me halfway, and grabs my elbows. Grip hard, his gaze searches mine. "Is everything all right?"

"Kiss me," I whisper, sinking in his ocean eyes. I could drown in them, and I know it would somehow be beautiful. "Make me feel like I'm really here."

Without an instant of hesitation, he leans toward me. Nick understands what I want, what I need. I breathe in his fresh scent, tasting something sweet on his lips—the toffees he likes to eat. I feel his kiss through every part of me, and I throb with yearning. I never knew a kiss could be this powerful.

I want more. I want all of Nick. Skin on skin, with nothing between us. I've never been with a boy before, but I want to be with this one. His long fingers slide up my arms to cup my face. He holds me firmly, but carefully. Nick presses his lower half to mine, and I lose a fraction of control. I twist the fabric of his brown tee shirt between my hands, anchoring him to me. Nick brings me to life, dispels anything that hurts. I could live off him alone.

"Nick. Lexie." The voice of the female worker commands, telling us to knock it off without actually saying the words.

We break away, staring at one another. His eyes are filled with lust, the pulse in his neck fluttering like the frantic wings of a hummingbird. Nick's hair is more unkempt than it was when I got here, and I vaguely remember running my fingers through it at one point. I can't get enough air. My skin feels unusually hot.

Using my thumbs, I smooth his furrowed eyebrows, then the sharp planes of his cheekbones. This face—God, this face—it undoes me. I dream of this face. I ache for this face. I could stare at it until I can't keep my eyes open. I press my thumb to his lips, and he kisses it, his eyes telling me a thousand stories I might never hear.

"Please greet me like that every time you see me." Nick's voice is rough, and a thrill shoots through my stomach.

I smile, taking his hands. They squeeze mine. "I'll try."

We move to the table I vacated upon his arrival, our chairs close, our knees touching. He doesn't release my hands. Nick levels his long-lashed eyes on me. "Is everything okay?"

"Right now it is," I answer honestly.

"But before?"

I shrug, avoiding his gaze. The words are there, but I can't say them. Not yet. Maybe not ever. If I tell him, what then? What will he think, knowing I'm not any better than the people who tormented me? Seeing him makes it easy to pretend the school, and everything that happens inside it, isn't real. "You know what I want, more than anything?"

"What?" he asks through lips that barely move. He seems to hold his breath.

"I want your arms around me as I fall asleep, and I want to hold you back as I do." I look at Nick, the intensity of my focus refusing to let him hide his eyes. "I want us to be free. I want you to be free."

Nick drops my hands, and his eyes fall to his lap.

"I want to know that in two years—seven, fourteen, twenty years—I'll still have you in my life." My mouth goes dry at the admission, at the barrier I knowingly remove by telling Nick this.

His eyes shoot to my face. "I want the same."

I swallow, unable to do much more. My hands shake, and I slide them between my knees to keep Nick from noticing. I've told him more than I planned.

"Alexis." Nick looks around the room. He brings his attention back to me, and I know it never really left me. He is painfully aware of me at all times, as I am with him. Whenever he entered a room while I was a patient here, I knew. Whenever I walked into a room he was already in, he found me with his eyes. Always.

"I want to tell you," he says slowly. "I want to tell you why I'm here."

"Then tell me."

"You'll hate me." He looks so sad, and I can't take seeing that expression on Nick's face.

"I don't think that's possible."

Nick's quiet is unnerving, worrisome.

The red-haired girl tells her boyfriend goodbye as they both stand, and a heated kiss is exchanged. Janice, the woman at the desk, watches them, but doesn't comment this time.

"Tell me something wonderful," I say quickly to Nick, desperate to take whatever camouflaged pain he has from his demeanor. I'm losing him. He's fading, going to that place we all have inside us to where we navigate when we can't stand reality. He grounds me; I want to do the same for him. I think I do.

Light comes back to his eyes, and he straightens. Nick lifts a hand, smoothing bangs from my forehead. Tingles shimmy along my skin at his touch. "I used to have nightmares every night, and I still have them often, but not every night. On the nights where I don't have nightmares, I get to see you. Sometimes, we just talk. Sometimes, we do...other things."

His skin flushes, and I bite my lower lip, able to guess at the "other things".

"Sometimes," he whispers, looking into my eyes like he sees his redemption in them. "I get to hold you, like you want me to. Those are the best nights. They seem the realest. On those nights, I can almost believe it isn't a dream, and that I'm really holding you. I hope, one day, they won't only be dreams."

I take a breath, and it sounds like a sob is trapped inside it. "I hope for that too," I tell him, my voice uneven. My eyes sting, and there is uncomfortable pressure on my chest.

A long moment passes. A moment where I look at Nick, and he looks at me, and we exchange hopes and dreams that may never come to be, other than in our minds.

Sixteen

NICK

CAN'T LET ALEXIS KNOW who I really am.

This is the prevalent thought in my head in the days between the times I see Alexis. As we get closer, it gets harder to keep the other Nick from her. I want to tell her, and that's what scares me the most. Yesterday, I almost told her. Yesterday, she pulled away another layer of me. What happens when she removes them all? What then? Will she find me repulsive, or will she see me?

My schoolwork for the year is done, and I can officially say I am finished with high school, although I'll have to take a test to get my G.E.D. I try to lose myself in books, or extra chores around the center, but nothing distracts me from the anxiety that's tied itself to me. It's a continuous woozy feeling in my gut; it's the surety of knowing something wonderful has a time limit. I'm supposed to take pills for anxiety, but I can't. Why should I have peace when I haven't earned it?

A lot of the time—too often—I find myself staring at the book about the half-man, half-alien Alexis gave me, or talking to the pink bear she loaned me.

I find myself wondering if I'm insane, and if I'd know if I am.

I wouldn't, would I?

It's Wednesday, and I'm in Dr. Larson's office. She always looks sincere. I know she cares about me, but I wonder if she looks like that with all the kids. I think she has to. Her brown and gold hair is pulled back in a loose bun, and she wears cream-colored pants and a top that matches the darker shade of her hair. I wonder if it's a requisite in her line of work to learn how to speak slowly, carefully, softly. To remain unruffled in the bedlam of her patients.

This isn't my regular counseling session time. I asked if I could see her now, knowing Alexis is due for her own therapy conference soon. I thought if I was already here when she showed up, maybe I'd be fearless enough to tell her my warped history. I know it to be a lie. I can't.

But I have to.

I am incapable of sitting still; even my eyes constantly move from one thing to another. I know the words I want to say, but something keeps me from saying them, even to Dr. Larson, who already knows everything. I want to tell her what Alexis told me about being bullied. I want to tell her my good dreams—the ones where I have a promising future, the ones where Alexis is in my life, the ones where I get to hold Alexis—but if I do, I'll have to tell her my bad. The ones where I never get out of this place. The ones where Alexis never speaks to me again, and eventually, forgets me.

"Did you have another nightmare?" Dr. Larson watches my movements with calmness.

"No," I say on an exhale. The bouncing of my leg turns violent. No new nightmare anyway. Just the boy; always the boy. He was particularly gruesome last night, telling me all my crimes with each slash of a tiny, deadly sharp blade across his wrists. Blood sprayed me, entering my mouth, my ears. I was awash in my sin. Choking on it.

"Nick."

I go still, like a line tugging at me suddenly stopped. "How do I get past this?" I whisper, shifting my eyes to hers. "How do I move on?"

Dr. Larson's brown eyes are compassionate, and seeing that makes me feel worse. "You forgive yourself."

"Yeah, right, I know that, but *how*?" I drop my face to my hands. "I don't know how."

"Whatever the circumstances, every person makes their own choices. You didn't make his for him."

"Didn't I?"

I'm crying. I don't even realize it until I feel the dampness on my face. The tears are warm, and lick my eyes with flames. I don't feel like this when I'm with Alexis. I can keep the monsters at bay. They're still with me; they'll always be with me, but they don't seem so close. They don't seem to be twisted around me, like they are now.

"Alexis told me," I rasp in a sandpaper voice, turning my burning eyes on Dr. Larson. "She told me what happened at that school. She told me what she did, what she tried to do."

Her brown eyes are pools of sympathy.

I have to look away.

"You have a choice too," the doctor tells me quietly. "You can choose to let it go."

"Choices are easy to make—living with them is entirely another thing."

She sits back, looking stunned by my words. The clock ticks off a minute before she speaks. "Why do you think you were drawn to Lexie?" When I don't answer, she presses, "Do you think it was because she reminded you of someone?"

157

"Yeah, she looks a lot like a five-nine male with short black hair and pimples."

"I didn't mean…" She frowns and looks over her notes. Even she, the professional, can't remember his name. Even she, the one person who knows me better than anyone else, has somehow forgotten the name of the boy who altered my life. The world may forget him, but I never will. His parents never will. His little sister never will.

"Jackson Hodgson," I say in a dead voice.

"I meant you," she says kindly, closing my file.

"I have to go." I abruptly get to my feet and spiral out the door before Dr. Larson can comment.

Because life hates me, at exactly the moment I don't want to see Alexis, she walks through the door. Her eyes light up like she sees *me*, but not the expression on my face. She does, though, and soon. The smile is wiped from her mouth, and a crease forms between her pretty blue eyes. I love her eyes. They're like the inside of a flame, intense and expressive. They talk, even when she doesn't. Right now, they're wondering what the hell is wrong with me.

"Nick?" Alexis moves to touch my tear-stained face. "What happened?"

I turn my body and avert my eyes, keeping myself out of her reach. "Nothing."

"I can see that."

"And I can hear your sarcasm."

"Are you sure? Because if not, I can try harder."

My eyes meet hers. She lifts one shoulder in a lopsided shrug, a small, understanding smile on her pink lips.

"You're early." My voice is thick, rough.

Her eyebrows shoot up. "And you're not in the library. We are conundrums."

I look toward the hallway on the right. A girl and boy walk down it side by side, their voices low murmurs. I want to follow them. My body tenses in preparation of flight. I want to disappear into my room until I have better control over myself. I want to redo this meeting with Alexis, redo this day. Hell, my whole life.

"Nick."

I face Dr. Larson, my hands fisted at my sides. Hysteria is pounding at me, shrieking at me to run, run, run, and never stop running. She stands in the doorway of her office, watching me. Dr. Larson knows I'm one step from a meltdown. *Not in front of Alexis. Please, not in front of Alexis. Keep it together, just a little longer.* The doctor looks at Alexis long enough to offer a friendly smile, and then her eyes are back to me.

"Nick, why don't you come back into my office for a moment?" Soothing. Her tone is soothing.

The receptionist stares at us—no, at me. I can't remember her name, but I'll never be able to forget the bulging veins that crisscross the backs of her hands or the astonishingly red shade of her hair. It looks like someone melted Red Hots on her scalp. Her hand hovers near a button on the wall. One push of that and I'll be taken away and put in a room with nothing but myself and my ghost in it. One wrong move, one wrong outburst. My throat closes on me as I try to inhale, and my eyes fill once more.

"Nick."

My gaze flies to Alexis'. Stays there. I could get lost in her eyes. I think I'd like that far too much. She doesn't look away, even now. *Stay here, with me, Nick*, she seems to say. I take a shuddering breath, and feel the tightness of my limbs loosen.

"I want you to come outside with me. We can walk on the path that runs around the center. Please?"

"Lexie—" Dr. Larson starts.

Alexis faces the doctor. "I'll be back in time for my appointment. I need to tell Nick something. It's important."

The tension around us escalates, throbs, and recedes.

Dr. Larson must nod, because Alexis takes my hand, and gently pulls at me. As soon as we're outside, being blasted by the sun and heat and the scent of blooming flowers, she drops my hand and instead grabs my face. Her eyes are blue lightning, electrocuting me to life. The kiss is unexpected, fierce, and fills me with an ache. Bittersweet. That is how I would define the kiss. I grip her wrists, but don't force them away from me. I hold them; I tether her to me.

Don't hate me. Don't hate me. Please, don't hate me.

The kiss turns desperate with my unwanted thoughts. I move my hands from her wrists to the small of her back. I enfold her. Embrace her. I angle my mouth. Our tongues collide, dance. It's hard to breathe. I keep kissing her. She tastes of sweetness and black licorice. Desire thrums through me, tautens my body. Her fingers curl around the sides of my face; she presses her body to mine. Too much. This is too much. She's going to kill me with need.

I break off the kiss, putting distance between us.

"Just so I know for future reference—walking the path is code for making out?" I rasp as I try to draw air into my lungs.

Alexis laughs, and it sounds odd. Ragged. Like she too is fighting to get her breathing under control. "That's just a perk. You asked me to greet you with kisses, remember?"

That was the best thing I ever said.

As if our bodies are in accordance, we reach for one another at the same time, lock fingers, and head for the dirt walkway that loops around the spacious land Live sits on. Alexis' fingers are slender, cold. I tighten my hold. I want to tell her how I feel about her. I want to tell her everything—that she *is* everything. Dust fans the bottoms of our legs as we walk the tree-lined path. A six-foot wooden fence separates us from the rest of the city. A fortress against reality. Reality sometimes sucks.

Not this one, though, not with Alexis.

"So, my dad and I, we sort of, kind of, had a talk."

The cautiousness of her tone gives me pause. "And?"

Alexis blows out a breath. "I think we're going to be okay."

"Good," I tell her, meaning it.

"It was the pants."

I give her a sidelong look, having no idea what she's talking about.

She smiles, using her free hand to touch the side of my leg. "Your fuzzy gray pants. I took one look at them and was out of control with lust."

"I'll be sure to always wear these then," I vow.

"It has to be the gray ones," Alexis informs me in a somber tone. "None of the others affect me in quite the same way."

"Got it. Gray pants. For all eternity. I'll get a pair for every day of the week, just in case I happen to see you."

I smile when she laughs.

"WHAT WAS GOING ON IN there when I showed up? You looked...haunted. Scared. Something."

We've walked the path twice now, in what is the accumulation of one mile. I thought she would have brought it up before now. I wordlessly shake my head, not wanting to talk about it. I don't want to break the serenity cocooning us. I know I have to tell her, and I know it will be the end of us. Why would I want to hurry that?

Alexis stops beneath an especially large tree. Her shirt matches her eyes, makes them brilliantly blue. The leaves dance as a breeze sifts through the air. The strands of her hair move as well. Her eyes are riveted to me, and I know whatever she is going to say, is something to which I won't know how to respond.

"Were you bullied too? Is that why you're here?" she asks bluntly.

Of course she would think that. Of course she would think we're alike.

My jaw stiffens. "I can't talk about it."

"Why? Why can't you talk about it? Why can't you tell me?"

Because you'll never talk to me again if I do.

She frowns. "What happened to you?"

My spine aches with how rigidly I stand.

"I told you about me. Why can't you tell me about you?" Alexis' voice is quiet with confusion, and beneath that, hurt.

I open my mouth to say something, anything, but Alexis is already talking again.

"Wait. That's a lie. I didn't tell you everything—I didn't tell you that I went back to the school to get even with my bullies," she blurts, her eyes widening at the confession.

The sun hides behind a cloud, and the air cools. It's unusually fitting to the moment.

"What do you mean?" I ask in a low voice, the hairs on my arms going straight up with trepidation.

"They hurt me, Nick, and now, I'm hurting them." Her expression is defiant, and also, still, confused.

"How?" It comes out inaudible, but she reads my lips.

Alexis shrugs, picking at the bark of the tree with her fingernail. "I'm doing to them what they did to me. Everything they did. I ridicule them; I fight back. I antagonize and stalk. I *am* them."

Vengeance snaps through the air, further chilling me. Thunder rumbles in the distance. It's as if the weather feeds off our discord, hones itself to it. I glance up, noticing the gathering clouds. They're moving fast.

"Stop," I say roughly, taking a step toward her. Alexis scalds my eyes with the infernos of wrath in hers. Beneath that, small and fading in the depths of blue, is shame. She knows. Alexis knows this is wrong. "Stop what you're doing. Stop it now. Leave it alone."

"Why should I?" Even as her voice is hard, it wavers. Alexis lifts her chin and glares at me, not backing up even though the space between us has disintegrated. "They picked on me for *months*. They made me feel like nothing, and then, I wanted to be nothing."

She blinks, swallowing. Her eyes are shot through with red, luminous with unshed tears. Alexis looks pale and drawn, and on fire with purpose. All at once. "They broke me, Nick. I can't let them get away with it. And I don't know what happened to you, because you won't tell me, but I think someone did the same to you. I thought you would understand."

I close my eyes, trying to keep the tears from forming, but the stupid things fill my eyes anyway. I rub my face, and then I blindly reach for Alexis. In each other's arms, we cry. I'm too damaged to care how this makes me look. That other me, he would sneer and mock at this display, but that other me, he hurt people. He broke them. And in the end, he broke me too. Just like Alexis' bullies broke her. I one-hundred percent understand her need for revenge, and I wish I didn't.

This is it. This is the end. It's too soon. I want more time.

The skies open up, obscuring our tears with rain.

"They don't even remember me. Can you believe it? I almost died because of them, and they don't even know who I am," she whispers in the grayness, her voice unusually clear under the torrent of rain soaking us. And then it hardens to steel. "They're regretting it now, and they're going to regret it more."

The tone of Alexis' soft voice chills me, and now I know what I saw in her eyes weeks before. I saw hunger, satisfaction, but I also saw menace. This has been growing for some time, working at her in the weeks since she's been back in school. Revenge destroys, and that's all it does. This darkness, if she lets it, will abolish her as well as her enemies.

"Who?" It twists my stomach to ask the question.

There is no answer.

"Who are they?" I demand, staring at the fence stained dark from the rain.

Her frame stiffens. Her voice is wooden. "Melanie Mathews and Jocelyn Rodriguez were the worst, but Casey Reed was almost as bad, in another way. She knows her friends are awful, and she lets it happen. She doesn't stick up for herself, or for anyone else. Then there's Clint Burns. There were others too, but they weren't as bad."

I barely hear her words. The names shoot through me, bringing up images and instances I'd rather forget.

"What you're doing—" I tell her slowly, my lips close to her ear. My hands shake where they touch her, and I drop them, hoping she doesn't notice. Hoping she doesn't wonder. "—is dangerous. To you. Please, Alexis, don't continue this. Stop now, before you can't."

"I already can't. I don't want to stop."

"What you're doing is wrong."

She shoves me, and I stagger over a dip in the slippery ground, my leg twisting and immediately throbbing with pain. I put my weight on my other leg. Hair plastered to her face, eyes blazing, with her mouth a slash of pale color across her white face, Alexis stares at me. The blue of her shirt is gray under the darkened sky, her jeans black. Rivulets of water make their way down her head and body. The sight of her takes my breath from me—in awe, in shock.

Alexis is fury incarnate.

"I thought you were my friend," she tells me bitingly. "I thought—I thought you were more than my friend."

"I am." I fight to inhale through the crushing pressure of my chest. "I am your friend—and...and more. I care about you, Alexis. A lot. That's why I'm asking you to not do this. If you keep trying to hurt them, who's to say you won't badly injure yourself along with them?"

Her mouth twists with suspicion, and it's like she's finally seeing me, all of me, but mostly, it's like she's seeing the badness I too carry. She looks at me like I betrayed her, and I guess I have. She despises the fact that I am against her on this. Maybe she despises me as well. Alexis can hate me all she wants, if it means her need for payback ends.

"Who are you? Who are you, really?" Alexis closes the distance she put between us with the force of her hands. The rain comes harder, fiercer. Louder. "Why do you hide who you are? Why don't you want me to know what you've done to get here? Why won't you leave this place?"

I watch her, helpless and mute. I want to become the rain, and drop to the ground. I want to dissolve.

Her eyes flash dangerously. "Tell me who you are!"

"Does it matter so much to you?"

"You're a coward." She trembles under the cold wetness trying to drown us from above. Alexis turns from me. "That's what matters to me."

Seventeen

Alexis

I AM A SOGGY MESS when I step into Live. One minute, Nick and I were laughing, and the next, I couldn't stand the sight of him. He was supposed to understand, not tell me I'm wrong. And it hurts—my heart throbs with it. Gladys takes one look at me and shakes her head, her eyes going back to the magazine in her hands. Water drips from my face, pooling around my squishy shoes on the nice floor. I open my mouth to ask for a towel just as Dr. Larson opens her door, as if she's been waiting for our return.

She looks behind me, a faint furrow between her eyebrows. "Where's Nick?"

Hell if I care, is probably not the best response.

"Still outside." I sound numb. I feel numb. I don't know him. I thought I did, and I don't. I was wrong about Nick, and I wonder if my feelings were wrong too. If he can't tell me about himself, then I'll never really know him. If he can't be brave enough to trust me, then I can't trust him either.

I almost gave it up. I woke up the day after my dad and I talked, and I looked at the answering response to my message on the chalkboard. And then there was seeing Melanie at the school, vulnerable and human. It was almost enough to make me decide to move on. Almost.

Before I went to bed, I wrote:

I used to wonder if you ever think of me, but now I know that it doesn't matter. Because I'm choosing to not think of you anymore.

Sometime over the night, the chalkboard exploded in letters. Words lined the black backdrop. Small words, large words, slanted words, almost unreadable words. So many words. I stood before it, staring. My eyes stung with tears as I read.

You forgot her sixteenth birthday. In fact, you forgot her fourteenth, and fifteenth too.
I blamed myself for you leaving me, but for you leaving Lexie? I blame you.
I failed as a husband, but I won't as a father.
I'll be the dad she needs, and I'll try to be the dad she wants.
Lexie is beautiful, and smart, and brave, and you're missing it all. But I'm not.

And now I know why I didn't stop. Even as I ran to him and opened up to him in a way I hadn't previously, I guess, somewhere inside me, I knew Nick was a mirage. I knew his secrets would destroy us. I just thought knowing them would do it, not the fact that he won't let me know them.

"Where?" I've never heard anything less than friendliness in the doctor's tone, but it's gone. "Lexie. Where is Nick?"

"He was near the path when I left him." My body quivers with chills.

Giving me a slanted look, the doctor says to Gladys, "Have Jensen and Zamora find me. I'm going to look for Nick Alderson. Page me if anyone sees him before I report that I have." She pauses. "Get Lexie some towels to dry off with too."

The woman already has the phone to her ear when Dr. Larson looks at me. Thunder shakes the walls. It's in her eyes too. "I don't know what's going on between you two, but I don't want to see it here anymore. From now on, you come to your sessions, and you don't go anywhere else inside these walls. If you want to see each other, it happens outside of Live."

"Nothing," I croak. My throat burns, and feeling left out, my eyeballs decide to join in. "Nothing is going on between us." Not anymore. He can't even tell me about himself. I told him everything, and he told me nothing. I can't care about someone I don't really know. And he doesn't know me either, not like he should.

Tight-lipped, she regards me for a moment. "Go into my office and wait for me, please. You still have a session."

Tossing on a neon orange rain poncho, the doctor's departure is as icy as the storm outside. Guilt coats my throat as I swallow; quickly followed by hurt at the harsh way Dr. Larson spoke to me, and the fact that she wasn't out of line. I shouldn't have left Nick. He was unstable when I came here, and I got angry, and whatever happened with us, I shouldn't have left him.

Lightning cracks the world outside, and with the towels from one of the laundry personnel in hand, I dry off as best as I can, and stumble into Dr. Larson's office.

I study the dimly lit room with its citrus scent and flower paintings, thinking it's too warm, too cozy, for my present mood. I want to be outside with the storm. I feel as volatile as it. My skin blisters when I think of Nick telling me to back off. I told him what they did to me, and he just thinks I should be able to move on. Like it's so easy. Like he can't possibly know how I feel, because he's never felt it. Anger takes over the hurt, and I allow it, better able to handle that emotion than the other. I thought we were alike. I thought he, of all people, would comprehend. I thought I meant as much to him as he does to me.

I thought a lot of things.

Fuming as I sit on the edge of the seat, my eyes land on the desk across the room, and linger there. I've seen Dr. Larson take files out of a drawer. My file is in there. Nick's file is in there. My pulse stutters. I glance to the closed office door. Even as a voice tells me to not do it, and my heartrate escalates to a dangerous thrum, I stand and walk toward the desk.

My hand reaches for the bottom right drawer. It'll be locked. I tighten my fingers around the handle, and pull. It opens without a sound. I let out a deep breath I didn't know I was holding, and suck in quick gasps of air to make up for the lack of oxygen. My fingers are close to useless, spasms going through them and the rest of me as I crouch on the soft carpet and search for Nick's folder.

This is wrong. Dr. Larson will be back at any moment. I wonder if I can be arrested for this, or at least charged with something. Thunder roars overhead, and I jump. My gaze flitters to the door and back. I pause on my own file, and keep going. I already know every messed up piece of my life. Nick's isn't in here, I realize with disappointment, and a small dose of relief.

I close the door with a small click, and go to the drawer above it before I can change my mind. His is one of the first folders I see. Waves of unease crash over me, and I blink to focus as my eyesight blurs. I feel sick. Once I see what's inside, I can't pretend I haven't. Once I know, I know. I shouldn't be doing this. This is a violation of his privacy.

That vicious part of me tells me this is Nick's fault for not telling me himself. That it isn't fair of him to want to know me, and not let me know him. It pushes that I am owed this. After all, didn't I tell Nick all the miserable details of what happened to me? Knowing I shouldn't, still, I listen to that voice. It's the voice that tells me it's okay to hurt my bullies, and that I haven't hurt them enough, not yet. It's the voice that I find myself listening to, more and more.

With silent movements, I pull the file from the drawer, opening it before my conscience is allowed to state its opinion. Heart beating in my ears, and all the blood in my veins turning to ice, I read. I see words like "bully" and "suicide" and "Enid High School", and for one instant, I think I must be looking at my own file. But although the words are similar, they're lined up in a foreign manner. Saying something entirely different than my own file would. And there is another name other than Nick's that I recognize. I've seen it before, at my school. It lives among the words "In Memory Of", and it is etched onto a bench beneath a tree, along with a birth, and a death, date.

Jackson Hodgson.

The ice is burned away, leaving havoc behind as my eyes drink in the letters, and their meaning becomes clear. I realize what I'm reading, and Nick's secret is unveiled. I know why he kept it. I wish I didn't know it. My heart sputters, stops, and careens into some wild beat to which the rest of my body cannot adjust. My limbs go limp, and I stare unseeingly at the wall on the other side of the room. I am in shock, and that's good, because I don't want to feel.

As if my fingers belong to someone else, they pick up the file, close it, and put it back in the drawer. They are ghost actions, noiseless and invisible. My feet move without any command from me. They take me from the room, past the narrow-eyed woman behind the desk, and into the restroom, where I throw up everything I've consumed today.

The hurt I carry for Nick evaporates as I sit on the cold linoleum floor with my back against the stall. Any good feeling I ever had for him is no longer there. Like I vomited it all out of me. My heart is empty, and then, it fills.

With something else.

It's cold.

Deadly.

Final.

Eighteen

NICK

I DON'T KNOW HOW I know Alexis knows about me, but as soon as our eyes meet as she steps from Dr. Larson's office, I feel it in my soul. That clear, undeniable truth of my dark heritage, staring back at me from cold blue eyes. Eyes I love, look at me with loathing. I shift my attention around her to Dr. Larson, knowing it couldn't have been her who gave away my secrets. Every word, every confession that passes between us, is confidential.

The doctor watches back, impassive. It wasn't her.

How, then? How does Alexis know?

After I dried off and changed into dry clothes, with the ankle I sprained giving me trouble the whole way, I limped my way down here to wait until she was done with her weekly counseling. She's right. I have been a coward. I hid myself inside these walls; I hid from myself. I blocked out the world because I never wanted to see it again. None of it. I wanted to pretend that other Nick Alderson didn't exist. I wanted to forget. I was fading away in here, and I didn't care. It was what I wanted.

Until I met someone who managed to shine around the cracks of her being.

As I made my slow trek through the hallway, I told myself I owed her the truth, however she responded to it. Alexis Hennessy, the broken girl who somehow made me feel closer to whole. Rightness hums along my skin, even as an ache grows inside me. I know what I have to do. I told myself I couldn't keep hiding my sins, not if I wanted us to be anything. But we won't be, not ever. I feel the inevitability of it in my bones. I see it in her frozen gaze.

We're over.

"Can I talk to you?" Hesitation muddles my words. *Why?* I ask myself. *Why even try to explain?* She's judged already. It would be different if she was wrong, if she unjustly loathed me. But everything Alexis is thinking and feeling toward me—it's all legitimate.

"Outside," Dr. Larson states, looking pointedly between the two of us. "And don't go past the sidewalk." Her gaze sears me. "You're still a patient here, Nick. Keep close to the building."

The warning is clear: Pull another stunt like earlier and you know what happens.

They found me sitting in the middle of the muddy walkway, head bowed, arms crossed over my wet hair, rocking. I was rocking like a crazy person. The ghost was there—Jackson Hodgson was there— watching me. He didn't speak. He just looked. What dropped me to the ground was the expression on his face. It was as if he pitied me. *He* pitied *me.* I started laughing, and then I started crying. Or maybe I never stopped. I don't know.

I give a sharp jerk of my head in affirmation.

Alexis glares at me as she passes, her steps careful and stiff.

It's interesting how different the elements are this time compared to the first time we came outside. No longer blue skies; there is no sunshine. The thunder and lightning have dissipated, but the rain is still at it. We stand under the lip of the roof, directly in view of anyone who happens to walk by the front door. I feel eyes on us, and glance up at the blinking red light of a camera recording everything. I wonder if there's sound for the spectators to get a real feel for the devastation of this scene.

"You're one of them," she spits out, turning on me. Hatred lines her face, morphing the pretty features into an unrecognizable mask.

"I'm—"

"You're a bully." Alexis' voice is a whip across my heart.

I can't protect myself from the verbal attack. I don't have time, or resources. All I can offer is the truth, however damning it is. I stand straight, even as I lower my head to keep our eyes connected. I force myself to gaze at her, to see the emptiness where softness once was. Maybe this is how it is supposed to end, maybe this is the ultimate payback for every shitty thing I did: me loving a girl who hates me.

"I was."

A broken sound leaves her, like a cry of denial and acceptance. Alexis shakes her head, arms wrapped around herself. The world pauses in the face of her pain, and I feel it pierce my chest like a bullet. I don't want to lose her. *She was never yours*, an answering voice tells me.

"I knew what you were going to say, but I still hoped."

"Alexis, *please*." Looking at her hurts, but walking away would hurt more. I can't sever our bond. She has to do that.

"Someone died because of you." Even though she whispers, she might as well have shouted, so deeply do I hear her words.

My body shudders. "Now you understand why I didn't want you to know."

"Tell me," she commands. "Tell me everything."

Jackson Hodgson stands behind Alexis, his form translucent. Still waiting. Waiting for me to acknowledge him, and what I did. He wears the same green and brown shirt he had on when I found him in his bedroom over a year ago, drained of life and blood. I glance down at his wrists, watch the blood drip to nothing. It's harder than it should be to look away, to look up at his face. His pale brown eyes look like pits of endless, horrible truth. I blink and the ghost is gone.

"Tell me."

I turn my gaze to Alexis, the girl who suffered at the hands of people I used to hang around. People I used to be like. I even briefly dated Melanie before moving on to Jocelyn. It makes me sick. I was one of them, and after I left, they continued on as if nothing tragic had happened. As if Jackson never mattered, and to them, Alexis never did either.

If not for what this will do to Alexis, I would say everything the kids at Enid High School get from her is warranted.

I roll my shoulders and I harden myself to the girl who made me want to live again. If I don't forget what she means to me, I won't be able to do this. It was stupid of me to think I deserved any kind of happiness after what I did. Borrowed happiness. That's all it was. A boy died because of me. I might as well have been the one to steal the scalpel from his dad's office and place it in his hand. I just as assuredly slit his wrists as he did. My hands shake and I pull a shell of self-preservation around me.

I start to talk.

"Jackson Hodgson was a geek." Even my voice is hard. It has to be, to talk about my past. Once, I spoke of it without holding anything back. Just once, and that was when I was first admitted to Live. But I was numb then, and I didn't feel the careening emotions like I do now.

176

"He played the trumpet and watched Pokémon—he even collected the cards. His black hair stood up around his head like he didn't know how to brush it, and his face was a mess of acne. Braces covered his teeth, and he always had food from his last meal stuck in them. He walked like a stork, his head bobbing forward and back, his eyes on the floor."

I laugh darkly. "Really, he made it too easy."

Her eyes throb with black fire.

"You can't hate me any more than I already hate myself," I tell her gently.

"I can try."

I nod and swallow against a hundred apologies I'll never voice. I've said them all, and they never changed anything. "I suppose you can."

"Keep going," she says flatly.

My fingers clench, and I stare at the slanted raindrops as they pummel the ground, creating pools of water. "We would make fun of his clothes, call him names. Brace Face was the most commonly used one. The girls thought it was fun to act like they liked him, and then laugh about it later."

"The girls." Bitter, she sounds so bitter.

I open my mouth to say their names. Melanie. Jocelyn.

"Don't. I already know who you mean." Disgust takes over the bitterness.

"I didn't know the teasing bothered him as much as it did, but even if I did know, I don't know that I would have stopped. He was there to be picked on. I told myself if he didn't want to be made fun of all the time, then he needed to stop looking and acting the way he did."

"Because he could help it."

Having no reply, I continue. "He asked me one day why I did it, why I chose him to pick on so relentlessly." My throat tightens. "You know what I told him?"

Alexis says nothing.

I smile cruelly, and my stomach painfully twists. "Because he was born."

Face stricken, she stares at me like I'm a monster. The coldness of the rain shifts my way, freezing me where I stand. With sickness in my soul, and leaking from my eyes, nose, and mouth in unseen disease, I know it too. I am a monster. Or I was. But if I once was, am I not still?

"Years, Alexis, it was *years* of bullying for him." I see the damnation in my eyes in the reflection of hers.

"Why did you do it?"

"I don't know." I run fingers through my hair in frustration. "Because he was different. Because it was easy. Because hurting him made me feel powerful. I don't know. And I should. I should know why I thought it was okay to make another person feel like shit."

The scent of damp earth blows our way with a sudden change in the wind. It makes me think of death, and graves, and I squint into the gray atmosphere, expecting to see Jackson. He isn't here. I visited his gravesite once, in the days before I was dragged to this place, and I wept. I lost my mind a little bit in the aftermath of the boy's death.

I'm not sure I got it all back.

I turn my attention back to Alexis. Even now, with the detestation emanating from her to me, I want to gaze at her. For a brief moment, she cared as much for me as I do for her. I know she did. I'll hang on to that in the black loneliness of nights to come, when the reality of all that's passed sinks in, and I know, in the end, Jackson won. I don't even feel bad about it. I'm glad. For him, I'm glad.

Penance for my sins, right?

"I suppose you want the bear back?" It's a stupid question, and I don't know why I ask it.

She snorts bitterly. "The person who gave it to me betrayed me. So did the person I gave it to. Keep it, and think of how much I don't think of you back."

Even though her words sting, I'm relieved that I can keep Rosie, however weird that is. My feet lead me closer to Alexis, and I watch her stiffen. Inches are all that stand between us. Inches and truth. Revulsion clings to her like a dark smudge upon her aura. The fruity scent I associate with her stands out, like something sweet among the vileness. Peaches, and blamelessness that will never be mine.

I look into her eyes as I tell her the worst of it. I want to see the moment she truly detests me. "I started a rumor around the school that he was gay. It didn't take long before everyone was talking about it, and you know the really macho guys? The homophobes? They beat him up one day after band practice. Cracked a few ribs, his nose, even broke his fingers so he couldn't play trumpet anymore."

My words are garbled as I say, "They carved the word 'faggot' into his forehead with a pocketknife."

A hand goes to Alexis' mouth, and her eyes are wide and filled with disbelief and agony. She looks like she's going to be physically ill. I see her expression change. The eyes narrow, the mouth hardens. Something dark glitters from her eyes. There. There's the look I imagined, only actually seeing the utter loathing in the eyes of a girl I cherish, hurts more than I could have thought possible. My heart is torn in tiny pieces.

"He was hurt bad."

Nausea hits me hard at the memory of finding Jackson in the school parking lot after they were done with him. Disgusting as it is, when he was broken and bleeding, I finally saw him as a human being. I was horrified at what they'd done, at what I'd put into motion. I called for help and a teacher dialed 9-1-1. An ambulance came to the school and took him away.

I drove to the hospital and paced the halls once he was admitted. I took the looks of hatred from his family with clear eyes and a clear head. I knew what I'd done, and I was sickened by my actions. When Jackson got out, I was going to make it up to him. That was my vow. That was my plea. *Let him live so I can make this better.*

I never got the chance.

I briefly close my eyes, everything inside me a pile of brokenness. "Turns out, the rumor I started was true." I open eyes that burn with misery, and shame. I didn't know. I didn't know Jackson was gay.

"The night he was discharged from the hospital, he snuck into his dad's dental office after hours, took a scalpel from the supply of them, and went home to kill himself. I stopped by his house to apologize, to just talk to him. His mom didn't want to let me in, but she finally told me he was in his room."

I blink my eyes, and tears drop. The memories haven't faded. I don't think they will. I don't know that I want them to. I need to remember this. I need to live this, and breathe this, and never forget. If I forget, Jackson's life has less value. If I forget, his death means nothing.

"I found him. He was lying on his bed, blood surrounding him, eyes staring at the ceiling. He'd slit his wrists, written on the wall with his own blood, and died in his bed. He wrote 'I wish I'd never been born'. And I knew, when I read those words, that it was my fault."

I look at the water on the ground, seeing blood in its stead. It's soaked through the soles of my shoes. I can never escape the blood. My throat is closing in on me, and I want to weep, but even that gets choked somewhere in my throat. "I have nightmares about it—and, sometimes, you. I guess maybe I always knew you and I were doomed."

"We weren't doomed, Nick. We were—are—nothing." Her words are vicious, and her tone is unrecognizable. "I could never feel anything for someone who could do the things you did to that poor kid. Anything I felt for you...it's gone."

"Right." My whole body gets heavier. The rain comes harder, sounding like millions of needles slicing into an unsuspecting victim. I refuse to think of her words, and how hopeless they make me feel. "I see Jackson, even when I'm awake."

"Good."

Half of my mouth lifts in mockery of a smile. "I stopped talking after that. I wouldn't eat; I couldn't sleep. The shock of it, of my role in his death—it was too much. I had a breakdown. Most days, I felt like I was drowning in remorse. Most days, I hoped I would. I hated myself. I hated the kids I used to call friends. My aunt brought me here, and I never once thought of leaving, of going back to face it all."

I look up. "Not until you came here."

Alexis slaps me, the sharp sting of her palm against my face welcome. "Forget I was ever anything to you, because that's what I'm going to do," she hisses. "I wish I'd never met you."

"I wish you'd never met me too." I smile sadly.

Nineteen

Melanie

WHEN OUR NAMES ARE CALLED, I turn to Jocelyn and Casey. Something warns me against this, tells me it isn't a coincidence that Lexie Hennessy isn't here on the day we are to read our group stories. Plus, she has been disturbingly quiet since last week, and anytime she looked at me, it felt like she was seeing someone other than me. She wasn't really here, but somewhere else. It was creepy.

I don't trust her silence, or her absence. I especially don't trust her.

Then there is the fact that the three of us never had any real part in the writing process of our project. I now realize how very, very stupid that was of us. What's even stranger than Lexie being gone is that three copies of our assignment were magically waiting for us on Mr. Walters' desk.

Like this was planned.

Am I overthinking this? My friends don't seem concerned, and I follow them to the front of the class. But my stomach roils, and my palms sweat, and this feels really, really wrong. I shouldn't be up here. I know I shouldn't read the words before me. Someone coughs, and I cringe. *Get it together.* Lexie isn't even here, and it still feels like she is in the room, watching me with wicked promises in her eyes. They're all watching me. All the kids are watching me, waiting for me to screw up.

You have two more days of school, and then you're free. Get a grip, and get through this. Remember who you are, and smile.

But I can't smile.

When did I long for the school year to be over? Not once, not ever, not until now.

With her black curtain of hair framing her bold features, and the red sundress that shows more than it covers, Jocelyn has the arrogant look of a queen ruling over her subjects, and Casey looks as ridiculously clueless as ever. Things have been tense between me and them over the last week. Especially with Jocelyn, who acts like kissing me on the lips in front of everyone wasn't a big deal, or like she isn't seeing Jeff. It doesn't do any good to hide it—I saw them making out by his car during lunch yesterday when I went outside to get some fresh air. Plus, the whole school knows.

When I saw them together, I expected to feel anger or hurt, but all I felt was empty.

Maybe I never really liked Jeff. The only boyfriend I've ever been serious about was Nick Alderson, and he dumped me for Jocelyn. That hurt. For months, I happily envisioned various ways of getting back at both of them. A lot of the daydreams ended with Nick begging me to take him back, and me shoving him into an unforgiving ocean full of hungry sharks, or off a cliff with jagged rocks below. Jocelyn lost her hair from a bad dye job, and got fat on protein bars, or was horribly disfigured in a knife fight over something ludicrous, like a tube of lipstick at the mall. The details depended on my mood at the time.

And then a boy died, and Nick went crazy before he altogether disappeared. I was glad about his mental breakdown, and I was glad that Jocelyn was boyfriend-less. Not that it lasted for long.

"Go. Read your part," Jocelyn whispers, nudging my side with her elbow.

"Don't touch me," I snap, thinking of the kiss, and what everyone is probably thinking as they look at the two of us. The gossip's died down, but there is still talk. And when a smooching sound breaks the quiet, and laughter follows, I know it hasn't died down enough.

Jocelyn purrs, "Careful, Melanie, it looks like you have competition."

Turning to her, I ask, "How can you joke about it?"

"Why are you so uptight about it?" she retorts, adjusting the strap of her dress.

Shooting her a dark look that she meets with a challenging one, I focus on the papers in my hands, scanning the part beside my name. Lexie assigned us roles? I look over the first sentence, my nerves whiplashing. If we don't read it, we'll get an incomplete for the assignment, and it will affect our final English grade. If we do read it, we'll be the laughingstocks of the school.

"This isn't right," I murmur, glancing at Casey. "This isn't what was originally written."

Lower lip locked between her small, white teeth, Casey stares back with wide eyes.

"Who cares?" Jocelyn answers with her gaze trained forward. "Just read it before we all get Fs on it."

"Miss Mathews, did you suddenly forget how to read?" Mr. Walters calls from his desk. "Too much time spent on fashion and not enough on books?"

Snickers erupt in the classroom.

I look around the room, and see kids who usually cower in my presence, or at least avoid eye contact, staring back at me like they see me as nothing special. My lack of importance has slowly progressed over the last month. It chafes like my lips having gone too long without lip balm. I can't take this. I can't do this. I need to leave this room; I want to get away from all the eyes. My hands shake around the papers they hold.

Don't look at them. I drop my eyes to the floor. "No," comes out weaker than it should.

"Then get started. I know it's hard for you to believe, but there are others in here, and they'd like to read their projects as well. Today. Before class is over."

Where is my snide comeback? Where is my head toss and eye roll? Where is my indifference to how I am viewed by others? Gone.

I don't know why I look up, but I do, meeting Jeff's eyes. He hurriedly focuses on his desk, his hands splayed across its top. Jerk. He didn't even bother telling me he was no longer interested in me. Like Nick, he just went from me to Jocelyn. At least Nick broke up with me first.

"I'll—I'll read it," Casey blurts, somehow standing taller and looking stronger than she ever has. She appears to have the backbone I lost. How did that happen? *When* did that happen?

"Fine. As long as *someone* reads it," is the teacher's exasperated reply.

186

This story is about us. I saw the names of the characters: Mel, Joss, and Cassie. The names are changed, but it's us. I want to tell Casey to not read it, but my lips won't open.

Her voice wavers on the first word, and Casey clears her throat. "My name is Mel. I think I'm perfect, but even I get pimples."

Clint guffaws from the back of the room.

"Quiet, Clint," Mr. Walters warns.

I turn to stone, even my lungs refusing to work.

Casey gives me a nervous look, and continues. "I'm not any better than you, but I act like I am. I tell myself everyone likes me, but I know, that really, even my friends...don't." She lifts her gaze to me as her pale face reddens, admitting her thoughts mirror the words she spoke.

I almost want to tell her it's okay, that I know I deserve this, and her fake friendship.

"What kind of a story is this?" the teacher demands, looking from the seated students whispering to one another to us standing near the blackboard. His eyes are suspicious, like we all planned this confusing scene merely to dupe him.

"It's an autobiography," Timothy Green, a kid with a pink Mohawk who spends more time on his skateboard than his schoolwork, says, and high-fives the boy sitting across from him.

"Keep going," Jocelyn urges, looking like she's enjoying this. The only thing I can hope for is that Lexie's written words are as true for her as they are for me.

"I'm a bully, and I like to hurt people so that I feel better about myself. You see, I don't like myself. But what I like even less, is that other people might notice."

187

It's true. It's all true.

My fingers unclench and the papers drop from my hands. The insides of my stomach spin, and the few grapes I ate this morning threaten to come back up. My eyes dart around the room, colliding with the sympathetic ones of the smelly kid, and it's the end for me. Seeing that look in the eyes of someone who is the lowest of the low is the point where I know there's no use in...anything.

It's over.

I briefly close my eyes, and take a long, cleansing breath.

Jocelyn clamps a hand around my forearm when I turn to flee, her long nails digging into my skin like tiny blades. Her brown eyes hit mine, and they are knives of contempt. How did I ever think she ever looked at me with anything but rivalry and malice in her eyes? "If you walk out of here now, you will lose any semblance of popularity you have left."

"I don't care." I wrench my arm from her grasp, her nails slicing open my skin. An ache forms where her nails marked me. "Don't you get it?"

I throw my arms up and spread them wide, encircling the room in my gesture. "None of this matters."

Around the chatter that erupts from my outburst, I hear the voice of Mr. Walters trying to get the room back in order. I hear him call my name. I hear laughter as I walk from the room, and it isn't until I'm out the front door of the school that I realize it's mine. I'm skipping school for the first time ever on the last week of my junior year. I'm not sure why, but I find that hilarious.

Twenty

NICK

THE LAST PERSON I EXPECT to see, or want to see, is the one I do when I enter the visitation room. Until Alexis came to see me, I denied all visits. After a while, it didn't matter whether or not I wanted anyone to visit, because the requests eventually stopped. Even my mom and dad haven't tried to see me for months. I wonder if they finally gave up on me. Do parents do that? Do they give up on their kids?

Call it boredom, or curiosity, but when I was told someone was here to see me, I was almost excited. I knew it wouldn't be Alexis. Part of me hoped, of course, as it always will. I think every time I go somewhere, or see someone, some small piece of anticipation will flare up inside me for a brown-haired, blue-eyed girl with a pretty smile.

I knew it wasn't Alexis who came to see me, but I never would have thought it would be Melanie Mathews.

I squint against the brightness of the lights in the neutral-toned room. Circular tables with chairs take up space without any form of order. This would displease Eric Winchester, a boy with nonfunctional obsessive-compulsive disorder. He rarely leaves his room due to the pandemonium of implied chaos around this place. A crooked painting on the wall set him off a few days ago. I can't even imagine the insanity of having everything out of my control, and desperately needing it to be.

It's uncomfortably warm in here, to the point where I wonder if I'll have to consider getting some shorts in place of my pajama pants. *Only if they're gray*, a voice that sounds like Alexis' teases. Her smile flashes behind my eyelids, scorching in its clarity. And then I see her face the last time we spoke, and there is nothing friendly about it. The taste of acidity enters my mouth, and I focus on Melanie.

Her eyes are bloodshot, and her brown hair seems lank around her shoulders. I look at her in her jeans and green shirt, and I see a faded out version of a girl who used to sparkle. Her physical appearance has changed, yes, but it's more than that, like the sourness of her soul has encompassed her. She's dull now. Good. She doesn't deserve to glow.

As I approach, she gets up from the chair she was sitting in when I entered, and tries to smile. I don't return it.

"I don't know why I'm here," Melanie says in a voice that sounds nothing like hers. It's softer, and I don't think I imagined the tremble. Where is the confidence, the disdain? Where is the Melanie I remember?

"Then you should probably go."

For the pain she brought Alexis, I hate her.

For the pain I brought Alexis, I hate myself.

There seems to be a lot of hate going around these days.

"I...stopped by your house." Melanie's throat moves as she swallows. She looks at her hands, and returns her attention to me. "Your mom told me you were here."

I can't say I'm shocked to find out Melanie had no idea where I was the last year. Everything was either about her, or it wasn't important. I want to ask her if she remembers Jackson. I want to ask her if his death mattered to her, because I know his life never did. She probably forgot about him. While I've been locked away in a mental rehabilitation center, unable to get past my role in Jackson's suicide, she most likely hasn't lost a single night of sleep over him.

"You look so different," she whispers, shifting her feet.

"What do you want?" My voice is hard, and I have to fight to keep my jaw unlocked. The thought of our entwined past, our shared intimacy, even the faint memory of my lips on hers—it causes a shudder of repulsion to pass through me.

Melanie blinks, looking around the room like she isn't sure where she is. "I don't know. I guess I just...wanted to see someone familiar. Someone from...before."

Alexis missed her last session with Dr. Larson. I know because I lingered near the waiting area, hoping for a chance to see her, maybe even talk to her. Dr. Larson caught me and informed me that Alexis is now doing her counseling somewhere other than Live. I told my aching heart that this is the way it has to be, but that doesn't make it hurt any less.

I called her. Multiple times. She didn't answer. She didn't call back.

Alexis is gone, because of me, yes, but also because of this girl.

And I am not that boy, the boy from before, that Melanie is hoping to see.

"Do you hate me too? They all hate me." Melanie hugs herself, her attention jumping from person to person. She looks at me with bleary eyes. "Am I a bad person, Nick?"

"Do you care if you are?"

Her forehead wrinkles. "I don't know. I never used to."

Even as she admits to her uncaring nature, the fact that she can, is somehow redeeming, in a warped way.

"Yes," I tell her frankly. I remember her running her fingers down Jackson's arm, winking at him, and then laughing about it with me and Jocelyn when she walked by him. I remember the pained look on his face, and how his shoulders slumped as our eyes met and he saw the grin on my face. "You're a bad person."

Rapidly blinking her eyes, Melanie looks down.

I take a deep breath. "But so am I. Or—I used to be. I'm trying to be better."

"I thought everyone wanted to be like me," she whispers, locking her fingers and releasing them, over and over.

I carefully study Melanie, noticing the shadows smudging the skin beneath her eyes, the nervous energy that makes it unable for her to stand still. Something about the way she's acting warns me to be cautious.

"What are you doing here, Melanie?" I ask in a quieter tone.

Someone coughs and Melanie's head whips around until she finds the girl in question. She stares at her with lowered eyebrows. "I'm not popular anymore."

I make a sound of disgust. "That's why you're here? Because you're feeling sorry for yourself?"

She looks from the girl with the rattling cough to me, her mouth pulled down.

Shaking my head, I run fingers through my hair. "You do realize where you're at, right?"

Some kind of clearness, maybe a hint of empathy, pulses through her eyes. "What happened with you? Why are you here? Is it because of that boy who died last year?"

Bitter laughter escapes around the tightness of my throat. "Do you even remember his name?"

An annoyed look passes over her features. "Of course I do. I only have to see it every day at school."

"How terrible for you."

"You don't belong here, with these..." Melanie cringes.

"There you are," I say softly, disdainfully "I was beginning to wonder about you."

Melanie crosses her arms. "I was happy that you lost it after he died. You dated me long enough to have sex with me, and then you dumped me for Jocelyn. Seeing you miserable made me happy." Her eyes flash.

I dated Melanie long enough to see that I didn't like her all that much, and the sex didn't make me like her any more. "So, in your mind, it's a good thing Jackson died, right? Because I broke up with you and dated your friend, and I deserved to lose my shit. Makes sense." It makes absolutely no sense, and I don't think I can stand to be around Melanie much longer. I might literally bash my head into the closest wall.

"That's not—I just liked seeing you unhappy, because I was unhappy. I didn't say it was right."

Scorn coats my next words. "Nothing about you is right."

Melanie uncrosses her arms. "There's a girl—Lexie Hennessy."

I stiffen, holding my breath. Hearing her name sends my brain and heart into shock, revives them, and kills me, all at once.

"I'm here because...because I think maybe she was here too. I thought you might know her."

She was here. She turned the gray of my reality to color. She gave me a teddy bear, and a book. I gave her my heart, and my untruths. Then I gave her the truths, and the world went back to gray.

"What about her?" comes out rough. My heart pounds in my ears.

Melanie watches as the coughing girl hugs her mom and dad, and they walk out of the room. "I couldn't figure out why she hates me so much, until a couple days ago, when in English class—it doesn't matter—but it finally clicked."

I wait.

"I picked on her, at the start of the year. It wasn't anything bad," Melanie hurries to defend herself.

"Right," I say agreeably. "It was probably like how we picked on Jackson."

"Exactly." She pauses, figuring out I'm being sarcastic. Her lips press together. "It wasn't something to die over."

My hands tighten into fists, and the veins in my neck go rigid. She says it haughtily, dismissively, and I'd give anything to be able to shove her little peanut brain into Alexis', to force her to watch, and experience, and endure everything Alexis has. I did that a lot when I first came here. I'd imagine I was Jackson, and I went through every incident that involved me or my friends, but I went through them as him. It was so much worse that way.

"Lexie overdosed on pills," Melanie says. "I remember the guidance counselor talking to us about suicide after she did it."

Nothing about bullying, of course. Why would anyone want to talk about that? Enid's school has its priorities disorganized, that's clear.

"I didn't recognize her when she came back. She looked different, and she acted different. She went out of her way to pick on me."

"How dare she treat you how you treated her."

Her eyes darken. "Shut up, Nick. Two wrongs don't make a right."

"No, they make a circle." My eyebrows lift. "What goes around comes around."

Sighing, Melanie taps her foot. "She didn't come back to school until a month ago. I know she was sent to some mental place. Was she here? Do you know Lexie Hennessy?"

"No," I tell her. Because Lexie wasn't here. Alexis was. Strong, not vindictive. Hopeful, not bitter. They are completely dissimilar people.

"I'm worried." Melanie shrinks in size. "She made the last month of school horrible for me, and I'm worried this isn't over yet."

"Why do you think that?" I ask slowly, my eyes trained on her.

"Because she left me alone the last few days of school."

My body shuts down at her words, and I stare at Melanie. I think of what day it is, and what this day always means for Melanie Mathews. Why would this year be any different? Alexis isn't done yet, I know that. I don't know if she ever will be, if she lets this consume her. If she does what I think she might. And if she kills all her light in the process, what's left? A girl living in the dark.

Lindy Zart

"Do you still do your silly parties the following Saturday after school is out?"

Melanie's eyes narrow. "They're not silly."

"Answer me. Do you?"

"Yes. It's tonight. Why?" She steps closer. "What is it?"

"Nothing." I avoid her eyes, glad that she can't hear the thunderous beat of my heart. "Go home, Melanie."

"You know something," she accuses.

I finally meet her gaze. "Go home."

"Thanks for being completely unhelpful."

"I'm not trying to help you," I tell her coolly.

"You're a jerk." Melanie glares at me and turns to leave. Her steps are wobbly, quick—unsure of where she should go, but knowing she should leave here. This place may be full of weirdos and freaks, but at least we're all real.

SPRINTING DOWN THE HALL IS a good way to get yelled at, and I do by the red-haired woman who sits at the front desk, but I keep going. Luckily for me, Dr. Larson is in her office when I reach it. I slam the door behind me and stand still as I try to catch my breath. She turns in her chair to face me.

"Nick?" Questions shift across her dark eyes.

"I want to be released. Today. Now."

She folds her hands in her lap. "We both know you are under no obligation to stay."

"Right." My voice cracks around that single word. I am not a patient here; I just pretend to be. Because that's all I've done since I found Jackson Hodgson dead in his bed: pretend.

"Do you feel well enough to leave?"

My smile feels as sick as my stomach. "I was never supposed to be here, remember?"

"Humor me." Dr. Larson brushes hair behind an ear. "Do you feel well enough to leave?"

Sighing, I fall into the chair and clasp my head between my hands. "Yes, Aunt Miranda, I feel well enough to leave." I let my hands fall and face Dr. Larson. "You know this isn't about me."

"I know it's about the girl."

"And the boy."

"Yes. And the boy. Always the boy," she says gently.

"I have to help Alexis." I force open my fisted hands. "I have to save her from herself."

She tilts her head, looking at me in a way that reminds me of how she used to watch me as a small boy when I didn't get my way and would throw a fit. "Why?"

Frustrated, I jump to my feet. "Because no one saved me, because no one saved the boy."

"And the boy died." Dr. Larson pauses. "You're talking about Jackson, but you're also talking about you. You were destructive to others, and you were self-destructive. You wanted someone to stop you, because you couldn't stop yourself. No one did. And you couldn't stop, not until it was too late, not until a boy's life was forfeit. The shame of that haunts you."

197

"Yes," I whisper hoarsely, tears filling my eyes. I attempt a smile, but I feel the twist in it. "You're not supposed to analyze your own relatives, Aunt Miranda."

"You shouldn't have stepped into my office then." She smiles, tenderness lightening her eyes, and points out, "Lexie didn't die."

"She almost did."

"But she didn't."

"I'm going."

She shrugs. "Go. I'll do whatever paperwork is required. Have you talked to your parents?"

"No," I admit.

My aunt sighs. "I'll talk to them. Give me two minutes, and I can drive you home."

"Thanks," I say around a swollen throat. I pause by the door with my back to her. "Jackson died because of me."

"No, Nick. He died because some souls are too kind for this world."

"I hate who I was." I look at my aunt, hoping she'll understand. "I had to kill that person. I had to kill that boy to become this Nick. That's why I shut down. I couldn't be that person anymore."

"I know. But don't you think it's time to stop feeling bad about being you, even the part of you, you don't like?"

My eyes sear into my aunt's. She took one look at me after Jackson died, and she knew I was broken. She knew I wouldn't survive if I stayed in that house of silence, if I stayed who I was. She brought me here when I asked for help; to hide, to change, to grieve. "It only matters what Alexis sees."

198

A soft smile tips her mouth, and the resemblance to my mom, her older sister, is striking. "Does she see you? I mean, really see you?"

"I think so." My voice is choked. "But some of what she saw was too much."

"The bullying?" she guesses.

I lower my eyes.

"Give her time."

I shake my head, my shoulders inflexible. "I can't. She's going to do something bad. I feel it. I have to stop her." Even now, panic crushes my chest, tells me to hurry.

"You're not responsible for the actions of others." Dr. Larson gets to her feet, crossing the room. She touches my shoulder. "Just like Jackson, and Lexie. Everyone makes their own choices. Remember that, Nick."

I know, logically, her words are true, but it doesn't make me believe them.

Twenty-one

Alexis

I AM THE SCHOOL PARIAH.

People sidestep me as I make my way down the white-walled corridor lined with lockers, afraid they'll catch the shunning defect if they touch me, or even make eye contact, for that matter. There were a few friendly kids my first days here, but as soon as it was determined I was not interesting enough, the smiles turned to vacant eyes, like I'm not really here. I am invisible, a translucent entity.

No one sees me unless it is to make fun of me. This cloak of my current truth is heavy and doesn't fit, yet it is how I am seen by others. I feel like an interloper in my own skin and the real me is suffocating, struggling to exist beneath the misconceptions. She is losing—I am losing.

And I can't help but think: what's this life for?

I park my car out of sight from passing traffic. The air is damp, and smells of rain. I walk through the small patch of woods that separate the cabin from the road, the memory of another girl, another life, another me, guiding me. She didn't understand how kids could be terrible to others, but I get it now. It's a lack of humanity. Maybe some are born without it. Maybe some, like me, have it stripped from them. I've been turned into one of them, and guilt has no place here.

My steps are purposeful, my eyes straight ahead.

The moon guides me, marking the path to the cabin on Murphy's Lake, and anticipation thrums through me. I had to lose myself to get to where I now am. I had to have my old life stolen from me to be able to live this new one. I'm tougher. I swear, even the bugs are afraid to bother me.

The reality of knowing who Nick really is, and what he's done, helps. I'm cold with the knowledge. Cold everywhere. But the pain— the pain won't go away, and it pulsates in time with my heartbeat, no matter how much I try to not feel it. And I miss him, more than I thought I could miss anyone. I stiffen my shoulders, redirecting my attention to what's before me. Each step gets easier. Each second brings me closer.

And there it is: Melanie's cabin.

Log-sided and sprawling, it boasts of money with its perfect landscape of shrubs, trees, and rock trails. Through the uncovered windows, the main level is visible, revealing plum and wood walls, dazzling light fixtures, and dark furniture. To the left of the cabin and down one of those rock paths is the lake, glimmering and softly rippling under the light of the moon. A dock sways with the water, and if it wasn't for where I am, and who is nearby, I would find it peaceful. But I don't.

I turn my attention back to the cabin.

This is it.

Everything has been leading up to this night.

Would I be here if not for Nick's confession?

I don't know, but I'm almost relieved he told me. It made the decision less of a decision when I found out about Melanie's yearly party, and more of an instinct. This is where I'm supposed to be. I am here, right now, to do this. They're all bullies, Nick included. They take, and they break, and they are without regret. They need to repent. Anyone they've hurt deserves an apology. I'll make sure they get it, even if I'm the only one who witnesses it.

Listening to Nick talk about how he treated that boy, and what that boy did to himself—it shattered my heart, including the part that cared for Nick. There's nothing left. I can't feel. I refuse to feel. If I let myself, I'll shatter too. I blink my eyes against unwanted thoughts, against Nick's smile, and his eyes, and how I can't see him as anything other than who he is now. It's a lie. He's a lie. He gave me hope, but that was false.

All I hear is the sound of my tennis shoes meeting with earth, and although there are lights on inside the cabin, it seems too quiet. Too still. My hands are empty, and I clench them at my sides. I feel like I should have a weapon of some kind—for what, I don't know—and then I realize, I am the weapon. My voice can be the knife, and I will cut with it.

That girl I used to be is here too. She clutches at me, and she won't let me go. She's whispering about all the times she was hurt, and she's so sad. Just...so sad. My throat tightens, my eyes blur with tears. I want her to disappear. I see her, I feel her, and as I stare at the cabin I'm standing before, she shows me how she died. It isn't like I don't already know. It isn't like I didn't experience it myself. But it feels new. Fresh. Raw.

It's strange how calm I am as I stare at the bottle, as I make my decision. I open it with trembling fingers, dump a handful of prescription pain meds into my hand. I wonder how I'll swallow them all. I carefully shut the door of the medicine cabinet and an image meets my eyes. The face is pale, blue eyes wide with fear and hopelessness.

It is my face.

Why? Why am I seeing this, remembering? Feeling the absolute bleakness. I jerk my head, as if I can dislodge the memories. But then I'm in the emergency room of the hospital, and I'm trying to die, or maybe I'm trying to live. I stumble over a log, slowing to a stop. I bend at the waist, pressing an arm to my ribcage.

A murky haze surrounds me as voices call over one another, hands grabbing at me. The world spins as I fight to remain conscious. And then I give in, and give up. Why am I fighting this? This is what I want. Male and female voices overlap as I'm shoved onto a bed. My eyes are out of focus and a ringing forms in my ears, drowning out all other sounds.

I moan and it sounds like a prayer. But to whom, and for what?

Don't save me.

Why are they trying to save me? I don't want to be saved. Sweat trails down my face and body, but I am cold. A tube is jammed down my throat, scraping it raw as it descends. I gag, instinctively wanting the foreign object removed. I claw at it, and my hands are restrained. A charcoal substance is forced down the tube and I am crying as I choke it down. I can't do this anymore. I want it over. I want this life over. The tube is removed, and I collapse, curling into myself. I retch and retch until finally, mercifully, I vomit.

The world goes gray, and I want to go with it.

I rub my face, not surprised to find it wet. *You're dead*, I tell the memory of a desperate girl. *Stay dead*.

Eyes forward, I stride for the front door of the cabin. Without allowing myself to hesitate, I grip the cool doorknob in my hand, and turn. The door opens to silence. It's supposed to be a party, right? It's the quietest, and emptiest, party I've ever encountered. I step inside, my eyes involuntarily widening as I take in the gleaming woodwork from ceiling to floor, the unending open space of the living room and kitchen, the stainless steel appliances, and sharp, minimalistic decorating. The collage of deep, lively colors.

My focus drops to the floor, and lands on Melanie.

She sits by herself in the middle of a room, playing with the string of a shiny purple balloon. Dozens more surround her, covering the floor like fake, fallen disco balls. Dressed in a cream-colored strapless dress with her hair pulled into a loose bun at the top of her head, she looks deceptively angelic. With her bowed head and slumped shoulders, she also seems somber. I don't know how to respond to seeing her like this.

Melanie's eyes are dim as they meet mine, even as her cheeks are flushed. "Hello, Alexis."

I jerk at the sound of my full name. I'm supposed to be Lexie to her, not Alexis. I am only Alexis to Nick. It made my name seem special that way. *And you hate him, remember?* Can I ever really hate him? I don't know that I can.

I shift my feet and study Melanie, wondering how I should respond. I decide to say nothing. She knows my full name, and that means, she knows who I am. Took her long enough. Melanie reaches for a brown bottle and tips its contents into her mouth. It hits the floor with a clang as she releases it. Tipping over, pale brown liquid forms a pool around the bottle on the hardwood floor. I count three more bottles lying on their sides nearby.

Waving a limp hand, she giggles and singsongs, "As you can see, all my friends are here."

Melanie is drunk.

"Where—" I swallow around a dry throat. I came for vengeance, not to find a lone drunk girl sitting on the floor. This whole scene has me confused. "Where is everyone?"

Melanie shrugs, "No one came." In a small, childlike voice, she asks, "Why do you think they didn't come?"

"They realized what a bitch you are?" The words are out before I can stop them, not that I would.

A sudden heat enters her eyes, scalding with intensity. "I had a feeling *you* would show up." Melanie's smile is at odds with her eyes. "You see, I finally figured out who you are. I admit, it took me far longer than it should."

Lightning cracks the world outside, sending pulses of white light directly over the lake.

"I was irrelevant to you. Why would you remember who I was?"

"True," she tweets.

I step farther into the room. "What tipped you off?"

"Nick Alderson."

The name strikes me with unimaginable pain, and longing—I might as well tear out my heart and offer it to Melanie. It hurts, and I don't want to feel it. I want to hate him like I tell myself I do, and yet, each beat of my heart pulses with need. He was cruel, and

205

inhumane, but I don't know that boy. I know the other one. I briefly close my eyes. *No. You don't. You don't know him at all.* Just a glimpse of his face, just a flash of his hesitant smile—like he wants to be happy, but isn't sure he's allowed—it has the power to drop me to my knees. It churns in my stomach, this need, this disgust, and in return, I am torn.

"Nick was one of the most popular guys in school. Before Jackson killed himself, and he went all crazy in the head. I guess he blamed himself or something."

I fist my hands and glare.

"I used to date Nick, you know," Melanie says conversationally, ignoring my silent simmering, or unconcerned by it. She lets go of the balloon, and it slowly falls to the floor. "But then he wanted Jocelyn instead. They all want Jocelyn."

A bad taste fills my mouth at the thought of Nick having anything to do with Melanie or Jocelyn. But then, he is one of them. Even though I know it to be true, it doesn't feel right. It doesn't seem like the Nick I know could have ever hung out with the bullies—or been one himself. I take a deep breath, and focus on the unstable girl.

"Jocelyn is supposed to be my best friend, and I think I hate her," she muses, a frown pulling at her cherry red mouth.

I stand stiffly, looking around our surroundings instead of at Melanie. This is all wrong, and I don't know how to respond. I expected a house full of people, and an antagonistic Melanie in place of the one before me. I expected to feel hatred, and rage, and when I look at her, all I feel is pity, and disgust.

Melanie meets my eyes. "Your story was true."

Blinking to break the stare, I take another step toward her. "What part?"

"All of it. Everything about me anyway. I didn't stay for the rest. I kind of wish I had, just to see what you had to say about Jocelyn." Her smile droops, and she sighs. "What do you want from me?"

"I want to know why you did it. I want to know why you think it's okay to treat other people like dirt." My voice is waspish, stinging with the force of my emotions. The beat of my heart grows stronger, louder. I can feel it against my chest; I can hear it in my ears. "You didn't like me because I was different. Admit it."

One dainty shoulder lifts and lowers. "I didn't care enough about you to like or dislike you."

"Then why did you treat me the way you did?" It always comes down to the why of things, and a lot of times, there isn't a good reason.

"Because it was fun," Melanie snaps.

Stunned by her callousness, even though I shouldn't be, I jerk my head back. "You really are an unfeeling monster."

Melanie's lower lip trembles. I'm sure I imagined it, because in the next instant, she straightens her back, defiance and resolve in her posture. "So, what's the next step in your quest for revenge?"

I stop when I am close enough to see the top of her head, and have to lower my eyes to look into hers. "I hadn't thought that far ahead."

She gets to her feet so suddenly I take a step back. She sways, holding her hands out on either side of her body to keep steady. With a lopsided smile and unfocused eyes, Melanie turns to me. The strangely sweet scent of beer seeps from her pores, and I wonder how many bottles made it to the garbage before she became lax and let them gather on the floor.

"How about this?" she suggests, her eyes sparked with unnatural light. We are inches apart, and nothing could separate us more. "How about we make things really interesting, and head to the dock?"

"What?"

Thunder rumbles, low and faraway. A storm is coming.

"Yeah. Come on. It's old, and rickety, and every year my dad says he's going to update it, and he doesn't." She turns and motions for me to follow. "It'll be fun, I promise."

Melanie plows over the balloons, kicking one viciously. It springs to the air, and back down, in a wobbly dance. This is hilarious to her. "Oh, God, Lexie," she guffaws, careening to the left before catching herself on the wall. "You're a bitch too, you know that? I think you're even better at it than I am."

My stomach clenches in denial of her words, even as they circle through my head with truth. I watch the spectacle of a downward spiraling Melanie Mathews as I stand in the center of an empty room. I should be enjoying this, right? Reveling in the mental meltdown of a cruel and selfish girl. Sickness swims where victory should.

I cross the room to her. Vibrating with anger, I stare at the pretty girl with the foul personality, and I lash out. "Don't you dare do this. Don't you take this from me. Don't you make *me* feel bad for *you*. You made my life hell; I'm just returning the favor."

She snickers. "A bully to the bully. How ironic." Melanie's face scrunches up as she jerks open the door and slants a look at me over her shoulder. "You're no better than me. We're all bullies, including you."

Twenty-two

Melanie

I STUMBLE THROUGH THE DOORWAY and toward the jagged path of rocks, glad for the shattered expression on Lexie's face. I can't be the only one having all the fun tonight. The wind is cool against my bare skin, and I close my eyes. I misstep, twisting my ankle as I land with my cheek on the walkway. Stone cuts into my flesh, and it burns, but I just laugh. Laughing is better than crying.

No one came. I don't understand how this could happen. Not one single person came—Lexie the loser doesn't count. I stay where I fell, the cold seeping into me, until I'm shaking with it. My ankle throbs, my face hurts, and I'm freezing. I have no friends. No one likes me. I'm a loser like Lexie. My throat tightens, and the laughter turns choked.

Lexie makes a sound of disgust. Hands dig into my arms and haul me to my feet. I'm spun around, finding my eyes level with her clear, blue ones. "You need to go to bed. There is no pleasure in getting back at you when I can't even enjoy it. You're too drunk."

"Would you like to reschedule to when I'm sober?" I smile widely.

"Yeah, why don't you pencil me in?" Her eyebrows lift when my mouth drops open.

"Get away from me," I snarl, shaking her off. "You've already done enough damage."

Her eyes are cool under the light of the moon. "It isn't anything you didn't already do to me."

"Right. Maybe I should be like you and just go ahead and *try to kill myself*! Did that make everything better?" I fling my arms in the air, almost losing my balance again. "Do you feel better now, knowing you couldn't even do that right?"

"I'm glad I didn't get that right," Lexie says softly.

Spinning away from her pain-filled eyes, I ungracefully make my way toward the dock. "Whatever. It's great that my party gets to be spent with the one person I would never invite," I continue, ignoring the pain in my ankle each time I put weight on it.

I don't know why I'm going to the lake. I just know that, right now, I need to be in control of something. I decided to go to the lake, therefore, I'm going to the lake. No one, least of all, Lexie Hennessy, is going to get in the way of that. I swipe at the dampness on my cheek, staring at the blood that coats my fingers. It looks black. My sandals skid on loose gravel, and I reach the bottom of the hill faster than expected.

"What are you doing?" Lexie asks from behind.

"You know what? Don't worry about it. Go home. I'm sure I'll have a better time without you." I stomp across the grass and dirt, cringing each time my ankle throbs, and stop before the dock.

I study the dark water, and the trees across the expanse of it. They look like murky creatures, moving with the breeze. I kick off my sandals. The moon seems especially bright here, and I squint my eyes when I tip my head back to look at it. Clouds roll past, gather and collect, as I watch. Looking at it makes me dizzy, and I shut my eyes and take a deep breath.

Lexie shifts behind me, moving closer.

"Why are you still here?"

"I can't leave you out here," she finally tells me, sounding supremely unhappy about it.

"Now you feel sorry for me? Is that it?" My voice is harsh, but my eyes sting with unshed tears. "You won. My life is ruined. Go home and gloat."

"I should," Lexie agrees, coming to stand beside me. "I want to."

I give her a sidelong glance.

"Seeing you like this should make me happy."

I roll my eyes.

"You hurt me, Melanie. You made me feel like crap, and for what? To get a few laughs? I was the new kid. I was shy, and worried, and I just wanted to make a couple friends. And you made that impossible. Every day I went to school, and every day, I feared it. I never knew what was going to be said, or done, and it screwed me up inside. Anxiety was my only friend, and it was slowly destroying me.

"And it wasn't just me, and you probably won't even learn a single thing from all this—because you obviously didn't learn anything from Jackson Hodgson, but I had to make you see that how you treat people—" Lexie grabs my bicep, her fingers hard against my arm, and yanks me around. Her eyes glow, and when lightning cracks the sky, it is reflected in the blue of the irises. "—is wrong. Some people can't handle meanness, and no one should have to endure it. Intentionally hurting people is *wrong*."

I feel my face crumple, and I avert my eyes. She's right. I am a horrible person. I guess I've always known that. I just never cared.

Not until I was the one being made fun of. Lexie drops my arm. I rub at the aching flesh, and move to the ancient dock as the sound of rain fills the air, and a downpour commences. It sounds crisp, and powerful.

The dock shifts with the water, and I plop to my butt on it. I move with the dock, and my stomach moves in the opposite direction. My throat prickles, and I break out in a sweat. I'm going to be sick. I move to my knees, my fingers gripping the edge of the wood plank, and vomit over the side.

"Lovely," Lexie comments when I'm done.

"Shut up," I get out around a ravaged throat. I flip to my back on the hard wood, and let the rain wash over me. Within minutes, I'm completely soaked.

"It's time to go inside." Lexie moves for me and I kick out a leg, missing her stomach when she smoothly moves to the side. "Impressive."

Anger flushes my skin, and I glare at a face I used to not remember, and now know I'll never forget. "Do you know what I call you in my head?" My upper lip curls. "Lexie the Loser."

Lexie pauses, and then sits down by my feet. Her tennis shoes squeak as she shifts, and the red top and jeans she has on are dark with night and rain. She wipes rainwater from her face and looks at me. I'm tempted to kick at her again, just to see if I'll get her this time. "Well, I have to say, that's really disappointing. You thoroughly lack creativity. Even Lexie the Lesbian tops that, and that's pretty sad too."

I stiffen, rising on my elbows to better see her shadowed face. "Did you make that picture?"

"What pic—oh, the one with you and Jocelyn lip-locked?"

My skin incinerates. "Yes. That one."

Smiling faintly, Lexie tells me, "No. Sorry. I can't take credit for that."

"Then…" My eyebrows lower, and I swipe at water as it tries to enter my eyes. The gesture sends me off balance, and I topple over, terribly close to the water, and where I puked. I feel like doing it again when I realize who it must have been.

Jocelyn.

With a brain that feels like a ship in the middle of an oceanic storm, I move to a sitting position. I tug the bottom of my dress over my knees, knowing this light color was a horrible choice. It makes sense—Jocelyn was too casual about it. And then she fed the gossip by kissing me. My head is pounding, and my mouth tastes like dirt. Elbows on my legs, I steady my head with my hands, and stare at the cabin up the hill.

"Jocelyn did it," I say out loud, wondering in what other ways she's tried to sabotage me.

After a drawn out moment, Lexie says, "You're an unlikable person, but Jocelyn is downright scary."

I feel betrayed, and utterly small. Even my friend is against me. I shouldn't be surprised. Part of me always knew she wasn't really my friend. I don't think I'd know what a real friend was, even if I ever did have one. Jocelyn competes, and Casey follows. That isn't friendship. Maybe I don't deserve anyone's.

"No one really likes me. They just pretend," I announce, and then immediately start to cry, my shoulders shaking with sobs. My throat hurts, and now my chest. I don't like how it aches. "Even my parents don't like me. I'm just this inconvenience to them. And yeah, I'm beautiful, and my family has money, and I have good taste in clothes, but what's the point if no one envies what I have?"

"Wow. You're pathetic, you know that, Melanie?" She sighs. "You get a little of what you've been giving for years, and you think your life is over."

"You're...pathetic." I sniffle. I shiver, the rainwater seeming to have cooled not only the outside of my skin, but the inside too. "You can't even...kill yourself...right."

Lexie snorts, and then she begins to smile. "Better luck next time, right?"

"Loser," I mumble, but my lips twitch. "Why am I talking to you anyway? I don't like you."

"Because I'm the only one here, and *no one* likes you, remember?"

I remember what she called me in the house. It's one thing to be named a bitch; it's far worse to be considered a monster. "You called me a monster."

Lexie traces a circle on her knee. "Maybe we're all monsters." She meets my gaze, and in it, I see a spark of hope. "What if...we try to be something better?"

The hope in her eyes causes a likewise emotion to sputter to life inside me. I start to smile around the tears dripping down my face with the rain, but then I look up. "What are you doing here?"

Lexie frowns, staring at me like I've lost my mind before realizing I'm looking behind her. She turns her head, and goes still at the sight of Jocelyn and Casey.

"We came to the party, but...there's no party. What are you two doing down here, and why is Lexie Hennessy with you?" Casey looks confused, which is nothing new. Her hair is in what was once a neat ponytail, but now is stringy and lopsided under the force of the rain. She looks like a ghost with her white skin and silvery hair.

Jocelyn, the cow, preens. The rain doesn't seem to touch her. Her hair is luscious locks about her shoulders, like a black cape, her lips red, and she has lots of skin showing in her microscopic shorts and tank top. I know, as I look at her gloating expression. I know she somehow did this too. Lightning takes over the world, highlighting her features and turning them sinister. Thunder joins in, and the area turns into a symphony of natural disaster.

It makes sense that the storm decides to turn ominous with Jocelyn's arrival.

I stand on unstable legs, reaching for one of the poles that frame the dock. It puts me directly beside the now choppy water. Up and down the dock goes, and I with it, like I'm on some lame ride at the fair. "How did you manage to keep everyone away tonight?"

Lexie slowly gets to her feet, seemingly unmovable as she faces Casey and Jocelyn. Of course, she probably hasn't been drinking for the last couple of hours like me either.

"What?" Casey blinks.

Jocelyn smiles, the bottoms of her sandals slapping the dock as she joins us. Casey, always waiting to be led, moves with her. "Jeff's having a bigger and better party. Sorry you didn't get the invitation."

My face goes tight. "You stole him from me. You knew I liked him."

Jocelyn looks at her nails, long and sharp. "He wanted me more."

"You always take them!" I don't sound like me. I sound...shrill. Hysterical. My fingers clench the pole hard enough to cause an ache in my joints. "Because you're cheap, and you're easy, and guys might want you, but they'll never want you for long."

Her face turns snakelike, and her eyes fill with venom. When Jocelyn strikes, I'll feel it. Still, I can't seem to stop the words.

"You made that picture, and you're glad I'm not popular anymore. You're not my friend."

"No. I'm not your friend. I've never been your friend." Jocelyn's eyes flash, and she fists her hands.

Lexie laughs. "Wait. What? You two have your own battle going on? This is rich."

Jocelyn's head snaps in Lexie's direction. "Nice English project. I especially liked the part about me calling myself a viper."

Lexie shrugs.

"You think everything is owed to you." Jocelyn's shoulders hunch as she makes her way down the dock, and to me. Her eyes glitter; her nostrils flare. She looks like a beast about to shred its victim. I'm the victim, I realize. "You get everything you want, and it isn't fair, Melanie. It isn't fair that you don't have to work for anything. It isn't fair that anything you want, you get. So yes, I take what's yours, because it isn't owed to you. Everything is easy for you, and it shouldn't be."

"Everything is not easy for me," I choke around a fresh set of tears. "My parents are divorced, my dad hardly ever sees me, my

217

mom makes me mad, like, every day, and now I am the school joke. And no one came to my party!"

"I want to date Lucas!" Casey's eyes dart between me and Jocelyn, and she looks as shocked as we do by the outburst.

"I hate you," I tell Jocelyn.

"I hate you too," she says back with a shrug.

"I don't hate you," Casey offers meekly.

"You three are...I don't even have the words." Lexie shakes her head and walks toward Jocelyn, and dry land. The wind turns violent, shoving at Lexie. The tail of her shirt flaps as she moves.

Jocelyn steps in front of Lexie, blocking her way. Her dark hair whips up and back, making her look mystical and unconquerable. "Where do you think you're going? I told you what would happen if you kept saying things about me."

"Right. You were going to rip out my tongue." Lexie's voice turns to granite. "Try it."

I don't know why I do it. Lexie is nothing to me. I should let Jocelyn do whatever she's going to do, and let it be. But something about seeing the strong-willed girl in a standoff against Jocelyn digs at a part of me. Lexie is brave—crazy, but brave. She's been shit on enough, by me and Jocelyn more than anyone else.

"Let her pass," I tell Jocelyn, letting go of the pole and trying to appear surefooted when I really want to fall and crawl across the dock to the safety of the cabin.

Jocelyn turns her deadly gaze on me. "No."

Twenty-three
NICK

I STOLE MY DAD'S CAR. He watched me take it, and I'm sure I'm going to be in a shitload of trouble when I show back up with it, but I was in a hurry. I left my aunt to explain after she dropped me off at my house. I'll feel guilty about that later. I drove like a maniac to get here, sure there would be cops on my tail. Only blissful darkness was behind me.

The wrongness of the empty cabin with its front door hanging open hits me hard. All the lights are on, and no one is here. It's eerie, and makes my stomach flop around. I go through possible scenarios, and none of them make me feel better. It's a shock to my system to stand here, to be in this place. I used to come here often, and when I think about that other me who drank and partied and acted like an entitled ass, he feels like a stranger.

My shoes squish with each step I take, and I leave puddles. I shove wet hair from my eyes and look around. My heart pounds, fierce and out of its normal rhythm. I see the empty beer bottles on the floor, the counters full of untouched food. It smells like unease in here, thick and volatile.

This cabin is large, and it's going to take a while to search it all. *Too long*, I think grimly, and start on the first floor. I don't find anything unusual, or anyone at all, and sprint up the stairs to the second floor.

I wrench open each door, my anxiety growing every time I enter a bedroom with no one inside. It doesn't help that I keep picturing Jackson whenever I look at a bed. I see his dead eyes with the unfocused stare, his parted lips, the blood. There was so much blood. Each room is the possibility of a similar scenario, and it's messing with my head. *Not now. Freak out later.*

True, I wasn't technically a patient at Live, but that doesn't mean I shouldn't have been.

In one of the rooms, I catch movement outside the window. I frown as I gaze in the direction of the lake. I squint, able to make out shapes on the dock, but I have no idea if they're male or female, or how many. Who the hell would be out there in the middle of a storm? Cursing, I dive for the door and stumble down the stairs, falling more than walking. I know who would be out there. Alexis. And the objects of her retaliation.

Rain pummels me, angled and unfriendly. The earth is soft with it, and ridden with holes. The hill looks like the rain wiped all the grass from it, and left muck in its place. I can't see well, not until lightning turns night to day. There are four figures, one somewhat separated from the other three, and all are on the violently shifting dock.

"Alexis!" The wind rips the word from my lips like I never shouted it. I sprint toward the girls, inwardly raging at my limbs to move faster, to get to them before it's too late. The ground is slick with water, and I slip a couple times.

When I reach them, my eyes quickly pass over Casey, Jocelyn, and Melanie. They come to rest on Alexis. She stares back, not appearing to breathe. Her hair is a whirlwind, her clothes soggy, and the sight of her lights me up. I didn't know how much I missed her until I am looking at her. White light streaks the blackness outlining us, and it doesn't compare with the spark in her eyes. I feel the jolt of her gaze all the way to my heart, and it thunders in response.

"What are you doing here?" she demands, her eyes moving over me. They flash with something, but not long enough for me to determine what it is. I'm going with abhorrence.

I approach slowly, my eyes shifting from one face to another. I note the placement of their bodies, how they're held. Jocelyn stands in front of Alexis, with Melanie directly beside Alexis. Casey is near me. An inhuman groan sounds, and I know it's the dock. This scene shouts danger, and I feel it cling to me as I get closer.

"You didn't come to Live for your therapy sessions," I tell Alexis. "You didn't answer any of my phone calls, which led me to believe you have caller ID."

Her eyebrows lower, and her lips part on a breath.

"You didn't call me back." Even I can hear the misery in my voice.

"Nick Alderson. Where the hell did you come from?" Jocelyn looks over her shoulder at me, her features set with toxicity.

"I thought you moved away," Casey adds.

I ignore them, my attention on Alexis. Always Alexis. "Whatever is going on, it can wait until you get off the dock."

Alexis glares at me, but I see the way her hands shake. "How did you know to come here?"

"You can let it go, Alexis," I tell her gently, pulling my eyes from her hands. "You can let the hurt, the anger, the vengeance—you can let it all go. You have that choice."

She looks away.

"Here's a better question: how do you two know each other?" Jocelyn asks suspiciously.

Again, I ignore Jocelyn. "It wasn't hard to figure out you'd be here, Alexis. I know these kids, remember? I know how they think, where they go. What they do. I used to be one of them."

"Plus, I told you about the party when I went to your group home," Melanie points out.

"It isn't a group home," I say absently, watching as cracks take over Alexis' face.

"Some party," Jocelyn scoffs.

"No thanks to you," Melanie bites back.

"She went to see you? *No one* sees you." Alexis tries to hide it, but her voice trembles. "You don't let them."

"He saw me," Melanie says, her smile turning savage as Alexis looks at her.

"Let me know when you're sober," Alexis says to Melanie.

"Why?"

"Because when you are, I'm going to hit you," Alexis tells her in a too-pleasant voice.

"It isn't important," I say impatiently, watching as the dock rocks to the left and right. It shudders, and makes another questionable sound. The lake is a tool of the storm, and it's getting strong. I remember jumping from the end of this dock, and entering water that never seemed to end. Even here, near the shore, it's deep. I look down, seeing the spiky rocks that live just below the surface.

In a voice like stone, I tell them, "Get off the dock. Now."

"No one's leaving this dock until I'm ready for them to leave," Jocelyn announces. "Lexie and I have some unfinished business. Don't we, Lexie?"

"Damn it, Jocelyn! Get off the dock," I holler, stepping forward.

"I think Nick's right. We should listen to Nick." Casey backs up a step, and another, until she's on the sand.

"Well, I think Nick is a moron," Jocelyn sneers, turning her attention to Melanie and Alexis.

"Don't call him that," Alexis commands, leaning toward Jocelyn. "I always thought Melanie was the worst, but I was wrong. It's you. You're like this evil, oozing, growing *thing* of puss. And you're ugly because of it."

Melanie's eyebrows shoot up, and a pleased expression takes over her features. "I'm not the worst?"

The rain turns piercing, to the point that it's hard to see or hear. It feels like needles prickling my skin. Wind is in my ears, causing them to ache, and rain partially blocks my view. I watch as, with an animalistic cry, Jocelyn swipes her hand across Alexis' cheek with nails like claws. Melanie moves for Jocelyn as Alexis stumbles back with a hand over her cheek. I react without thinking, racing toward the three, and yet, I don't seem to get anywhere. It plays out in slow motion. Jocelyn lunges for Melanie, shoving her out of her way. Melanie falls to her knees. Alexis straightens and moves for Jocelyn. She's too close to the edge of the dock, and Jocelyn is livid.

I have to get to Alexis.

I have to get her safe.

I have to get her off this dock, and away from these girls.

I have to, I have to, I have to...

Lightning follows my movements, and the sky roars. The storm is angry, but I am determined. I race onto the dock, and am immediately yanked to the right as it rears up and slaps against land and water like a captured beast bent on its escape. The dock lifts again, crashing down forcefully. Casey screams from the safety of the shore, and so does Melanie from where she crouches, her hands splayed on the wood.

Alexis stumbles back, and back. And back. My heartbeat stutters. I heave a choked breath of air when she finds and clings to a pole, her form small and gray under the blanket of rain. She's too far away. My chest twists with the knowledge.

Jocelyn is closest to me, and I firmly grab her around the arm, swinging her toward land. "This dock isn't safe. Get out of here," I shout at her, giving her a shake to hopefully get some sense in her head.

I turn, shuffling toward Alexis. There is nothing to hold on to as the dock lurches, and I brace my legs until the water calms enough to move. As the shudders turn stronger, and a splintering sound fills my ears, I focus on Alexis. She seems miles from me, out of reach, like she's already been taken by the storm. I bypass Melanie, who seems more or less steady as she attempts to crawl her way to land.

"The dock is going to give!" Blinded by rain, I rapidly blink to keep Alexis in sight. "Come to me. I'll meet you halfway!"

Alexis shakes her head at me, jabbing her index finger toward the sand.

I shake my head back, and take another step. "I'm not leaving without you."

224

"Not me. Her." Alexis points effusively, her voice reedy against the wind. "Get Melanie. She's drunk."

"No," I argue. "She's fine."

"She is not fine!" I feel her glare on me, even if I can't see it. "Help her, Nick. Please."

"Alexis—"

"This is my fault," she whispers, but I somehow hear it.

"Meet me in the middle," I urge, only five or so feet from her now.

"The dock isn't going to make it much longer."

"Neither are you if you don't start moving!" Fear makes my voice harsh, and my body is strung taut. Something shifts beneath us, and grinds. The waves are bigger now, and I don't think it will take much to bring this thing upside down. The lightning is closer, with less breaks in between.

I curse, staring into Alexis' shadowed face. Her features dim and brighten with the natural light, flashes of sad blue eyes and firm lips. She is a paradox.

"Please, Nick."

That pleading note in her voice breaks my resolve. Frustrated, my very being telling me this is wrong, I nod with agreement. "Stay there," I tell her.

"I'm not going anywhere," she jokes feebly.

Even as I lean down to retrieve Melanie, my body wants to straighten, and turn in the other direction. Gritting my teeth, my fingers fumble against her wet, limp body. "Melanie, come on, help me out here."

"I'm good. Just give me a minute."

"We don't *have* a minute." My neck strains with the chaos battling inside me. *Leave her*, a voice roars. *Leave her and get to Alexis!* I almost do.

Melanie waves me away with a hand and attempts to navigate on her knees and hands. She's literally moved maybe an inch since I got here. I take a deep breath, briefly close my eyes, and haul her over my shoulder. I careen to the left as the dock rolls, and Melanie pounds at my back with her fists, screaming at me to let her down, and then screaming at me to not let her go when I slid toward the edge of the dock.

I fall to one knee, her elbow knocking into the side of my head. Pain slashes through my temple. "Hold still!"

She goes limp, and I shake the ringing from my head. Staring straight ahead, I force myself back to my feet. My muscles burn. Jocelyn and Casey sit huddled together, two dark shapes waiting in the sand. Casey shoots to her feet, her mouth open and her eyes large. She cups her mouth and shouts something.

Hurry.

I'm close to land.

Knowing I shouldn't, I shift my head and look back.

I'll never forget it.

Never.

Alexis is slowly making her way toward me, her eyes locked on me, her features set with concentration. She focuses on me like I am her destination, and she only has to reach me, and then everything will be bearable. She meets my eyes as I look at her, and I feel the force of her essence all the way to my core. I don't think she's ever realized how alive she truly is. I don't think she knows that death could never really be an option for her. Alexis burns brighter than anything as small as mortality.

The corners of her mouth dip. I see forgiveness and regret in her eyes. She takes a deep breath. I see every dream she had that involved me, every hope. Her mouth wobbles. I see her heart. Her eyes shine. I see me in her eyes, and I don't see what I expect to see—I see something that has to be close to love.

As if knowing what is about to happen, she mouths, "I'm sorry."

Multiple waves, bigger and fiercer than I'd ever expect a lake to produce, crash over the dock with unapologetic savagery. The middle of the dock disintegrates, an unnatural sound taking over the noise of rain and thunder. It splits in two, separating us. The end Alexis is on immediately goes under.

Gone.

She's just...gone.

I blink, not believing what I see. My grip loosens, and I almost drop Melanie. I want to drop Melanie. I stare in horror at the emptiness where Alexis stood. It's nothing but choppy, furious water. I can't hear anything, and then I hear a siren. It's Melanie.

"Put me down!" Melanie shrieks, pounding at my back. "Put me down and *get her*!"

Practically throwing her the last few feet, I spin around, searching the black depths for a slight, pale form. I sprint back and forth, up and down the broken dock, looking, looking. My chest is crushing under the pressure of being unable to draw air. The fractured part of the dock bobs in the distance, and there is no one with it. A horrible sound fills my ears, and I realize it's me, sobbing.

She can't be gone. She can't be gone.

I hear voices, see flashing lights through the trees near the cabin. I make out the forms of people running this way, one frame looking a lot like my dad's. I turn away, diving into the icy, tumultuous water.

Twenty-four

Alexis

THE COLD IS THE WORST.

I go down, falling through the water, and I wonder if it will ever end. Is there a bottom, or does it go on forever? Will I never stop falling? I jerk with shivers, and they take over my body I open my eyes to black. I am weightless, like I'm part of the lake instead of separate. When I stop spiraling down, I float in limbo before kicking my legs to try to get to the top. Even as I struggle to the surface, and find it blocked by the floating piece of dock that broke off, and unable to draw much needed air into my lungs, it's the cold that is the worst.

I think of impossible moments as I fight the lake. The feel of Nick's arms around me, the certainty that I was special to him, and still am. I think of the time my mom decorated my room in pink and frills because I was sick, and she wanted to make me feel better. My dad carrying me through the darkened house after a long day and night at the fair, and how he tucked me in bed and placed a kiss upon my brow. I think of all the things I want to do, should have done, and regret steals whatever air I have left in my lungs.

Regret knows me well.

I wasted too much time on things that didn't change anything, instead of focusing on the things that could, for the better.

The wood of the fractured dock has become a weapon, and we do a fatal dance of chance. Each time I try to be free of it, it seems to follow. On and on this goes, until I fear my lungs will burst. When I think I'm finally around it, and shoot upward, the water slams it into me. It hits my head, and around the agony pulsing from my temple, I see stars. They're so pretty, but they don't belong here, not in the water. My head is heavy, and my lungs are on fire, and I finally close my eyes.

As consciousness slips from my grasp, I think of Nick's dream, the dream where I died. It would be cruel to escape death once just to have it take me now, but then, that is exactly what I know life to be: cruel. I would laugh if I could, but instead, I do nothing. Death is easy; life is cruel. I still want life.

But I am so cold.

Twenty-five

Melanie

I T'S THE FIRST DAY OF my senior year, and like I pledged at the end of my junior, I'm going to be better and more spectacular than ever before. Enid High School won't know what to do with me. I smirk at my reflection in the full-length mirror, and add in a wink, just because. I look good. I cut my hair over the summer, and highlighted the brown with sun-kissed blond. It now haloes my face in wisps and waves.

"Melanie, breakfast's ready."

Giving my black high-waist shorts and navy blue and white striped shirt one final look, I twirl around. I snag my backpack off the floor and skip down the stairs. I have a good feeling I am going to kill today. The kitchen smells like coffee and spices, and I breathe it in with a smile.

With her back to me, Mom opens the refrigerator door, pulling out a gallon of milk. She turns with a smile. Over the summer, we went for walks almost every day, and in turn, she's looking slimmer and happier than I've seen her in years. She even streaked her graying hair with white, and got it cut in layers around her face. She looks awesome.

"What is it today, Mom?"

"Pumpkin muffins." Her smile grows.

I groan. "Mom, you know those didn't turn out right."

"I think they're good."

"They taste like egg."

She opens a container and pulls out the final product from my latest infamous baking attempt, and pops a chunk of pumpkin muffin in her mouth. "It's good," she assures me, setting a look of bliss on her face.

I laugh and toss a grape at her. My mom catches it and pops it in her mouth. "It's close to inedible."

"It's a work in progress. Don't be so hard on yourself." My mom winks and sips from her cup of coffee. She lifts her eyebrows. "Want some?"

"Mom, you know I cut back on caffeine." I removed a lot of things from my diet over the last few months, and my life. I spent the summer alcohol, sugar, and caffeine free, and other than when my mom and I were together, I spent it alone. And I didn't mind it.

"It's decaf."

When I nod, she pours me a cup.

"Are you going to your dad's this weekend?"

After what happened at the cabin, and my dad appearing as Lexie was taken away in an ambulance, I have since been forbidden to be there without his supervision. Old me would have thrown a fit; new me gets it. When I told him I wanted to see him more—after throwing up on his shoes—he agreed that he hasn't been around as much as he should be. We've fallen into a schedule where I stay with him at the cabin, just the two of us, once a month. It's something. It's more than I used to get.

"Yeah. I think so."

"Good. That's good." She sounds like she means it. "I thought I could grab a pizza on my way home from work today. We could watch Supernatural."

I smile around the coffee mug. "Deal."

I introduced my mom to Sam and Dean Winchester in July, and she's since become obsessed—or she's just pretending interest in the show to do something with me. I know that the initial time she barged into my room and plopped down on my bed with the demand that she was going to watch whatever I was, was a means to connect with me. The show happened to be Supernatural.

She made an effort. I decided I should do the same.

I set down the coffee. "I have to go. Don't worry about the dishes; I'll get them when I get home from school."

Blinking, my mom asks, "You're sure?"

"I'm sure."

The total one-eighty I recently pulled was shocking to everyone, including my mom, but mostly, me. That night at the cabin changed me. It changed us all. Since then, I've been trying to figure out who I am, and the kind of person I want to be. I want to be a good person, someone Lexie Hennessy would approve of.

I blink as an image of Lexie's lifeless body being dragged from the water by Nick enters my head, bringing the cool kiss of icy death with it. In spite of the warm temperature, I shudder. I think of her often. In a messed up way, I'm glad I met her. She saved me that night, in more ways than the obvious. I'm kind of sad that she's gone. I think I could have liked her.

It was evident a part of Nick died as he wept over her frigid and limp body, clutched within his arms. She had to be pulled from him

233

by the EMTs, and she wasn't breathing. He sat in a daze in the sand, looking at the water like he was waiting for it to bring back Lexie. They say death is never the answer. Maybe someone should ask Alexis Hennessy about that.

"It's okay, Melanie." My mom places a hand on my shoulder, knowing exactly where my mind has taken me. "It's okay to think about it."

I shake my head, dispersing the memory, and give her a quick hug. "I'll see you later."

"Have a good day," she calls after me. "And take a muffin!"

I wave, and leave the house, minus the muffin.

My house is a ten-minute walk to the school. I wonder why I never bothered to walk it before. It's already hot out, and I'm glad for my shorter haircut, knowing it's only going to get hotter as the day goes. The breeze is nice, and I slide sunglasses onto my face to help block out the sun. Less potential for wrinkles when I'm not squinting.

A car of teens drives by, and I face forward, not wanting to know whether or not I know them. My mom's car appears at the four-way stop, and she honks. Making a face, I wave as she heads in the direction of her workplace. The houses on either side of the street become sparser, and then the school stands before me.

I pause for a moment, taking in a lungful of air. I lift my head, straighten my back, and walk.

The first person I see upon entering the building is Jocelyn. She looks the same—same long black hair, same heavily made-up face, same suggestive outfit that's probably inappropriate for school. She stands near Jeff Oliver in the hallway, a palm on his chest. His lightning blue eyes touch on mine, shifting away before mine can. Jocelyn doesn't notice me until I'm almost past her, and when our eyes briefly meet, it's like looking at a stranger. We both avert our gazes, and I continue toward my locker.

With my backpack inside the metal nook, I'm about to close the locker door when I smell familiar cologne. I shut the locker door and turn to face Jeff. His hair is longer than last year, and the rumpled waves soften his features. With his head tilted, he studies me like he can't figure me out. I could end the mystery and let him know that he won't. I am no longer paper thin like Jocelyn. I'm working on adding some depth.

"Jocelyn isn't here," I say pointedly when he continues to stare.

He tries to smile, but it doesn't touch his blue eyes. "I liked you, you know."

I cross my arms and rest my back against the cool lockers. It makes my skin break out in goose bumps. "Yeah, I could tell by how you went on a date with me, and the next time I saw you, you were with Jocelyn."

Frustration tightens the skin around his eyes. "You didn't act like you were interested."

"I guess you should have asked," I reply coldly.

Jeff opens his mouth, and I hold up a hand. "It doesn't matter. I wouldn't date you now, no matter what. I hope you have a good year."

With those parting words, I head for the cooking class I chose as an elective. I promised Mom I'd make dinner most nights, and I need some serious help if I want to make anything decent.

Farther down the hall, I see two boys shove a boy back and forth between them. The girl standing with them knocks papers from his hands. They laugh as the boy scrambles to pick up the papers from the floor. I slow my footsteps, watching as one of the boys kicks a paper out of the kneeling boy's reach. With a sigh, I hurry my pace to get to them before the group disperses.

"Hey." My tone is commanding, and four sets of eyes snap to my face. "What are your names?"

The boys stutter responses, but the girl remains quiet. Even the boy on the floor tells me his name. I focus on the girl, taking in her wavy red hair, challenging green eyes, and the magenta top I almost bought a couple weeks ago. "I like your shirt," I tell her.

Suspicion clears from her gaze, and she brightens. "Thanks."

"What's your name?" I ask again, and this time, she tells me.

"You're all freshmen, right?" When they nod, I continue. "I'm Melanie Mathews, and I'm a senior. Being freshmen, maybe you aren't aware of certain rules, so I'll be helpful and tell you the most important rule." I pause, meeting three pairs of eyes. "You don't treat other kids badly."

The girl rolls her eyes.

I grab the front of her shirt and yank her to me as she sputters and tries to get away. Transforming my expression from friendly to wicked, I hiss, "If I see you picking on anyone, *anyone*, you'll get to see my nasty side." I smirk into her wide-eyed face. "You don't want to see my nasty side."

I open my fingers and she staggers back, tugging at her shirt. When I look at the boys, they blanch and start to turn. "Where do you think you're going?" They freeze. "Get these papers picked up. *Now.*"

They scramble to do my bidding. I look at the blond-haired boy with brown eyes crouched on the floor. He looks young, and innocent. He looks like the kind who won't fight back. He'll be eaten alive if he doesn't change his ways. I offer a hand. Looking relieved and much too grateful, he accepts.

I squeeze his hand as he stands beside me, and he meets my eyes. "Stick up for yourself. Bullies hate that."

AS I GO THROUGH MY classes, and steer through the halls, I feel Lexie. It's hard to explain how exactly I do, but it's like her mark is on the walls. Her ghost walks these halls with the students. She was here. I knew her. I won't forget her. I smile ruefully, thinking of the crap she pulled on me in retaliation of the crap I pulled on her first. I wish I hadn't been such an awful person.

So don't be, I hear her say inside my head.

In Art, my last class before lunch, I hesitantly take a seat at the same table as Casey. I'm not sure what to expect from her, but I owe her an apology. I treated her wrongly.

Other than one time when we bumped into each other at a clothing store at the mall, I haven't seen her since the night of my disastrous party. She was with Lucas when I saw her, and she looked happy—well, she looked happy until she saw me, that is. I said hello. Her reply was less than friendly.

Dressed in a pink top and black shorts with her blond hair in a side-braid, Casey looks sweet and pretty. She stiffens when I say her name, avoiding my gaze. Feeling my chest deflate, I look around, contemplating sitting somewhere else entirely, but then she speaks.

"I always thought you and Jocelyn were better than me."

I go still, staring at her lowered head.

Casey looks up, her mouth tight. "You were, but only because I let you."

"I'm sorry," I whisper, meaning it.

She gets to her feet and walks to a table across the room, but not before saying, "You should be."

Lunch isn't much better. I stand in the cafeteria, surrounded by hundreds of kids, and I have nowhere to go. The noise level is earsplitting, and it smells like tacos and cheese. Kids are talking about what they did over the summer, and the air is thick with excitement. I feel displaced. Grabbing a tuna fish sandwich and a bottle of water, I quickly leave the mayhem of the lunchroom and head for the picnic tables outside.

There's a handful of students making use of the picnic tables, while others sit in the grass. One girl sits alone at a table, eating a sandwich as she watches traffic go by. I can't remember her name— I think it is Anne—but she's in my grade, and I saw her with Lexie last year. I wonder if she knows what happened to her. If she doesn't, I'm not telling her.

Swallowing my pride, because, really, it needs it, I keep her in sight as I approach. The girl has limp brown hair, and dresses in jeans and tee shirts that are too big. Her face is pale with small features. She isn't popular. She will never be popular. In fact, she's one of the kids who are usually picked on by others, a kid I probably made fun of at some point. And I want her to be my first new friend.

"Hey...Anne. Can I sit here?"

"It's Anna." Her eyes are wary upon my face as she looks up.

"I'm sorry, Anna. For...that, and for, well, for me. You know, how I acted last year." I roll my eyes. "Okay, all the years."

I didn't realize I'd spend most of my first day of school apologizing to people, but maybe I should have.

"It's okay." Her smile is small but real.

"Really? Just like that?"

Anna shrugs. "Holding grudges hurts the person holding them more than anyone else."

I think of Lexie Hennessy, and when I see the unease pass over Anna's face, I wonder if she's thinking of her too. In the end, though, Lexie had the right idea. She chose to forgive me. I knew it when I saw the flicker of hope touch her eyes. She was thinking past the hurt, and our history. Lexie chose to move on.

"Right." I let out a low breath. "I know it's shocking, but I seem to be in need of some friends. Real friends," I add, giving her an expectant look.

Anna's grip tightens on her sandwich to the point where she mashes the edges, her eyes shifting from me and back. "What about Jocelyn and Casey?"

"We don't really talk anymore," I say carefully, wondering how much she knows about what happened between me and my previous friends. I plow forward, out of my element in this type of situation. People used to want to hang out with me; I didn't have to campaign myself. "I'm nowhere near as popular as I used to be, but there are certain perks to having me as a friend."

"Oh?"

My face heats up. "I can't think of any at the moment, but I know they're there."

Anna laughs softly, and I smile.

"Maybe we can hang out this weekend? There's a movie playing downtown that I wouldn't mind seeing."

"Sure," she says after a pause. "I would like that."

A light feeling overtakes my apprehension. "Great! And what about Chinese? Do you like that? We could get some before the movie."

"I love Chinese," Anna assures me. She scoots over. "Want to sit?"

"Yes," I reply immediately. "I do."

After a couple silent minutes pass where I pick at my sandwich and Anna nibbles on hers, she turns to me. "Is this a joke?"

My smile drops. "No."

Anna nods, looking away. She faces me once more. "Are you sure?"

"I'm completely sure. I don't..." I swallow the bite I took of tuna fish sandwich overloaded with mayonnaise. "I seriously don't have any friends, Anna, and the ones I had...either I didn't deserve them, or they didn't deserve me."

Our eyes meet.

I shrug, the sun burning the back of my neck to match my face. "You seem nice. I'd like to know someone who's nice."

Anna takes a breath, swallows, and nods. "Okay then." With a smile, she offers me a bag of chips. "Do you like sour cream and onion chips?"

If this was last year, I would have knocked the bag from her hand in disgust. If this was last year, I'd still dislike myself. I don't want to be that girl anymore.

"Thanks," I tell her, and take a large handful.

Twenty-six

Alexis

"DAD." MY VOICE COMES OUT in a squeak, and every breath I take makes it harder to take another, like they're all trapped inside my lungs.

He looks up from the book he's reading, blinks, and slowly lowers it to his lap. He doesn't say anything for such a long time that I fear I look hideous, and he's remaining quiet to keep from telling me. My dad stands, and crosses the room to me. I fidget, wanting to touch my hair and face, and knowing enough to keep my hands at my sides.

Gripping my clammy hands in his dry ones, he raises them, and spins me in a slow-motion circle. I smile, the material of the dress making a swishing sound as I move. He steadies me, drops a kiss to my forehead, and tells me, "You look extraordinary."

I exhale, lightheaded with giddiness. "Is it too much?"

Crinkles form around his pale blue eyes as he smiles. "I wish I could tell you, but I don't know what he plans on doing with you."

"Me neither," I grumble.

"It better not be anything I'll have to kill him over."

I laugh, but swallow it down at the look on his face. I clear my throat and smile weakly.

My dad's bald head gleams like it's been freshly polished. "He told you to dress up, correct?"

"Yes." My heartbeat picks up, stalls, and careens madly to the promise of Nick's turquoise eyes. I'll see him soon. It's been two weeks since we last got to spend time together. It seems like it's been much longer.

"Then it's perfect."

I look around the dimly lit living room with its country blue and cream walls. I'm scared to sit anywhere. I'll probably wrinkle the dress, be unable to stand once I'm seated, or both. This house is smaller than our old home in Ridgefield, Iowa, and it's older than the one in Enid, Illinois. It lacks the memories of each, and I'm glad for it. It's a new beginning in my old town, and we can make new memories here. Start over. Life is an endless chance at do-overs, I've recently discovered. As long as you're alive, you have choices.

High school is something you get through to get to the good stuff. It's a chapter, a start. It isn't your life, and it isn't forever. In the larger scheme of things, it doesn't even matter. I know that now.

"Do you need anything?"

I shake my head, and my hairstyle shifts, but holds. It is now long enough to pull up, and my friend Carrie stopped by this afternoon to French braid it, leaving strands loose around my face. "No. Nick said I only needed a dress, and to not worry about anything else."

"Hmm. I'm sure I'll worry enough for the both of us."

"Dad." I give him a look, and he smiles—barely, but he smiles.

In the hospital bed as I was treated for a concussion and received six stitches on the side of my head, my dad told me he would get a transfer back to the factory in Ridgefield, allowing me to graduate with my friends. I didn't tell him all the details of that night at the lake, but he figured out enough to know it would be best. I don't remember everything that took place on the dock, but I was told I stopped breathing at one point. My last memory is of me falling into the water with the broken piece of dock, and the cold. I still feel the cold.

Death and me, we need to come to an understanding. As in, I won't be needing its services for some time.

Dad allowing us to move back to Iowa was a happy surprise, and the retransition into my old school, with my old friends, was seamless. I think of the Enid kids, though, and often. I'm sure Jocelyn is the same as always, and Casey—well, I hope she's learned to be an individual. I know Clint will think twice about messing with anyone. After the rock incident, he fled anytime I was near.

Melanie Mathews sent me an email a few weeks ago. It read: *I stole your friend Anna. Keep yourself out of hospitals.* I replied with: *I stole your boyfriend. Stay away from booze.*

I guess that means we're okay.

"What time is it?" I've looked at the grandfather clock across the room three times now, and it doesn't matter—I still don't know the time. I'm nervous, and excited, and I really, really hope I don't get sick.

Although we've talked a lot, and have seen each other every few weeks since I moved back to Ridgefield, Nick and I have both been holding back—because of our pasts, because of what happened between us. Because we're scared. I don't want to hold back. I had no right to judge Nick based on the person he used to be. That isn't who he is anymore. I don't even know that person.

He shared his darkness with me, and I bolted. It was too much, too close to my own wounds. It was the start of my junior year all over again. But I have my own darkness as well, and he stayed with me through it.

The doorbell rings, and my nerves skyrocket.

"Dad," I say again, my voice close to inaudible.

"I'll get it. You just...stay there." My dad bustles from the room, putting on his intimidating face as he does.

I sigh, imagining how the greetings will go.

"I'm here for your daughter." That will be Nick.

"Hurt her, and I'll cut you." That will be my dad.

Over the last couple of months, my dad has gone from distant to proactive. It's nice, and overwhelming, at times.

With my back to the entrance of the living room, I still know when Nick arrives. The air prickles, and my pulse zigzags. I close my eyes, and open them to see my dad watching me from directly in front of me. I jump, and he chuckles. I give him a look, and luckily, he understands that it's his cue to disappear.

"Have a good night," he says, and looks over my shoulder. "One at the latest." The "or else" part is implied. Nick must nod, because with one final look at me, my dad grabs his book and heads for the stairs.

Once his footsteps recede, only then do I turn.

My breath is stolen as our eyes meet. I look into his aqua eyes, and see how they widen as they start at my hair and travel down my glittering dress to my matching silver shoes before coming to my eyes. I just stare at his face, wondering how it's possible to ache for another with the entirety of my being. A missing piece of me is now back in place, and I feel whole. This is the boy who holds me during the night until I fall asleep, and I get to hold him as well.

I love Nick. The knowledge is scary, and wonderful.

"You shine like a galaxy full of stars," Nick murmurs. The blond is back in his hair, telling me he's been outside a lot. Telling me, if I didn't already know, he's not hiding anymore.

My cheeks warm. "It's the sequins on the dress."

A half smile takes over one side of his mouth. "It's you."

When he approaches, I finally take in his outfit. Silver tie, black button-down shirt, and...gray fleece pants. Laughter bubbles forth. With a grin curving his lips, Nick's hands frame my jaw. He looks down into my eyes, and I fall into his. The kiss is soft, lingering. It causes the blood within my veins to soar, and my body to spark to life. Nick is magic, and my essence reacts to his.

"Where are you taking me?" I whisper when the kiss ends. My fingers dig into his shoulders, wanting to pull him closer.

With a secret smile on his lips, he takes my hand and turns toward the doorway. "Everywhere I never thought I'd be able."

THE BUILDING IS NONDESCRIPT—A rectangular slab of gray stone without adornment, and minimal windows. Gravel surrounds it, along with a handful of trees nearby. I look around as I get out of Nick's older black Toyota Camry. We're in the town where Nick goes to college thirty-seven miles from Ridgefield, but I've never been in this part of Hamilton, Iowa. I haven't a clue as to what could be inside this place, and I feel supremely overdressed.

In spite of the sun glaring down at us, the September breeze is cool, and I rub my bare arms. "What is this place?" I ask as we meet near the hood of the car.

"You'll see." The sun catches the color of his eyes, turns them indescribably captivating. I see hints of gold among the blue-green.

I eye the structure doubtfully before returning my gaze to my boyfriend.

Nick winks and starts toward the building. I watch his lean frame for a moment before following. He's gained muscle since he left Live, and his skin is golden, which makes his intriguing eyes stand out that much more. During the week, he goes to school and works part-time at a bookstore. On the weekends, he is with me when I'm not working myself at a local diner, or his aunt, Dr. Larson. Never saw that one coming. Nick doesn't talk of his parents, but I know it's because he isn't close with them, and not because he's hurting.

We are both healing, slowly, on the inside. I absently touch the wound that will leave a scar on my forehead. I'm healing on the outside too.

Nick stops before the gray steel door, staring straight ahead. His throat bobs, his profile fierce and strong. He looks nervous, glancing at me. I slide my fingers through his, locking our hands together. "I am afraid," he confesses in a low voice.

"Of what?"

He just smiles.

I know the feeling.

I am afraid to ask if he specifically chose Hamilton to pursue a career in guidance counseling because it is close to where I am.

I am afraid to hope he wants to see me as much as I want to see him.

I am afraid, if I don't tell him every thought I have, I will later regret it.

Life is unpredictable, and I want to live mine without doubts.

Silence stands between us, and I ask something I've wondered, but didn't have the courage to voice. "Did I ruin us?"

The color of his eyes changes from blue to green as he focuses on me. "No."

"I mean, the old us. I know...I know, right now, we're okay." I frown. "I think. But...it was all so perfect at first—well, as perfect as any budding romance between two mentally unstable people in a treatment center can be—"

Nick makes a sound that seems halfway between laughter and choking.

"—and now...I don't know. I wish I'd made different decisions. I wish I'd trusted what was before me, instead of doubting it." I shrug helplessly. I'm not sure how to explain. It was simple between us, and then, it turned very, very complicated.

"We're okay, Alexis. I think, there isn't a way for us to *not* be okay. Unless you, I don't know, stab me in the heart with an icepick or something."

I blink. "Icepick?"

Nick smirks. "Did you have another weapon in mind?"

"*What?* No."

He laughs, repeating, "We're okay."

I let out a relieved sigh. "Oh, good. I thought—" I shake my head. I thought I hurt him too much. I thought I blew it. I thought I didn't deserve to know this Nick. The Nick I fell in love with. My eyes sting.

His jaw flexes, and light dances in his eyes, intense and powerful. "I don't want a perfect love." Nick gently touches the jagged wound that lines my temple, his smile bittersweet. "I want this. I want you."

Love. Nick said love. Butterflies erupt inside me, and I press a palm to my jumbling stomach. I try to smile, but it wobbles. "That's good, because perfect is the farthest thing from what I am."

Taking a slow inhalation, Nick turns back to the door. "Ready?"

I think he's asking himself more than me, but I nod.

Chuckling, he shakes his head, takes another breath, and opens the door to shimmery lights, low-playing music, and silver streamers and balloons. Nick waits, looking like he doesn't breathe. I freeze, taking in the scene before me, and then I turn to look through the doorway to the normalness outside. I turn back to the twinkling lights and silver decorations.

It's like standing on the precipice of a never-before-seen world.

It's amazing. And super clever. I have a smart boyfriend. This is good. Smart is good. And creative. Also good. I feel a goofy grin take over my face as I look at Nick, my cheeks hurting from being stretched so wide. With his hands in the pockets of his gray pajama pants, he watches me, revealing nothing of his thoughts with his blank expression.

"What is this?" I whisper, stepping carefully into the spacious room.

The door closes behind me, and Nick talks over my shoulder, his breath tickling my neck. "This is prom, and homecoming, and anything else you didn't attend but should have."

I whirl around, my eyes burning, and slap a palm to his chest. "You're...you're..."

Eyebrows lifted, Nick stares at me, looking apprehensive.

I spin away from him, my head back as I turn in a slow circle. Shadows of light dance on the high ceiling, and clear, tiny lights cover the white walls, roping around the room. There is a circular table with two chairs. A long table with a white tablecloth stands along one wall, laden with a crystal punch bowl and plates of miniature snacks. My stomach grumbles, and I realize I forgot to eat lunch. I was too nervous about seeing Nick.

We stand in the center of the room, and the walls seem to shift around us. Straining my ears, I pick up on the song, hearing the familiar chords of 'Lost Boy'. It's strangely appropriate. Nick was lost; I was lost. And when we met, we no longer were. My chest hurts. I understand the anxious look I caught on Nick's face, because I feel it too. Too many emotions are vying for dominance, and it makes me dizzy. Foremost, I want to cry.

"You did all this yourself?" Even my tone is thick, waterlogged with unheard sobs.

"I had help," he admits when I look at him. "My aunt and your dad—"

"*My dad* helped you?" Shock turns my voice into something unnaturally high. He acted like he didn't have any idea what Nick had planned, the sneak.

"A little." He shifts, looking everywhere but at me. "Do you like it?"

I turn back to him, grab his face, and kiss him with all the heat of my being, and all my heart. With every part of me, I kiss him.

"You must like it," he says in a sandpaper voice.

"I love it."

Nick lassoes me with his arms, holding me close against his front. We leisurely shuffle to the slow song. Nick says he doesn't want perfect, but right now, we have it. This is a perfect moment. That's all you can hope for. Little instances of amazement that make the sucky ones dim.

For the first time, I really feel like everything will be okay. We went through a lot of bad. It's nice to have some good, and to be able to see it for what it is. I can't forget the past, but I can focus on now. I wouldn't be where I am, at this very moment, if not for the collage of terrible events.

I should send Melanie a thank you letter. I smile. But probably not.

"Thank you for doing this, for bringing me here." I hook my arms around his neck, my front flush with his. My skin is on fire, and I only want to be closer, always closer.

Nick gazes into my eyes, and smiles sweetly. "This is where I tell you that you make me happy. This is where I tell you that you helped me be brave. This is where I tell you that you made me want to stop hiding."

His voice drops. "This is where I tell you that I love you."

"In your gray pants," I add quietly, my pulse spinning at his words, at the way he makes me feel. He makes me feel like there is true possibility in each day, and that all you have to do is go after it.

Nick laughs, and holds me tighter. "In my gray pants."

I brush my lips across his neck, and feel him shudder. "I love your gray pants," I whisper on his skin.

"I know. They're my signature sex appeal."

We turn in an unhurried circle as I laugh.

"This is where I tell you that you showed me it's okay to forgive. This is where I tell you that you made me want to hope. This is where

Lindy Zart

I tell you that I will always love your gray pants." I grin, feeling his smile against my forehead.

His heartbeat picks up when I tell him what else I love.

A NOTE FROM THE AUTHOR:

When I was sixteen years old, I went to live with my dad's parents. It was in a different town, and a new school. Mediocre interest was shown in me at the school, and the unseen barrier was firm. I was not one of them. I did not belong. Naturally quiet, and not all that outgoing, I quickly became invisible. It didn't help my social status that I wasn't into sports—sports were major in this school.

But then something changed. I wasn't invisible anymore. Instead, I was singled out. Mocked. Kids would pretend to be nice, but they were really making fun of me. It didn't take me long to figure it out. An ugly drawing of me was dropped on my desk in passing; a cutting remark about my car, said with a smile. Someone stating that the lunch I brought from home looked like shit. No one would sit by me. No one would ask me to sit by them.

No one talked to me.

It was like I wasn't a person.

I'd never been bullied before. Sure, there were minor incidents at school, but nothing to this level of meanness. Nothing that made me wonder why I was even living. I didn't know how to deal with it.

I lost weight. My skin was washed out, colorless. My smile became forced, and it wasn't happy. I was slowly dying while living in that atmosphere. It was months of feeling like I'd lost myself, and didn't know who I was. I would tell my grandparents I was sick, and ask to stay home, just so I wouldn't have to go to school. And my nerves were frayed to the point that I did feel sick a lot of the time.

I remember crawling into bed with my grandma in the middle of the night, and telling her I wished I was dead. I was crying. She hugged me and told me that, no, I didn't.

But I did.

I don't talk about this often. In fact, hardly ever have I spoken about this. Do you know how people react when you tell them you tried to kill yourself? Sometimes, it's as if you never spoke. They won't look into your eyes; they might even visibly step back. Like it's contagious. It's not something people talk about. Therefore, those of us who have hugged the darkness, and been embraced by it in return; we hide our black secrets. And it makes us feel even more alone.

One morning, the thought of going to school made me panicked to the point that I decided enough was enough. It was destroying me—going there, being there. I was at a breaking point. No, I *was* broken. I couldn't do it. I wouldn't.

After my grandparents left for the day, I took my grandpa's bottle of insulin pills from the kitchen table, and I swallowed them. I don't know how many, but it was a lot. I was finally going to be done with it.

But then, you see, I became scared. The world was turning gray, and everything was muted, and I was close to passing out.

I called someone—my aunt.

An ambulance came.

I was taken to a hospital.

I had a tube of charcoal shoved down my throat.

I prayed, or I cursed—I'm not sure which. "Oh, God." That's what I said.

And I vomited, repeatedly.

I don't know if I lost consciousness. I think I had to have, at least partially. It's mostly a blur, like even my brain doesn't want to remember it. I had to stay in the hospital for days. I can't remember how many. People came to visit, all to witness the almost death of Lindy.

My sister came, looking stricken, and like she had so many words to say but couldn't. My little niece wanted to be held, and when I complied, she pulled at the tubes connected to me. She didn't understand what was going on. I remember an aunt, different from the one I called, bringing me a penny with an angel shape cut out of it, and I carry that angel penny with me to this day. It's on the keychain to my vehicle—has been for over twenty years.

I had to go to counseling. The counselor was kind. I liked her. When she asked me what I would do if I had to go back to that school, I told her I would run away. I meant it.

I was allowed to finish the remainder of the school year from home; I had to hand in projects every so often. I wasn't left alone. All the pills were out of sight. You see, I wasn't to be trusted after that, and I understand that. I understood it then. I was a liability. The unstable girl who tried to kill herself. I knew they feared I would do it again. But I wouldn't. Not after that. Because I realized something.

It takes more courage to live than it does to die.

More than anything, I was ashamed. That I didn't deal with what was going on in a healthier way. That I let a group of insensitive kids destroy my value of myself. That I forgot who I was. That I wasn't strong enough to fight back. I'm grateful that I was given another chance at this ugly life, and I don't regret learning how sacred it is. Ironic, right? I could have died. And I didn't. I'm here until I'm not, and I have no say in it. As it should be.

I'm telling you all of this, because that is where this story came from—from me, and my time at a school where I was treated like dirt. Based on fact, with fiction morphing it into something more than just the sad story of a bullied girl.

I hope you aren't bullied. I pray you aren't a bully. I want you to know that if you're suicidal, you can make another choice. You can choose to live. You can talk to someone, even a stranger. Even me. I hope you know that every life is worth something. If you need help, and you feel like you have no one, call the phone number below. There is always someone.

Lindy

NATIONAL SUICIDE PREVENTION LIFELINE
CALL 1-800-273-8255

If you enjoyed this book, please consider leaving a review on the site from where you bought it. If you did not enjoy this book, please consider leaving a review on the site from where you bought it. Keep it classy—all hateful posts will be framed and hung on a wall in my home for my kids to read. Please don't traumatize my kids.

Lindy

Acknowledgements:

Tiffany Alfson, Jen Andrews, Jacinda Owen, Kendra Gaither, Megan Stietz: Thank you for being my beta readers for 'bullies like me'. Hugs and love!

Thank you, Wendi Stitzer, for editing once again! You're great.

Sarah from Sprinkles On Top Studios—the cover is epic, and it epically goes along with the story. Thank you.

About the author:

Lindy Zart is the *USA Today* bestselling author of Roomies. She has been writing since she was a child. Luckily for readers, her writing has improved since then. She lives in Wisconsin with her family. Lindy loves hearing from people who enjoy her work. She also has a completely healthy obsession with the following: coffee, wine, bloody marys, peanut butter, and pizza.

You can connect with Lindy at:
Newsletter signup form: http://bit.ly/1RqPP3m
Facebook Reader Group:
https://www.facebook.com/groups/335847839908672/
Google.com/+LindyZart
Twitter.com/LindyZart
Facebook.com/LindyZart
Instagram ZartLindy
Lindyzart.com
Lindyzart@gmail.com
YouTube channel: http://bit.ly/1Qs6wXr

Made in the USA
San Bernardino, CA
28 December 2016